Searching for Ever Land

KAREN SLOAN-BROWN

BROWN REFLECTIONS

Searching for Ever Land
Copyright © 2013 by Karen Sloan-Brown

All rights reserved.

No part of this work may be reproduced or transmitted in any form or by any means, electronic or mechanical, including photocopying and recording, or by any information storage or retrieval system, except as may be expressly permitted by the 1976 Copyright Act or in writing from the publisher. Requests for permission should be addressed to Brown Reflections, Nashville, Tennessee, Brown-Reflections.com.

This book is printed on acid-free paper.

ISBN: 978-0-0991551743

Library of Congress Cataloging-in-Publication Data on file.

MANUFACTURED IN THE UNITED STATES OF AMERICA

Searching for Ever Land

KAREN SLOAN-BROWN

BROWN REFLECTIONS

*This book is dedicated to my husband,
Cornelius, for all the support
and space to accomplish things
I never dared to dream about.*

Chapter One

Honestly I don't know if I would describe it as a downward spiral or a shot off in a wild trajectory but the direction of my life was unexpected altered on a hot and muggy afternoon in June 2009, the 25th day to be exact. It started off as a typical Thursday with me apathetic about showing up for the rest of the week and feeling like a couple of extra days on the weekend would make all the difference in the world. The expected monotony of my daily eight hours at Scott Edwards Investments was taken over by the buzz of Bernie Madoff's imminent sentencing for his $65 billon Ponzi scheme and the Dow Jones Industrial Average gaining 172 points. In spite of all the uproar, I moved through the day on auto-pilot as I performed the repetitious duties that my job had become. By 5:05, I was out of the door and behind the wheel relishing the calm of my car in contrast to the steady hum of the office. It was a short drive home and I'd just walked in the house with my arms and hands filled with my messenger bag, a carry-out of left over wings from lunch, my purse, keys, and the mail when I heard the telephone ring. It rang two more times as I attempted to rearrange all the things I was carrying to free up a hand to pick up the phone in the kitchen.

"Hello," I said casually.

"Mama," she said with anguish in her voice.

My heart nearly stopped hearing the intense emotion in the first word of her response. It was my daughter Pam on the other end and she was hysterical. I couldn't make sense of the rest of her tirade but the high volume of her voice and the jumbled words mixed with tears and upset were clues enough that something horrible had happened.

"Pam, what is the matter?" I asked worried, but trying not to panic prematurely.

"Turn on the TV, Mama," she yelled frantically through the receiver.

I rushed into the den dropping my bags, keys, and everything else in my hands on the floor all along the way and grabbed the remote and pressed the power button. The channel was still on CNN from when I'd watched the early morning news and there it was flashing in words moving across the bottom of the screen while an anchor gave live updates, Michael Jackson had died. Between the words of the news anchor I could hear Pam hollering something else in my ear but I was distracted.

"Hold on, relax for a second, sweetheart," I said hesitantly as I tried to catch up to the breaking news, my shock building with each word. "One of the reporters has said that he might be in a coma," I rapidly repeated into the phone trying to calm her with that possibility.

"No, Mama," she shrieked inconsolably, losing patience with my inability to make this all right for her. "He's dead."

Chapter One

It was true. Sadly, there was nothing I could think of that would make sense of the situation as it was broadcasted from corner to corner on the screen in high definition color. Michael Jackson was gone forever.

Pam was my only daughter, the mirror image of her daddy with clear almond-colored skin, bright brown eyes, lean arms and legs, and a smile so filled with joy it almost made you laugh. Whenever I heard her cry it tore me up inside. She was living on campus, a junior at Tennessee State University majoring in theater, but she had been an ardent fan of Michael Jackson from the first moment she saw my Moonwalker video playing on the VHS recorder in the den when she was only four years old. Lord knows she was just one of millions around the world but from that day she had to have all of his music and videos and she knew every word and every move by heart. She had watched his tapes more times than all of her Disney tapes put together. Yet, the fact remained that she was simply a second generation fan, I was an original, and now the first hit song of the Jackson 5; "I Want You Back" and its lyrics suddenly took on a whole new meaning.

I couldn't believe it, how could this have happened? Michael Jackson was an icon, he couldn't have been a mere mortal like the rest of us. I stared at the TV dumbfounded, in distress, as if I was a full-fledged member of the Jackson family; after all we had grown up together. I watched and listened intently as the anchor gave another update, "The world has lost the greatest entertainer of all time," he announced solemnly. I rifled through my mind desperately to find something consoling to say to his biggest fan. Through the receiver I heard her mumble something in irritation and then she hung up the phone.

I stood there, transfixed, for another half-hour before I pulled myself away to the kitchen to make a quick salad for dinner and then I came back to eat it in front of the television. I watched the news reports late into the night hours while I lay in bed until my eyelids refused to stay open and then I turned it back on again as soon as I woke the next morning. It was tear-jerking when the camera zoomed in on the gurney carrying his thin body under the sheet as it was wheeled out of the hospital. The sadness of it made me lose my appetite and I sat there with my toast and egg growing cold in front of me while I was hypnotized by the unbelievable news on the screen. The images held me there for over an hour until I was late for work.

***

I had been employed at Scott Edwards Investments for twelve years as a broker and financial advisor for individual investors. I was the Department Leader at the Nashville branch office located in the North Hamilton Mall. My associates, Suzanne and John, had both been there for less than five years, late to the party of high flying stock prices and commissions, and disconcerted about the recent bear market.

The television in the reception area of the office, usually tuned in to the business reports of MSNBC throughout the day, was on CNN when I walked through the door.

"It's so sad, its surreal," Suzanne said, wiping a tear from her make-up free face and pushing her mousy brown hair off the top of her heavy rimmed glasses.

Suzanne was our branch office administrator. Raised in Boston, she was a recent Vanderbilt University graduate with an MBA who obviously had been told to tone down her personal appearance to appear more professional.

"He was a drug addict. I don't feel sorry for him," John added.

He was our resident ass-hole in the office, pompous and narcissistic. He had climbed his way down out of the Appalachian hills of Eastern Kentucky by way of technical schools and community colleges and was determined to make the trek all the way to Wall Street as a broker. He still hated anybody who had, in his opinion, undeservedly achieved more success than he did.

"Have a heart, the man lost his life," I said, giving John a disgusted look as I paused to listen to the latest report.

"He did it to himself," he said dryly.

"How do you know? Do you have psychic powers we don't know about?" I asked without masking my displeasure with his attitude. "There's a whole different perspective when you're on the outside looking in."

I shook my head in annoyance and continued on into my office. I left the door open to the lobby so I could hear the ongoing news reports. Throughout the morning I kept hearing words like "propofol" and Benzedrine and accusations of his hired doctor's negligence and incompetence wafting in the air.

"It doesn't make any sense; the man had all that money and he still wasn't happy," John said, standing in front of the TV screen in an off-the-rack khaki-colored suit that barely hung over his wrist and ankles.

"Money isn't the answer to everything," Suzanne told him, wearing the frown she couldn't shake whenever he was around. "Haven't you heard it can't buy happiness?"

"Yeah, I have, but why should I take the word of a poor man," he said, smirking and running his hand over his reddish blonde hair.

"Is the monthly report ready to forward to the main office?" I shouted out to them, tired of hearing them bicker over things their young asses had yet to learn about.

Michael Jackson's death was a colossal media sensation and they played the story incessantly over the next few days. There were reports that he had been addicted to pain killers and drugs that he needed to help him sleep ever since the infamous Pepsi commercial where his hair inadvertently caught on fire. There were countless interviews on TV and in the newspaper with people who'd worked for him, his friends, and family, and they all referred to his dependence on prescription drugs for more than ten years. His doctors and medical caregivers provided further insight to his health and frame of mind. There was one television interview with a nurse who worked for him for some months that fascinated me.

"Did you know that he was using Dipravan?" the reporter asked.

"No, I didn't," the nurse answered, "Although he did tell me he needed something to make him fall asleep right away to get

Chapter One

through the rehearsals for his upcoming concert."

"Do you know if he was taking the Diprivan or any other prescribed drugs for sleeping when you were treating him?"

"No, he wasn't, we discussed the situation and then we tried some holistic treatments and eliminated some stimulants that he took that could have been keeping him awake."

"Was he satisfied with the results from those treatments?" the anchor asked.

"He followed my directions and he was able to sleep for about five hours."

"That sounds like a reasonable amount of sleep for a man his age."

"I thought that I had proven to him that he didn't need any drugs but he wasn't satisfied," the nurse replied.

From the interview I could see that the nurse felt she had demonstrated to Michael Jackson that the propofol was just a physical addiction and he didn't really need it. Nonetheless, he continued to rely on it regularly. The more I thought about the conversation I was further convinced that it was more than sleep that he was dependent on.

The interview played over and over in my mind for days because in many ways I sympathized with Michael's situation. I could relate to what the nurse said about him not being satisfied. It's not about just being able to sleep or getting a certain amount of hours sleep; it's the quality of the sleep, the restfulness of the sleep, the tranquility of the sleep, and how you feel when you wake up. The nurse discounted what he may have experienced when he was asleep. There was no mention of any disturbances or dreams that could have troubled him. She obviously didn't understand the lack of peace in his sleep that maybe he didn't get without the drug. I understood how that peace could become so valuable and what lengths you might go to achieve it.

Nothing was supposed to go wrong. He always hired doctors to monitor his vital signs while he slept. In so many ways it was a gamble, he laid his life on the line every night, and most people would never consider taking that chance, but they hadn't walked in his shoes, for him it was more than worth the risk.

His desperation would resonate louder in my mind on the nights that I laid awake, wanting to sleep but afraid of my own dreams. I began to empathize with the man who I now thought was a kindred spirit. He had found his way to rest through the night and somehow I could feel it was more than that. I needed to know more. Over the following months my simple curiosity turned into an obsession. I had been struggling with sleeplessness and nightmares of my own for several years and that made this personal for me. I had grown weary of the nights I couldn't sleep and the nights when my sleep was neither peaceful nor restful. I wanted my serenity back, I wanted to dream sweet dreams, and I believed Michael Jackson had found the answer.

***

I had lost my peace of mind three years ago when I received another startling phone call. It was from the coach at Harrison High School.

"Is this Mrs. Portia Roberts, Nicholas' mother?"

Chapter One

"Yes, it is," I answered inquisitively.

"Mrs. Roberts, there was an incident at football practice this afternoon. Nicholas is at St. Luke Hospital, I've spoken with your husband and he is on the way there to pick you up."

"Oh Lord, what happened? What is it? Is Nick all right?" I asked anxiously, even though I was afraid of the answer.

The coach hesitated for a moment before he started to speak. "We were at practice this afternoon and Nick ran out for a long pass, caught it, and started running full speed across the field, then he stopped suddenly and dropped the ball. Nick seemed confused for a second and then he collapsed on the thirty-five yard line. Two of the coaches and a few other players rushed over to him and saw he wasn't breathing. One of the assistant coaches did CPR until the ambulance came around seven minutes later."

I couldn't stand to listen to him anymore. Trembling with the horror of it I dropped the phone and ran out of the office just as Raymond pulled up in the front.

"Oh my God, Raymond, what's happening?" I said, jumping into the car.

"I don't know, Portia. We need to get to the hospital," he said, speeding back into the intersection.

We got to the St. Luke emergency room in less than ten minutes. I burst out of the car door and ran ahead of Raymond pushing the sluggish automatic door out of my way.

"We're the parents of Nicholas Roberts," I declared to the woman sitting behind the glass at the entrance between my quick breaths.

"You can go through those doors into the waiting area," she said indifferently, looking back at her computer screen and pointing to her left, "The medical team is still working on him."

Raymond grabbed my hand before I could break the glass to strangle her and pulled me into the waiting room where we saw the two football coaches were waiting. I sat down on a wooden chair covered in blue vinyl while Raymond went over to talk with them. I closed my eyes and prayed, and prayed, and prayed some more, rocking back and forth until I felt hot like I had a fever.

Twenty minutes later, although it seemed like forever, two doctors in long white coats came out, one was tall, Hispanic, and older, and the other was short, Indian, and younger with thick glasses.

"Hello, Mr. and Mrs. Roberts, I'm Dr. Gervis and this Dr. Jindal. Your son, Nicholas, went into sudden cardiac arrest during his practice today. Has he had any history of heart disease?" the tall and older, Dr. Gervis asked.

"No, he hasn't," Raymond answered quickly.

"How old is your son?" the short Dr. Jindal asked, looking between the both of us.

"He's seventeen years old," I said, leaping to my feet, terrified, tired of the questions, and needing to hear that he was out of danger.

"Your son, Nicholas, is on life support right now," the tall one said.

My legs buckled under me and I dropped back down into the seat.

Then he sat down beside me to explain, "His brain has gone without oxygen for an undetermined period of time and we will have to wait for more tests but it doesn't look good right now."

"Can I see him?" I asked with my hands still pressed together from praying.

"Certainly," he said, standing on his feet.

Raymond and I held onto each other with both doctors leading us into the intensive care unit where Nicholas was. I nearly fainted when I saw my baby hooked up to all those tubes but when I got closer to the bed he just looked like he was sleeping. Raymond and I stood at the side of the bed distraught and stared at our son in silence; it was too much to comprehend. We hadn't been in there but a few minutes when the door opened and there was my meddlesome next-door neighbor Cynthia standing with Pam.

"I heard what happened to Nick, Portia, so when Pam came home I thought I should bring her right to the hospital."

"Thank you, Cynthia, for bringing her," I said, meeting her at the door, putting my arm around Pam, and blocking her from coming any further. She backed up and I closed the door. I truly appreciated her help but I also knew she was too nosey for her own good.

"Daddy, is Nick gonna be okay?" I heard Pam ask Raymond.

"He's got to be, baby," he said, wrapping his arm around her and pulling her close.

I moved over next to them and we pulled the chairs close to the bed and sat there in the room with Nick, holding hands in the quiet not knowing what to say to comfort each other.

The tall Dr. Gervis came in a few hours later and said, "I think it will do you all some good to go home and get some rest."

We didn't want to go but it was becoming too much on Pam to see her brother like that. We decided to take the doctor's advice and drive her home where she could eat, shower, and get some rest.

The whole thing was beyond my scope of reality. My son was healthy and strong, he'd played in sports from the time he could walk. He'd had all his physicals; he'd never shown any signs of heart trouble. When we finally got home we were all exhausted, unable to process what had happened, and unable to talk to each other. Neither Raymond nor I were much support to Pam who was in her senior year of high school. I watched helplessly as she closed her bedroom door behind her. I tossed and turned in our bed with my world crashing down upon me. I prayed to wake up from this unspeakable nightmare, I prayed for the survival of my family, and I prayed for a miracle.

Neither Raymond nor I slept for even a minute that night and in the morning he spoke. "Portia, Nick is already gone; the doctors already informed me that there wasn't any brain activity. I think we should take him off of the ventilator today, waiting for a few more days or a week won't make it any easier on any of us. We have to accept what has happened."

How was I supposed to respond? Never in a million years would I have imagined this dreadful circumstance. All I could do was nod in agreement. We went to the hospital early before Pam woke up and gave them permission to take our child off of the life support.

From that day when I had to let Nicholas go my night hours were torturous from which I had no relief. I had gotten over the questions of whether we had done the right thing. I had accepted

Chapter One

the fact that it actually happened and that he was in a better place like everybody kept telling me, but I couldn't bear not seeing him again, not talking or touching him again for the rest of my life. I spent my days begging God to give me one more opportunity to talk to him.

The hours that I lay in the bed before falling asleep were the most heart wrenching. That was when my mind was filled with painful memories of him laying in that hospital bed. Then there were the nights when I slept and the dreams where I saw Nicholas again but he never spoke, the connection between us was always out of reach. They were the kind of dreams where you'd rather just stay awake.

The hole in our family grew bigger in the following months and Raymond and I were 180 degrees apart. Pam graduated from high school and moved on campus at Tennessee State University at the end of the summer, probably relieved to be out of the perpetual grieving that had become our new normal. We carried on with our lives like robots programmed to go through the motions of our daily activities. I still remember the conversation we had before he left.

"Portia, I'm drowning," he said one morning after he got out of the shower.

"What are you talking about?" I asked him, confused, since he was out of the tub.

"I have to get away and be by myself for a while until I can get my head above water."

"We're all drowning Ray, not just you. Why do you think

you're so special that you can walk away?"

"I can't help you, baby, if I can't help myself. Half of me is dead and the other half is slipping away. If I don't leave now, you'll be burying me next."

"So that's it, you're giving up."

"I'm sorry, Portia. I won't be coming back home this evening."

"You what, where are you going?"

"I don't know and it doesn't matter. There are too many memories for me here."

"Do you want to sell the house?"

"It's not just in the house."

"So you want to leave me, I'm the problem now."

"It's not that simple and I don't have any answers. I only know I can't live like this anymore."

That was that. True to his word Raymond didn't come home that evening. That was over two years ago that he left. He called pretty often to check on us at first but then as time went on the calls came further and further apart. Our split was amicable, not as enemies, I didn't blame him. We just weren't able to connect with each other anymore. So much had come between us, so many old arguments, so many unresolved issues, so many communication obstacles, and all of that with the added grief; we couldn't get through it and we couldn't get past it. We let it go.

Chapter Two

I watched an endless parade of television shows looking back over Michael Jackson's life in the following weeks. It was no secret that Michael was tormented in his waking hours by the media who refused to let go of the ridiculous child molestation accusations. We've all seen it before, it's always the same, some people build you up just so they can tear you down. The higher the height you attain the more intense the desire to see you fall.

I sensed there was something that he got during those drug-induced hours that sustained him, something that was worth the incredible risk that he took every night. I had to know what it was; it became a preoccupation for me. I wanted to experience it just once. I needed to test it for myself. I couldn't explain my fixation except to say that I felt it would make all the difference in my own life. I had to get some of the propofol, but how? It wasn't like I could buy it over the counter or get my doctor to write a prescription for me. In my desperation I even considered scheduling some type of procedure like a colonoscopy or something else where it was used, but that wasn't the way he did it. He used it at home in his own bed and that was the way it had to be for me.

For weeks I pondered the first step of my plan. How was I going to conduct my new research project? Where could I get some of the drug? It wasn't like weed, crack, or even pain pills that were easily available in the hood any time of the day. I would have to get a doctor to get access just like Michael did, but how could I do that? I made a decent living but I didn't have the kind of money to hire a private physician. Clearly I couldn't go into the hospital or a doctor's office and say give me some propofol. So then began my master plan to find my doctor, one I could convince to take part in my private experiment.

Now I had something to focus my life and energy on, I was on a mission, I had a purpose in this new journey of mine and its success would have to include a doctor. I wasn't really interested in dating but I had to make contact in some way to get to know some of them personally. So there I was trying to think of ways to connect, trying to find my doctor. Where do doctors hang out? Where do they go for recreation? Don't they play a lot of golf or do they play tennis? I wondered if I should learn to play golf. I had a dilemma. How was I to enter that exclusive social circle? I didn't want a long term relationship with anyone. I wasn't interested in getting another husband. I just wanted to meet someone who would help me get what I wanted.

I was sitting at my desk at work on a Friday afternoon when the light bulb came on. It was so simple; I needed to work in a hospital. That was an environment where I would be in close proximity to a large population of doctors. Except that was a major negative aspect, changing jobs was a huge step. I had pretty much withdrawn myself in a tiny world where I only came in contact with a few people each day. It was a comfortable

Chapter Two

retreat when I didn't feel like dealing with the daily drama of the universe. I bounced the notion around in my mind for the rest of the evening and early in the morning, around 7:00, I called my sister Paula; she was my sounding board whenever I got ready to make a big decision. She and I are two years apart, she's the older one but most people think we're twins. Our mother passed away when we were teenagers and ever since then we have always been there for each other through hell and high waters.

"Hey, Paula, how are you and Charles doing?" I asked congenially.

Charles is my brother-in-law. He and Paula are one of the few couples I know that are still as much in love as they were twenty years ago. I have wondered on many occasions if it had anything to do with the fact that they had chosen not to have any children.

"We're sleeping," she answered dryly, "What are you doing up so early?"

"I'm just restless; I feel like it's time for me to make some serious changes to get out of my rut."

"There you go," she said, waking up and sounding optimistic, "Now you're talking, what's on your mind?"

"I'm thinking about switching jobs, getting out of my comfort zone and doing something new in a totally different environment."

"All right, Portia, I heard that. The stock markets are beginning to recover. Are you thinking about making a move to a larger firm?"

"Maybe, I don't know, but I'm going to put some feelers out and see what comes up."

"Well you got my vote, sister; I'm for anything that gets you motivated and thinking about you and your future."

"I hear you. Well, thanks for listening to me before you've filled your belly; I know that's a tremendous sacrifice for you."

"Stop your mess, girl. Anyway, how's my niece doing?"

"She's good, staying busy, moving from classes to internships, I hardly get to see her anymore."

"Well, if you feel like you're getting that empty nest syndrome, do yourself a favor and get a dog or a hobby or something."

"I'll keep that in mind, sister. Now go back to sleep."

"Bye, girl," she whispered before she hung up.

***

By Monday morning I was committed to leaving Scott Edwards Investments. Sitting there idle for the better part of each day, apart from pink sheet orders, was starting to bore me. Now that I had a new mission I was beginning to see my cushy job as a huge waste of valuable time. The majority of our clients were individual investors who were making their own trades on line without any advice from us. That coupled with the slow recovery from the stock market crash my commissions were down and I hadn't seen a decent bonus in a dozen quarters. Giving up my position wouldn't be a great financial loss at all. Besides, I would probably be open to doing something completely different even if I didn't have a specific purpose.

"Good morning, Portia," Suzanne said when I walked in, "Did you enjoy your weekend?"

"It went by too fast but it was a productive one. How about

Chapter Two

yourself?" I asked, feeling a tinge of guilt about my plans to leave her there alone with John.

"I started a new diet, it's a part of the new self-improvement program I'm beginning. I think it's time to make some positive changes. I'm ready for a new me."

"Good for you, Suzanne, it is always the perfect time for a make-over, don't get discouraged no matter what," I said, the words meant for her as well as myself. "By the way, where's John this morning? He's usually here complaining about something by now."

"Car trouble he said, I guess he'll be in later."

"I'll let you savor the peace and quiet for as long as you can," I said, shutting the door to my office behind me.

I turned on my computer and got busy. Three hours later my laptop was hot to the touch and had started blowing air out of its back. I had searched through every available position at all the major hospitals in the city. Then I found the ideal job at Metropolitan General Hospital.

The job description was for a financial advisor for retirement and estate planning for employees. That was right up my alley and I hastily registered on their website and applied for it. Where else could I find a plethora of eligible doctors to choose from? Granted, some of them would not be eligible but they were certified and suitable candidates for my experiment.

I was pleased that my plan was progressing nicely when I received an e-mail for a phone interview from their Human Resources Department before the week was out. I locked my office door ten minutes before the appointed time to ensure I wouldn't be interrupted.

"Hello Ms. Roberts, this is Mr. Patterson calling."

"Yes, Mr. Patterson, I have been waiting for your call."

We talked at length about my education and job history including my present position and then he provided me with the full job description of the position. The subject drifted to sports and entertainment and by the end of the phone conversation I was scheduled for another interview at the hospital in the following week.

Chapter Three

Doubts and fears started to fill my head like storm clouds when I pulled into the visitor's parking space outside of the hospital and I was having second thoughts. The bad memories flashed back and my first instinct was to back my car out and speed away. All of sudden I wasn't so sure I could work in a hospital environment after the traumatic experience I had with Nicholas. From that terrible day when we resigned ourselves to the inevitable, turned off the machines, and I had to walk out without him I hated hospitals; all I could think about is the suffering of the patients and their families. I knew first hand that there was so much sadness and misery inside the walls. I had since avoided them like the plague.

"Get it together," I scolded myself, making an effort to calm my nerves. I was determined to continue on my quest. I took a few moments to psych myself out since I was early for my interview. I tried to think about all the positive things that happened in hospitals, all the fortunate people who were healed and found relief there. I had to remind myself about the birth of my children in the hospital and all the miracles that take place there every day. Five minutes later I got out of the car with a renewed perspective and prayed that I would find the miracle I was searching for in there also.

"Welcome to Metro General, Ms. Roberts," Mr. Patterson,

Director of Human Services, said with a firm handshake. "It's a pleasure to finally meet you in person."

"Thank you, sir, I'm glad to be here," I said as I followed close behind his heels to his palatial office.

Inside, he took a seat behind his desk and I sank down deep in one of his plush office chairs facing him. He smiled at me before he began to talk.

"Can I offer you some coffee or water?" he asked politely.

"No, sir, I'm fine, thank you," I answered.

"Ms. Roberts, I've read your resume and we've talked extensively on the phone. I have no reservations about your ability to be an asset to this hospital and our staff. Are there any questions or concerns that you would like to address?" he asked as he reared back in his chair with crossed his legs and the fingertips of his hands touching.

"No, Mr. Patterson," I answered as self-assuredly as I could while being swallowed up by the chair. "You have been very thorough and informative in our conversations and I feel confident that it would be a smooth transition for me."

"In that case, I'd like to offer you the executive level administrator position in the Financial Benefits Division of our Human Resources Department."

"That's wonderful, thank you, sir," I said with a smile spreading across my face, "I'm very happy to accept this opportunity to work with you here at Metro General."

"You may find it to be a little less exciting here at the hospital than trading stocks on a regular basis but I think you'll adapt

Chapter Three

well to our more laid-back environment."

"That's exactly what I'm hoping for," I said, "I'd like to get out of the pressure cooker and simmer for a while."

"As stated in the job description your responsibilities will include advising our employees on their insurance needs and retirement accounts."

"That sounds unproblematic, I'm anxious to get started," I said, pleased about being one step closer to fulfilling my plan.

"Fantastic, now let me show you to your office down the hall."

With some effort I dug my body out of the chair to accompany him. He had a long gait so I lengthened my steps to keep up. We marched stride for stride with our heels clicking loudly in unison against the marble floor. At the end of the hallway, Mr. Patterson opened the door to the office suite that had Financial Planning painted on it and handed me a set of keys. Inside, there was a young woman who looked around twenty-five years old sitting at a desk in the outer office.

"Ms. Roberts, this is Keisha Manning, your administrative assistant."

She was nice-looking and fashionably dressed, even though her style leaned towards ghetto fabulous with a light brown and blond streaked weave, low-cut blouse, and earrings that draped down to her shoulders.

"Nice to meet you, Ms. Roberts," she said, standing up to give me a light hug.

I couldn't help but smile when she towered above me in her seven-inch platform heels.

"It's a pleasure to meet you too, Keisha," I responded and trailed Mr. Patterson to the office behind her desk.

"Keisha can help you get oriented and if you have any other questions or need anything I'm right down the hall," he said, stopping at the door.

"Thank you again for the opportunity, Mr. Patterson."

"You're most welcome," he said as he turned and walked out.

I sat down in the huge burgundy leather chair at my new desk and admired my lavish new office. It was amazing to me that I had come to this point in my mission. I swiveled around in my chair to face the window and took in the view of the parade of white coats walking across hospital courtyard and it looked promising.

***

It turned out to be the perfect situation, more than I had dared to expect. Traffic through the office was always brisk with the greater portion of the professional employees being concerned about their portfolios and anxious to make adjustments they hoped would recover the losses in their 401K accounts. Within my first month on the job I had met nearly every medical person on staff. The majority of the doctors on staff were extremely assertive individuals who walked around the hospital like they were rock stars. I imagine you have to be that type of individual with a huge ego to take the lives of so many people in your hands. Some were condescending when they came into the office and talked to me like I was one of their nurses, and then there were those who were particularly personable.

Chapter Three

"Excuse me, Ms. Roberts," a heavy voice said with a gentle knock on the door.

I looked up over my reading glasses into the face of a very attractive man wearing a long white coat. He was just shy of six feet, pecan-colored skin with dark brown eyes, his head was bald but he had a thick mustache and beard. I could see from his muscular arms and shoulders under the coat that he worked out on a regular basis.

"Your assistant isn't at her desk at the moment; do I need to make an appointment to speak with you for few a minutes?"

"No, that's not necessary, I have some time, come on in," I said, taking off my glasses to give him my full attention.

"I'm Dr. Keith Whitman; I spoke with you on the phone a few weeks ago and requested that my insurance beneficiary be changed."

"Yes, I remember our conversation, please take a seat, Dr. Whitman, I had that done for you, all I need is your signature," I said, looking for the file on the computer. I found it and clicked print for a paper copy. "The only beneficiary will be Miriam Whitman, is that right?"

"Yes," he answered, staring deep into my eyes making me a little uncomfortable.

"One more thing, I need to check the relationship of the beneficiary. Is Miriam your spouse?" I asked, glancing over the paper work.

"No, that's my mother, I'm single and available he said with emphasis.

Those were the magic words that turned him into my first prospect.

"A handsome doctor unattached, how does that happen?" I asked jokingly.

"I'm very particular about the women I get involved with," he answered with all seriousness.

"I guess you have to be discriminating as a successful man in your profession, Dr. Whitman."

"Please, call me Keith," he said, sitting back in the chair.

"So what type of doctor are you, Keith?" I inquired.

"I specialize in Orthopedics and Sports Medicine."

"That sounds interesting you must work with a lot of athletes."

"I do, but believe it or not most of my patients are overweight with bad knees and feet."

"That's surprising," I remarked with a smile.

He sat there for another minute staring and smiling back at me and I started to feel embarrassed, it was like he had super human powers that allowed him to see through my clothes. He wasn't shy about letting his eyes wander.

"Is there something else that you need to address today?" I asked, attempting to finish up with the business at hand.

"Yes, you can let me take you out for drinks."

I looked down at the paper work on my desk again and quickly scanned it with my eyes to find his date of birth. It was a drawback; he was only thirty-three years old, twelve years younger than me.

"Are you sure you wouldn't prefer to take my assistant out,

she's closer to your age?"

"If I wanted to take her out I would have asked her. Personally, I prefer a woman who's already got her act together."

"Good answer, doctor," I said with a nod, "I'll think about it."

"You do that, Ms. Roberts," he said, standing up to leave.

I could smell his fresh clean scent as I escorted him to the door.

"Please call me, Portia," I said as he walked out.

I was hesitant about getting close to Keith, he was young and cocky, but it might mean he would be less rigid to my request. Nevertheless, after that day he came by every morning to say hello and flirt with me for a few minutes. I let him enjoy the chase for a while, and I must admit I enjoyed it myself, but from the change in Keisha's mood I could tell she was feeling jealous of the attention he gave me. It was time to take our friendship outside of the office.

"Thank God it's Friday," he said, peeking in my office door at the end of the day.

"Amen to that," I said, shutting down my computer, "It's been a long week."

"Why don't we get the weekend started right?"

"How do you propose we do that?"

"Let me take you out for drinks after you get done."

"How about I meet you there?" I said, giving him a knowing look.

From the rise in his eyebrows I knew I had surprised him. He had been diligently asking me out for nearly a month and I had consistently declined.

"Now that's what I'm talking about," he said, nodding his head in agreement, "The Zanzibar around seven."

"Okay, I'll see you there."

I usually dressed in conservative professional attire at work but I knew how to turn on the charm when I wanted to. I decided that for my serious mission I needed to go home, change clothes, and bait my hook as they say. I put on a form-fitting gold colored dress that was sexy but still classy with shoes to match. I usually kept my hair held back with combs or pinned up because I don't like it hanging in my face but this evening I chose to let it hang down. I put on lip gloss instead of lipstick thinking it would give me more of a youthful glow. I stood in front of the full-length mirror and took a long look. I still looked good, even if I say so myself, but I hadn't been out with a younger man since the time I was a younger woman and I felt a little self-conscious.

I walked into the dimly lit bar with the air of confidence that I called on whenever I needed to command a situation. I did a swift search of the room and saw Keith sitting at a table near the window with a drink in front of him. Strategic move, I thought, remembering the long ago days of dating and tactical game-playing before I was married. He had chosen a spot where he could see whoever came in. I knew then that he had been watching for me and had probably given me the once-over as I walked in.

"No problem," I said silently, "I'm dealing with a player. Fortunately for me he's somewhat young in the game." He stood up behaving as a gentleman when I approached the table.

Chapter Three

"Good evening, Ms. Roberts," he said as he pulled the chair out for me to sit down. I moved toward the seat with him standing so close behind me I could feel his breath on my neck.

"Being that it's after hours I insist that you call me Portia."

He smiled, sat down across from me, and took a sip from his glass.

"What would you like to drink, Portia?" he asked, licking his lips.

"An apple martini would be nice," I answered and he grinned as if I had revealed some inner secret about myself with my drink selection.

That was one of the things you lose as you get older, the false sense of knowing more than you actually do. He motioned for the waitress who'd just brought drinks to the next table.

"An apple martini for the lady and another one for me," he said, pointing at his glass.

"Sure thing," she answered.

She looked like a cute college student and she smiled at Keith as she took the order and then gave me a quick up and down critique before she walked away. It didn't bother me one bit, I was well past the point of petty jealousies that some women have when they're competing for the attention of a man.

Waiting for my drink to come I took the opportunity to get to know Keith a little better.

"Nearly all of the doctors working at the hospital are from out of town or out of the country. Are you from Nashville or someplace else?" I asked.

"Someplace else, I'm from D.C., born and bred, I went to Howard for undergrad and medical school," he said proudly, and then he barked like a dog for an exclamation point that let me know he was an Omega.

"I hear you," I said with a nod, "Another successful product from a HBCU."

"That's right, but this is all about you tonight. I want to hear something about you that I don't know," he said as the waitress set our drinks down on the table.

"Okay, I'm also a HBCU grad; I went to TSU for undergrad and my MBA. Right now I'm separated and I have a daughter who's a junior at Tennessee State."

"Separated," he said thoughtfully, "I don't understand how a man with half a head on his shoulders would let you get away."

"It's complicated, different things come between people and they grow apart, that's life."

"You seem like you dealing with it, I mean you're looking very good," he said with a sexy smile.

"I guess I'm proof that the way you feel doesn't have to show on your face," I said, returning his sexy smile. We had a few more drinks and talked some more before I told him, "There comes a time when women need their beauty rest."

"You definitely don't fit in that category," he said.

"Thanks, but I get cranky without it," I said as I stood up to leave.

"When can I see you again?" he asked.

"Whenever you want, just call me," I said, handing him one of

Chapter Three

my cards with my cell number and e-mail address.

Driving home I felt energized, I had taken the second step and it wouldn't be long before I would be under the euphoric sedation of propofol and the intriguing mystery behind it would be revealed to me along with pleasant dreams that I prayed included Nicholas. The complication of my plan and its shortcomings surfaced when my cell phone rang as soon as I closed the door behind me at home.

"I want to see you now," Keith said on the other end using his deep sexy voice.

"You've got to be kidding," I said to myself before I answered him. "You've already seen me several times today. Be patient, good things come to those who wait," I said in my alluring voice before I hung up.

This was definitely going to be a challenge to get his mind to move away from the crotch, it seems these younger generations fuck first and asks questions later.

For the next week every time Keith had a break in his schedule he was in my office trying to get next to me. I don't think he was interested in anything serious, he just wanted to date, which was fine by me, but he was always talking about when we were going to hook up. It was not a good look and very unprofessional. I am a firm believer in keeping work and private life separate.

The 'Taste of Nashville' food festival was coming up on the weekend so I invited him to go. It would be a chance to relax and talk without all the anxieties and Keisha listening in at the door. I wanted us to take our own cars and meet downtown but he insisted that he was a gentleman and wanted to pick me up at my house, so I gave him my address. I decided to tone down my outfit because this fish was already on the line and I might have to throw it back. I put on a sequined tank top, a pair of Capri jeans, some flat sandals, and pulled my hair in a ponytail.

Keith got there around 6:00, pulling up in a big white Hummer. I came to the door with my cross-over bag on my shoulders and my keys in hand, ready to walk out. He was dressed casual in jeans and a muscle t-shirt that fit tight around his biceps and hugged his six-pack. I have to admit he was enticing; the problem was I had a different agenda. It wasn't that I was against Malcolm X's philosophy of "by any means necessary," I just needed to be assured that he could be persuaded to go that extra mile to get what he wanted.

"Nice, you're wearing those jeans," he said, opening the door and helping me up in his jeep.

"I'm not all business; I like to kick back and relax sometimes."

He turned the ignition and Drake leading a quartet of rappers in "Forever," the explicit version, blasted through surround-sound speakers. I clicked my seatbelt and prayed for consecutive green lights to cut the ride short.

We parked in the parking lot of the courthouse and walked to the entrance of festival where he bought us a big stack of tickets and handed them to me.

"So what kinds of things do you like to do in your spare time?" I asked him as we walked toward the vendors.

"I like to make love to a beautiful woman," he said, flashing me his perfect row of bright white teeth and flexing the muscles in his chest.

"That much I've assumed, now what else do you like to do?" I asked, trying to keep the conversation on the light side.

"I like going to movies, I spend a lot of time working out in the gym, and I love sports, especially football," he answered.

I felt a shiver run through me, just the word football could send me off the deep end sometimes, but I composed myself, took a deep breath of all the mixed aromas on the street, and headed over to one of the vendors who was serving samples of barbeque ribs.

"I see you like to go for the meat," he said, watching me bite into the juicy pork.

"As a matter of fact I like it all," I said, "The meat, potatoes, the veggies, and the desert. Now I need something to drink."

He laughed and we walked a few more feet where they were serving wine.

"Ten tickets!" he exclaimed when he saw the price of a glass. "It better be good," he said while the bartender poured. "You never told me what type of things you like to do in your spare time?"

"As you can see, I like to eat good food. I'm a music lover, so I like going to concerts and listening to live music, but I really love to travel."

"That sounds nice, I'd like to take you away for a weekend," he said.

"Maybe in time, first let's see if we enjoy each other's company enough to go out of town together," I said, smiling.

We had a good time at the festival, drinking all the different wines and sampling all the food was relaxing, and we really got a chance to talk without any pressure. Keith told me about his family, he had two brothers, one older and one younger, and how his relationship with his father had been strained after he abandoned them when he left their mother for a younger woman. As he talked about it I began to understand his attraction to older women a little more.

He said he had never been in any serious relationships in college and now he preferred to concentrate on his career for while. He got bonus points for that because I wasn't looking for anything deep, just access to a certain medication. Around 9:30, I was full, had a buzz from the wine and beer we'd sampled, and my feet were tired from walking on the concrete and asphalt in my no-arch-support sandals.

I grabbed onto his arm to hold myself up and he asked, "Are you ready to go in?"

"The heat and all that alcohol is taking a toll," I said with a laugh.

We made it back to the jeep and we drove to my house with the windows down. I leaned back against the headrest and closed my eyes trying to imagine how I should broach the subject that I needed so much to discuss, but we were in my driveway before I even had time to sober up. Keith opened my door, helped me out, and escorted me to the door. I got out my keys, unlocked the door, and when I walked in he stepped in behind me.

Chapter Three

"Portia, I'd like to spend some more time with you," he said, "I've had a nice time and I don't want it to end yet."

"Have a seat," I told him in the living room, thinking it would give us some more time to talk. "Would you like something to drink?"

"Yeah, I'll have beer and some dessert," he said, licking his lips again.

He never stops I thought but I went into the kitchen and got a beer. I needed him relaxed and off guard while we talked. However, the truth of the matter was that he didn't want to talk anymore. As soon as I sat down beside him he grabbed the back of my ponytail and starting kissing me deep down in my throat while his other hand was working nonstop with the skill of a trained doctor to get me out of my clothes.

I hadn't anticipated things getting this far until I knew if he and I were on the same page in terms of my plan but the cart had gotten in front of the horse. Keith was exploring and touching my body and I was feeling turned on by him and the idea of being wanted by a younger man. His body was tight and muscular and it wasn't the worst thing that could happen to me. It had been a long time since I had been with Raymond and even though I had my issues, I now realized there were other needs that hadn't been attended to. My greatest concern at the moment was Keith seeing my body. I worked out and did some yoga in attempts to renew my mind, body, and spirit as I had been advised after the tragedy but I hadn't been in my twenties for a very long time. Suddenly I felt insecure about the age difference between us.

I stopped him and said, "Why don't we take this to the bedroom and get more comfortable."

Not to mention the free condoms they handed out at work were in my nightstand and I didn't need anything else to worry about.

Sex with Keith was a flashback of my twenties and early thirties, the sheer energy and desire without all the passion and love, satisfaction for satisfaction's sake and nothing else. Yet, it felt good to get lost in the experience and excitement of a different man after twenty years. He was a generous lover, except it seemed like he had something to prove, not to me, but rather to himself. After the second round he lay asleep beside me. I watched his body rise and fall with each breath and wondered if he was dreaming or if his subconscious rested in the afterglow of his climax. I stirred around in the bed until the movement finally woke him up.

"You okay?" he asked.

"Not really," I said, "I have problems sleeping most of the time."

"Really, what's that about?"

"It started about three years ago and there's nothing that seems to help."

"Have you seen a doctor, because I think I can help," he said, reaching for me again.

"I have," I said in serious tone to put him off.

"Well, what was the diagnosis?"

"They prescribed some sleep medications, but I was told that there is no medical explanation for it and I should try some diet

Chapter Three

changes or yoga."

"That sounds like good advice."

"I've heard that during the residency a lot of the interns suffer with insomnia from being up so many hours at a time."

"That's true," he said, "The body clock gets confused and it's very hard to rest."

"How did you deal with it?" I asked, glad that we were finally on subject.

"I had some friends who did some pretty radical things to get some sleep but I would never do that. I've never taken drugs of any kind; I think it's a sign of weakness."

"Did you have a problem with your colleagues who weren't as strong as you?" I asked.

"Yes, I did," he answered, slightly agitated, "Once you take the Hippocratic Oath there are things you can't do or condone."

"I hear you," I said as I slid down under the covers and closed my eyes. This was a dead end and there was no way around it.

I didn't blame Keith for his high principles; I even admired them and hoped he'd be able to sustain them through all this life has to offer. Once upon a time I had steadfast principles of my own but I know that this life can take you through some things that will have you compromising yourself in ways you never thought you would just to survive. It's easy to be strong when you've never had to suffer, pain is the game changer, and those of us who have to endure it are forever trying to find ways to soothe it.

In my life I had experienced so many levels and intensities of pain, mental, physical, and emotional like most people, but when a circumstance combines all three there is a breaking point. I didn't think I was the type who would ever need a crutch; I'd been standing on my own two feet without help from anybody, but losing Nicholas pulled the rug out from under me and now I have a disability. I don't like feeling like a victim or one of the walking wounded but I hurt. The one thing that renews the body and mind is sleep and I feel deprived because it's not working. If there's anything that can be done to get me out of this trap I'm going to find it.

Chapter Four

Now I had another dilemma, how to cool down this fire I started with Keith. He had come by the office everyday this week whenever he had a break. I feigned that I was overrun with a backlog of work and would most certainly have to work through the weekend. When the next weekend approached I told him it was homecoming at TSU and I would be spending most of it with my daughter Pam. Keith was an intelligent guy and after a few weeks he walked in my office, shut the door, and pulled the chair close up to my desk and sat down.

"Portia, what's the deal?" he asked, "Ever since we got busy you've been out of pocket. You don't have any time and I feel like you're playing me off. I thought we were cool and enjoying each other's company?"

I was cornered, he wanted an answer and I needed a way out. Then the lie fell out of my mouth so easy that it even surprised me.

"Keith, there is something going on with me and it has me really torn up. My husband came to see me right after you stayed over and we had a real conversation. He wants us to go into counseling and try to save our marriage. I was shocked because he never wanted to get counseling before so I feel like I owe it to my daughter and us as a family to try. You are such a dynamic man and I have enjoyed all the time that we spent together but you aren't really looking for anything serious so I think its best we chill for now. I don't want to get you mixed up in my complications."

He sat there for a while nodding his head up and down. Finally, he stood up, "I can respect that and I'm glad you decided to be honest with me," he said, and then he walked out.

I was relieved that the situation was resolved but I was feeling a tinge of remorse. I knew I misled him for my own personal reasons but then I thought it over for a few minutes and deduced that he hadn't really been hurt in any permanent way. I almost wanted to send him a thank you card for the night we got busy. It was refreshing to be up against a hard young man again, I thought those feelings were behind me. However, it was evaluation time; I had to figure out if I was willing to confront more possible tricky situations in my quest or should I abandon the mission and go back to business as usual. It didn't take me long to conclude that I was going further, I could feel it in my gut that this was going to make all the difference for me and I could move on and heal.

***

I looked over at the calendar hanging on the wall in my office and my heart sank. It was halfway through the month of November and Thanksgiving and Christmas were just around the corner. I had a ton of e-mails with party invitations, sale discounts, and donation requests to sift through. If I had my choice I'd just skip them all and start the New Year. I used to love all the holidays, planning, decorating, and seeing how much the kids enjoyed them. Now the happiest times of my life were over leaving me with only memories, and the saddest times of my life were painful flashbacks of which I couldn't escape.

"Time will heal your hurt, honey, just give it time," my sister Paula told me whenever we talked on the phone, but how much time would it take I wondered. If I didn't have to try to hold it together for Pam over the holidays I would probably get out of town to some place in the Caribbean where I could forget all about the season.

I was still hosting my pity party when Dr. George Reynolds tapped on the window. When I glanced up he walked in the door. I smiled to greet him even though I suspected it was slightly twisted. I liked Dr. Reynolds; he was always charming and owned any room he walked into. He was tall, about six-feet-two inches with broad shoulders. His hair was cut in a short fade and he wore reading glasses on a neck chain that he looked over whenever they were on his face. I had sat at a table with him at one of the employee recognition functions a few weeks ago. He was Chief Physician of the Intensive Care Unit. He had the combination of good looks mixed with maturity and that sexy dignified air that's only seen in men over the age of forty. He was from St. Maarten, Virgin Islands, and with his accent he could make Sean Connery fade into the background and disappear. He always made me think of an Almond Joy candy bar, dark, sweet and tropical, and with an added treat.

"Ms. Roberts, I have some serious major changes that I need you to handle for me and they have been a long time coming. I have been in what turned out to be a lengthy process of divorcing and yesterday I got my freedom papers."

"I would give you my condolences but you don't seem to be torn up about it," I said, looking him in the eye.

"Actually I am ecstatic, and once I make the necessary changes on my insurance and retirement accounts I can close the book on that drama. I would hate to die and have that woman benefit from my demise. Hell, she's probably making plans to take me out as we speak."

"Come on, Dr. Reynolds, it couldn't have been that bad."

"You weren't there my dear, although I wish you were," he said, flirting with me.

"Well, let's get this done for you as quickly as possible before she gets her posse together."

He gave me his social security number and the computer pulled up all his vital information. I removed her name from all his accounts and he named his son as beneficiary.

"Will any portion have to be paid out to her as part of the settlement?"

"No ma'am, she has gotten all she's going to get from me, case closed."

"All right, sir, then you are good to go," I told him after I printed out his copies of the paperwork.

"Thank you, my dear, if only my attorney had been so efficient."

"You're welcome," I said as I stood up to walk him out.

"Ms. Roberts, I'd like to take you to dinner to show my appreciation for you handling that urgent business for me," he said, turning around at the door.

"That's not necessary; I'm just doing my job."

"I understand that, but I just got divorced and I want to take a beautiful woman out to dinner. Is that a problem?"

"No, it's not, I'd love to have dinner with you," I said, inhaling his scent of Polo Blue; it was the familiar scent my husband used to wear.

"Perfect, I'll pick you up around seven-thirty."

"Don't you need my address?" I asked.

"I already have it," he said and walked down the hallway without looking back.

"Was this just a friendly dinner or was Dr. Reynolds interested?" I asked myself, wondering how he knew my address. He was a doctor and he had access to what I wanted but he was older and not so easy to manipulate. I decided not to read anything into the invitation, relax, and have a nice dinner; if nothing else it would probably help my mood.

That evening I looked through my closet for something more conservative to wear than sexy. I chose my short-sleeved black sheath dress and I pinned my hair up in a French roll. I definitely didn't want to give the wrong impression and move things too fast again. The doorbell rang at 7:30 on the dot. Dr. Reynolds was punctual and I liked that in a man, it showed consideration.

I hurried down the steps and opened the door.

"You look beautiful," he said.

I couldn't help but smile. "Thank you, doctor, and you look quite dapper yourself," I replied as I took notice of his charcoal black suit and purple paisley tie.

"I neglected to ask you to call me George," he said as he stepped inside the foyer.

"Welcome to my home, George, and you're welcome to call me Portia, give me a second while I grab my coat."

"I took the liberty of making reservations at Stoney River, is that fine with you or would you like to go someplace else?" he asked.

"That sounds fine," I said as I handed him my coat to help me. He was 'old school' and they appreciate a woman who lets them be the man.

"Your perfume smells divine," he said as he adjusted the coat on my shoulders.

"I wore it especially for you," I said, smiling again.

He opened the door and we stepped out in the crisp air and he put his arm around me to shield me from the brisk wind and we moved quickly to the curb to get inside his car. He opened the passenger side of his black Mercedes CLS550 and I slid onto the butter soft leather. George lifted the bottom of my coat that hung below the door into the car before he shut the door.

"Who said chivalry is dead," I mused, looking at all the bells and whistles across the dashboard while he walked around to get in on the driver's side. "Your car is gorgeous."

"I like nice things," he said, making eye contact.

"Don't we all," I said as I drank in the luxury.

The hostess at Stoney River led us to a private booth in the low-light area of the restaurant and George helped me take off my coat before we sat down. When the waiter came to greet us

Chapter Four

George ordered a bottle of red wine.

"I'm glad you came out with me tonight," he said "I didn't want to celebrate all by myself."

"I couldn't in good conscience let you come out and drink that bottle of wine alone."

The waiter returned in a flash and poured a small amount into George's glass. He swirled it, sniffed it, he took a sip, and then he nodded his approval.

"Are you all ready to order?" the waiter asked as he poured the wine.

"We'll have two filet mignon topped with jumbo crab," said George.

"Very good, sir," the waiter responded as he took away the menus.

"Let's toast to new endings and happy beginnings," he said with his glass raised.

"George, you are too much," I said before I touched his glass with mine and sipped some.

"I mean to be," he said with a chuckle, "I can't deny I'm feeling good, I just lost about 250 pounds."

"You're so wrong for that one; I've got to come to a sister's defense."

"What if I told you she wasn't a sister?" he said.

"Are you telling me you were a deserter?"

"Yes, I was, and it was a mistake from the beginning and a long story I might add."

"How about you make a long story short?" I asked, curious to know why so many professional brothers went there.

"Okay," he said, putting down his glass, "We met in college at the University of Pittsburgh, she was cute, intelligent, and I was looking to add a serious player to my team. She was a graduate student in a research lab where I was doing a fellowship. There was some jungle fever going on and we started dating. Long story short, she got pregnant during my residency, I married her, she quit school, had the baby, and she spent the next fifteen years gaining a hundred pounds. The good thing is that her family insisted we have a prenuptial agreement so that if we separated we would leave with whatever we brought to the marriage."

"Are you saying you were never in love?" I asked him.

"Probably not, things started off wrong and I couldn't make it right. Now what's your story?" he asked as the waiter brought the food to the table.

"My turn, okay, that's fair," I said. "We met in college, married for love, raised two children who are now on their own, but things happened, we grew apart, and we couldn't bring it back together. We've been separated for almost three years and we haven't spoken for two of them but I haven't taken the next step to divorce."

"Are you afraid of letting go and moving on or getting into a relationship with someone new?"

"I don't think so, I just needed some time to clear my head and be by myself for a while."

"To tell the truth, Portia, I liked being married, I'm a family man, it's just that we weren't compatible."

"You sound like you're ready to sign up for Match.com or BlackPeopleMeet already."

"I am, but I don't think I need their services just yet, I plan to go out with you again if you are interested."

"I think you should say what's on your mind and don't hold back," I said with at laugh to lighten the mood a bit.

"I'm serious, Ms. Roberts, I'm a busy man and don't have time to waste. I'm used to having a woman in my life and I think you're very special."

"We've gotten real personal this evening; you're not going to go back to calling me Ms. Roberts again are you?"

"I'll call you whatever you want, as long as I can keep calling you," he said, lifting up his glass for another toast.

George intrigued me, I'd never met a man who was this open and talked about his feelings so easily, he said what he wanted and what he needed. He renewed my faith in the male species. After dinner we drove around Centennial Park and it was so mellow in the darkness that I had to stop myself from kicking off my shoes and placing my seat in a serious lean.

He looked over at me and asked, "When can I see you again?"

"Don't you think we need to let this gel for a while first?"

"No, I don't, I've spent so much of my life compromising and now I'm going to live like there is no tomorrow. Now, I'll be out of town for the holidays, can we go to the movies on the Saturday after the holidays?"

This man kept me laughing and that was something that I didn't get a chance to do very often, so why shouldn't we go out again.

"Sure that sounds good to me."

He nodded his head and kept looking ahead as he drove. When he pulled up to my house, he opened my door, walked me to the door and kissed my hand and said, "Till the first Saturday."

It had been a pleasant evening and I enjoyed his company but I hadn't gotten any vibe that would have let me know if he would eventually be receptive to my proposition.

***

Pam came home for the Christmas holidays and I did my best to be upbeat, we hit all the malls on Black Friday like we always used to do. Even though I never let on to Pam, the sickening music over the intercom and the crowds of shoppers feverishly buying things that would probably be returned got on my nerves. No matter how hard I tried to stay positive it hurt whenever I saw some things that I would have bought as gifts for Nicholas. We even bought a live tree to decorate but it was difficult to maintain my Christmas spirit realizing that the holidays would never have the joy they had before we lost Nick.

On Christmas Eve I baked her favorite chocolate cake, placed her gifts under the tree, and went to bed early. My head had barely hit the pillow when the grief came in like a wave and covered me. I lay awake most of the night reliving all the nightmares that were my life three years ago, the phone call, the rush to the hospital, him laying there connected to all those tubes, turning off the life support, the funeral home, the coldness of his arm, and how he looked like somebody else.

The next morning I pasted on a happy face for Pam's sake and

Chapter Four

made a big breakfast. We exchanged gifts and called Paula and Charles with the phone on speaker to say Merry Christmas.

"Happy Jesus birthday," Paula answered cheerfully after the second ring.

"Merry Christmas to you too," I laughed, feeling better. Paula could always lift my spirits.

"We have to remember the reason for the season," she said, singing her words.

"Hey, Aunt Paula," Pam squealed into the receiver, "Thanks for the gift, I really needed it."

"You're welcome, niecey, don't spend it all in one place."

"She won't," I added, "She's tight with her money like her aunty."

"As she should be," Paula said, happily. "Anyway, I want you both to have a good day today."

"We will," Pam assured her.

"All righty then, we'll talk again before the New Year," Paula said.

Bye, P, tell Charles we said hello and Merry Christmas," I told her before hanging up.

Later on after dinner Pam got dressed and went to meet some friends. I changed into my flannel nightgown, spooned myself a big bowl of ice cream, and watched "It's a Wonderful Life."

***

I was feeling positive about the New Year beginning with the hope that it would be bring me the breakthrough I was hungry for. George was turning was the man that I'm sure many women fantasize about. Even though he had gone home to St. Maarten for the holidays he still sent me flowers on the job and called me the first thing in the morning and the last thing before he went to sleep just to say hello.

On the first Saturday of the New Year he called and said, "I'm back; it's time for us to see that movie today."

I could surely use a pick-me-up so I said, "How soon can you get here?"

He laughed, "I'll be there in a couple of hours."

Pam was having a lazy afternoon eating cold cereal in her pajamas in front of the television in the den.

"Guess who's going out to the movies on a date?"

"Who," she asked absentmindedly, crunching and staring into the TV screen.

"Me, that's who," I said in a higher volume over the TV.

That got her attention, she turned around and asked, "With who?"

"One of the doctors from work," I answered.

She just looked at me not knowing how to respond so I said, "It's nothing serious, he's just a friend."

That eased some of the shock and she said, "Have fun," and went back to watching the screen.

I showered, put on corduroy jeggings and a heavy sweater, and kept watch through the window for George with my coat in my hand not wanting to make any introductions today. When he pulled up I rushed out of the door before he had time to get out of the car.

Chapter Four

"You are ready to get out the house," he said jokingly as he got the door for me and I slid in the warm comfort of his Benz. He put in a smooth jazz CD and asked, "How was your holiday?"

"I've had better ones but it's good to have my daughter home."

"I hear you; this was certainly a lot different for me than last year, but it's going to get better."

"I hope so," I said, looking out the window at all the cars speeding along the interstate wondering if he would be the one.

We drove out to the Opry Mills Theater where he let me out at the door and then parked the car. I stood inside the door and looked up at the choices on the marquee.

"Have you seen "The Tourist," the critics say it's a good movie?" he asked, joining me.

"No, I haven't but the next show doesn't start until 4:00."

"We can kill an hour walking in the mall," he said, unperturbed, taking my hand.

We converged with the crowd of other restless souls in town who were out shopping or browsing to pass the time in the remaining days of the holiday break. Huge markdown and sale signs hung in most of the stores to attract buyers but we were content to window shop.

"You would look good in that dress," George said, pointing to an outfit in the Saks Fifth Avenue window.

"It's pretty but I don't know, it looks a little dramatic for me."

"What's wrong with that, don't hold yourself back, you're a beautiful lady."

"That was a boost for my self-confidence, thank you," I said, forcing a smile.

"You're kidding; you must really be having the blues. I'm going to have to fix that," he said, patting me on the back.

"I'm fine; the holidays just take a lot out of me."

"More than just money?" he chuckled.

"A lot more," I answered softly.

"Cheer up, pretty lady, you made it through and they're behind us for now."

He checked his watch and we turned back toward the theater. At the concession stand he bought popcorn, cokes, goobers, and a hot dog.

I smiled at the large order and he said, "I don't want you to get hungry."

George was always thoughtful and considerate, he even volunteered to go out for the drink and popcorn refills, but I was looking for something extremely specific in a man right now and it was non-negotiable.

Chapter Five

Pam had gone back on campus and George and I had been out at least twice a week for a month now and he wanted to take me away for a weekend in Las Vegas for Valentine's Day. He said he wanted to getaway to some place warm, and with the temperatures hovering around freezing and below in Nashville, that sounded like paradise. Besides, it was time to see if he would be the accommodating partner in my objective before things went any further, I had already been down one route that led to a dead end and I needed to know where we were headed.

I thought about calling my sister to tell her about George but then I decided to wait until I knew if he would be the one I was looking for. In the past, whenever I've talked to women at work, or old friends of mine from college, and even family members, they were always saying how hard it was to find a man who wants to commit, and now that I'm trying to find a way to get to the medication I feel will open up a secret world for me I keep meeting men who want to start long-term relationships.

I canceled my standing appointment at the beauty shop and invited George over for dinner. I hadn't been doing much cooking lately since Pam had gone back on campus, it was only me at home and I'm not that particular about what I eat. There wasn't much in the fridge so I stopped at Kroger to pick up some groceries to make spaghetti and a salad, they were always quick to put together. George rang the doorbell at 7:00 and when I opened the door he gave me a hug and a kiss and I noticed how good he looked in his khaki pants and loafers.

"Dinner is ready and on the table unless you need a few minutes to unwind," I said, leading him into the dining room.

"I can unwind while I eat if you have a bottle of wine."

"I do, if you don't mind doing the honors," I said as I handed him the bottle and a cork screw.

He opened the wine and poured it while I served the food. Then I said a quick blessing.

"So you can cook too, a woman of many talents," he said, enjoying a big mouthful of the spaghetti. "It's been a long time since I've had a home cooked meal."

"Well you have been wining and dining me so much I wanted to do something for you. I also asked you to come over this evening because I wanted to tell you that I would like to take the trip to Vegas with you."

"Now you've really made my day," he said, tapping my glass with his, "I'll make all the arrangements, I want to surprise you."

There he went again, reminding me of an Almond Joy.

I took Friday off from work and we boarded the early morning non-stop flight and George had gotten us first class seats. He gave me the inside seat by the window and as the plane gained altitude I tried yawning to clear my ears. I kept trying every few minutes without success.

"What's the matter, didn't you sleep well last night?" he asked.

"That's one of my issues, I never sleep well," I said, looking out into the clouds.

"That's not good, what's the problem or have you even checked on it?" he asked, speaking like a true doctor.

"It's not anything physical," I said, not wanting to share my sad story, "It's just a bad case of chronic insomnia."

"Have you taken any meds for it?"

"I've pretty much tried everything, all the over-the-counter meds and they left me feeling groggier than I did without the sleep. I saw my doctor and he prescribed Ambien and then Xanax for a while but they gave me headaches that were worse than feeling tired."

"There's always something else to try, we'll look into that when we get back," he said, "Not getting enough sleep compromises your overall good health."

Now was time to put the bait out there and see if he would go for it.

"I've heard about some resident doctors using propofol for their insomnia and how refreshed and good they feel when they wake up even after only a few hours sleep. That's what I wish I could try, just once, and get that feeling of being re-energized and rejuvenated again."

"Baby, that stuff will kill you, I wouldn't mess with it. It's some seriously dangerous shit."

"It's used in the hospital everyday without any problems and the residents use it safely."

"Portia, drugs aren't to be played with, prescription or illegal.

I've seen the repercussions first hand. There are several non-medical treatments that I can recommend for you that might help."

I could see he was becoming agitated so I said, "Don't worry about me; I've dealt with it this long, I'll work it out."

George ordered some wine from the flight attendant and I chugged mine down, let the seat back, and closed my eyes to hide my disappointment that there wasn't a future in our relationship.

***

The limo ride from the airport to the hotel was delayed in traffic on the strip and moved slower than the pace of the many hopeful gamblers that walked from casino to casino in anticipation of hitting the jackpot. I couldn't help but think that I had already lost.

"What's on your mind?" George asked, nudging me on the shoulder.

"I was thinking that the city looks so different since the last time I was here, there are so many more casinos in the skyline of the strip."

"They do what they have to do to keep the people coming back."

"I'm sure, but how many of them are satisfied customers."

"It's not always about winning, Portia; it's as much about just being in the game."

He had a point, so I decided right then that I would contain my mood and try hard to enjoy the moment and have a good weekend in Vegas.

"Welcome to the Venetian," the driver said as he pulled up at the hotel.

Chapter Five

The entrance was majestic; it was the hotel that would have been my own choice. If you couldn't fly to Italy this was the next best thing to being there. We got registered quickly and rode the elevator to the 31st floor.

"This suite is gorgeous," I said, looking at the décor of the lavish suite from the bedroom to the deep Jacuzzi in the bathroom.

"I'm going to order up a small snack from room service and I want you to take a few hours and relax, take a nap, take a bath, whatever you want, doctor's orders."

"That nap sounds good to me," I said, walking in the bedroom.

"Close the door behind you, I don't want to hear all that snoring," he shouted behind me.

"Oh, so they have comedians in the rooms too," I said with a chuckle, grateful for George's consideration in giving me some time to myself.

The bed felt like a cloud and I sank into it and fell asleep. I woke up about an hour and a half later when George opened the door carrying a tray of fruit and hors d'oeuvres.

"That looks so good," I said, sitting up and making room for the tray on the bed.

"Don't eat too much; you know you're my dinner date."

"I'll try to hold back," I said, filling my mouth with a loaded cracker.

It was a great night; we pigged out on the buffet at the Paris Casino, caught one of the comedy shows at the Improv at Harrah's, and gambled up and down the strip. I even won a few hundred dollars playing craps despite the fact I wasn't feeling very lucky. We practically crawled back to the hotel just before daybreak exhausted but in a good way. We fell across the bed as soon as we got back to the room.

"I'm so tired my bones ache," George said, kicking off his shoes.

"I wish I could kick mine off but they're strapped on."

George rolled down the bed and unbuckled the straps and my feet rubbed against his leg in gratitude. We were a sight wriggling around like two helpless turtles on our backs trying to pull off our outer clothes while we were stretched out. Somehow we got between the sheets before we passed out.

"Wake up, sleepy head," I heard George say from outside the blanket later in the morning.

"I'm not ready yet," I said with my head still covered.

"I hate to miss breakfast; you know it's the most important meal of the day."

"So I've heard," I said, rolling over.

"You can always go back to sleep after you eat," he said, holding the hotel robe out for me to slide my arms in.

Outside the bedroom there was a table set with French toast, sausage, fruit, and orange juice. "That looks perfect," I said, and my stomach growled in agreement. "First you're a comedian, now you're a magician, what else do you have up your sleeve?"

"You're right if you think this is the prelude to the main event."

"There's the comedian coming out again," and we laughed. George was good company.

"I hope you're not afraid of heights," he said with a smile.

Chapter Five

"Sometimes I am," I said with a little apprehension.

"You'll be all right. I'm gonna take a quick shower," he said, going into the bedroom.

I sat there at the table for a few minutes letting my breakfast settle and looking around the fabulous suite he had chosen.

"What's wrong with you, Portia?" I whispered to myself, "Here you are in Vegas with a man who's treated you like nothing less than a queen and all you can think about is moving on to the next person to get some stupid propofol that you don't know anything about. I'm sorry," I said, apologizing to myself, "I can't help it, I'm fixated, so sue me."

"It's all yours," George hollered from inside the bedroom.

I walked in to see him wrapped in a towel rummaging through the closet and pulling out a pair of jeans. I could smell the scent of the soap on his skin and I envied the drops of water that rolled down the center of his broad shoulders. His whole body looked fit and well-toned for a man his age; he obviously took as good care of himself as he did of others. I walked past him into the bathroom and gently closed the door without a word.

The shower was heaven sent; water pulsed out from both sides in six different directions. I wanted to linger there for a while but I didn't want to keep George waiting. I followed his lead and put on some comfortable jeans for the day.

"I'm not going to ask where we're going," I said as we climbed into a shuttle in front of the hotel.

"Good, that way you won't get frustrated when I don't tell you," he answered.

"Not a problem, there's nothing I like better than people watching, so I'm just going to enjoy the sights of Las Vegas."

"I knew you could get with the program," George said, satisfied.

I spent the next thirty minutes humming along with the radio until we pulled up in front of a sign that said Maverick Tours of the Grand Canyon.

"No, George, I'm drawing the line on this one."

"Come on out of the van and we'll talk about it," he said, pulling me by the arm.

"Let me just say that I am scared of heights."

"That's okay, I feel like you're a woman who conquers her fears."

"No, I don't know that woman, I'm the woman who lives with her fears, and I mean lives."

"Now look who's making jokes."

"I'm not making jokes, George, I'm for real."

"If you can get on an airplane you can get in a helicopter."

"Not necessarily so, a plane is much bigger, large enough to absorb some impact."

"Relax, trust me, we'll be fine."

George just stood there patiently beside the helicopter unmoved by my protests. I gave up. The pilot opened up the door and I crawled in. Who was I, on a mission to experiment with a controlled substance but scared to get in a helicopter.

"Do you want to squeeze my hand?" George asked sarcastically.

"Yes I do," I answered, meaning every word of it.

I heard the motor rev up and the whirr of the propellers begin

Chapter Five

and I knew this was actually going to happen. The helicopter stirred up its own cyclone and lifted up into the center of it.

"My stomach is thinking about jumping over the side," I said, afraid of spilling my guts and embarrassing myself.

"Take deep breaths," he said.

"You're a doctor, why don't you have something to calm my nerves?"

"You don't need anything, I'm here," he said, cool, calm and collected, like he was my private superman.

We rose to an altitude and leveled off and I settled down and dared to look out at the ground below us.

"The first part of the tour will be over Hoover Dam," the pilot said into his receiver from the front, and I released George's hand to get out my camera phone.

Once the thought of imminent death faded from my thoughts I took in the landscapes of Las Vegas and Arizona on the way to the Grand Canyon.

"It looks like the background from an old western movie out here, it's deserted," I said to George, looking at all the cactus bushes and rough dry terrain.

"Land is really cheap out here if you want to put up stakes," he said, being funny again.

"No thanks, I've gotten rather fond of civilization."

About an hour later the pilot said, "We're approaching the west side of the Grand Canyon."

I moved closer to the window, humbled by the mixture of colors and textures in nature.

"It's awesome, magnificent, and scary at the same time," I said.

"Consider the works His hands hath made," George said, and I had to agree, it was truly a wonder.

The pilot flew over the Grand Canyon Skywalk and we could see the tourists walking around on the glass platform. My heart rose higher in my chest, the depth of the canyons was unbelievable and it looked like it had been intricately carved by an artist. It took my breath away along with the words that could describe it.

I relaxed on the way back to Vegas but I can't say I wasn't relieved when the helicopter landed and I placed my feet on solid ground again.

"I don't know what to say George; you amaze me, that was so special," I said as we drove back to the hotel.

"It was my pleasure, I'm glad I could share it with you."

"You have to let me take you to dinner this evening."

"I would, except I've already made reservations for us at the Pinot Brasserie inside the hotel."

"You're going to make me cry if you do one more nice thing for me."

"Pull out your tissues, girl; I'm just that kind of guy."

"I don't know what I'm going to do with you."

"Are you taking suggestions?" he said with a sexy smile.

"You are too much," I said.

We got back to the hotel, freshened up, and changed for dinner. We ordered the duck and the lamb. The food and wine were delicious, it was the most romantic meal that I have ever had.

"Here's to a lovely evening," George said, raising his glass.

Chapter Five

"Not just the evening, it's been a fantastic weekend, thank you," I said, tapping his glass.

We walked through the casino trying our luck and playing a few slots and watching the high rollers at a blackjack table.

It was around 11:00 when George took my hand and said, "You know we can't leave without trying out the Jacuzzi."

"You're right; it wouldn't make sense to let that go unused."

We caught the elevator up to the suite and when we walked into the bedroom there were champagne and chocolate-covered strawberries waiting. This man was a true romantic. I was bowled over when George ran the bath for us.

I started to feel nervous listening to the sound of the water rushing into the tub. Up until I began this mission only one man had seen this body in the past twenty-five years. George had seen me in my underwear last night but I couldn't wear them in the Jacuzzi. He had been generous and attentive, showing me the best time I'd had in years. I'd come this far and I didn't see any reason to spoil the end of a magical weekend.

I watched George out of the side of my eye strip down and climb into the Jacuzzi. I could feel his eyes on me as I took off my shoes, dress, and everything else. What the hell, I grabbed the champagne and glasses and stepped into the bubbling water.

"Feel good?" he asked, taking the glasses and pouring the champagne.

"Feels great," I said, sliding deeper in the warm water.

"I'm really glad you decided to come, I needed some down time with a pretty sexy woman in a hot tub," he said, moving closer and putting his arm around me.

"I'm glad you asked, I needed some time off with a handsome man and a glass of champagne in a hot tub."

"You are too cute," he said, covering my lips with his in our first real intense kiss.

Things got even hotter in the tub and after a while George said, "We need to get out of this water before we hurt ourselves."

I stood up and grabbed some towels and threw him one while I dried off. I pulled back the covers and climbed onto the cool sheets.

"I love your body," George said before lying down beside me.

It made me feel so comfortable and sexy that I opened my arms for his embrace. He was a passionate and experienced lover, tender and strong, more turned on by my pleasure than his own. I wanted to make him as happy as he had made me this weekend. The long anticipated lovemaking between us lasted for hours. It was a testimonial to the fact that if you do it right the first time, there's no desire or energy to do it again.

I stood at the window afterwards while he slept and took in the brilliance of the lights on the strip afraid to lie down and take the chance of having my mind darken with despair. I lost track of time. The blue of the sky had brightened and my legs threatened to give out on me by the time I crawled back into the bed.

***

There was time for a relaxed breakfast before our afternoon flight.

"Portia, I want you to know how much I enjoyed this weekend with you. I feel like there's something very special between us,

Chapter Five

and since we're in Vegas I've got to put my cards on the table. I want us to be exclusive."

"I always have a great time whenever we're together, George, you're flawless. I don't know how your wife let you get away, but I don't want us to move too fast, I'm still married. I don't think it's fair to ask you to invest too much into this relationship until I get divorced. I just don't know what I'm doing right now. You have been so wonderful and I feel like I'm making a big mistake asking you to slow things down."

"Baby, it's cool, I'm not making any big moves for a while, I just got free. Take your time; I'll be here as long as no other fine, sexy, intelligent woman who can cook turns my head."

We both laughed and he put his arms around me when we got on the shuttle to the airport. After we boarded the plane back to Nashville I couldn't help thinking that if we had met at another time in our lives it might have been a happy ending for us.

Chapter Six

George and I continued to talk on the phone at least once a week and the sound of his sensual and exotic voice always reminded me of the exceptional couple of months that we had spent together. There was no mystery of how he had become so successful in his field, he simply gauges a situation and if the prognosis isn't good, he doesn't get emotionally involved. He didn't waste his time trying to change my mind, he accepted my decision. He was practical, something I used to be, and I was sorry that he had given up on me so easily. There were many evenings that I was tempted to call him and take back all the ridiculous things I said. I wanted him in my life, if only I didn't want to get the propofol even more.

It was April's Fool Day and tax season was in full bloom. I was bombarded with phone calls and e-mail messages from what seemed like the entire hospital staff for additional copies of their tax statements for their retirement contributions. It was the worst time for Keisha to take a vacation; I was getting overwhelmed with the requests. Probably from past experience she knew just when to take off to dodge the overload of work. I didn't know enough at the time to deny her leave request; she had taken advantage of me yet again.

I needed to get out of the line of fire for a few minutes so I could pull it together. I took the stairs down to the cafeteria to get my blood flowing. A large extra strong cup of coffee might be just what the doctor ordered to get me through the rest of the afternoon.

I was standing in line inhaling the soothing aroma of dark roast in my cup when the cashier said, "Two dollars," and I realized I hadn't brought my purse or any money. "I am really losing it," I thought as I stood there unsure of how to tell her I forgot to bring any cash.

"I got it, just add it to mine," a voice in a white coat behind me said.

"That's all right, you don't have to do that," I said, turning around to face the voice, "Maybe that's a sign that I don't need it."

"It's no big deal and you look like you need it," he said with half a smile.

"Thank you for rescuing me," I said, breaking the top to get my first sip of the precious caffeine.

"David Tucker," he said, holding out his hand.

I reached for it and said, "Portia Roberts."

"Now the least you can do is sit with me for a minute," he said, "I've had a crazy morning and I want to take my mind off of it by looking across the table at a very attractive woman."

"Good line, David Tucker, but that's a lot for just a cup of coffee."

"I'll buy you whatever you want, tell me and I'll get it, a donut, a sandwich, lunch or dinner."

"I'm not hungry," I said, smiling at his humor, "Let's just sit down, I'm stressed out."

"Aren't we all?" he added.

I followed him to a table and sat across from him. He appeared to be close to my age, around forty-five years old, the studious type, café au lait-colored, about five-feet-nine inches, good hair cut close in waves, thin wire glasses, and in reasonably good shape despite a small belly that stressed the buttons of his white coat.

"Looking at you, I'll assume you're a physician here, what's your area or specialty?"

"I'm a cardiologist," he answered.

"That's impressive, except I probably need to bump into a psychiatrist."

He laughed and said, "You don't look like you have a worry in the world."

"I've heard that before but looks are very deceiving. I'm totally stressed out."

We sat there for a minute drinking our coffee in silence before he asked, "So what do you do to decompress, Portia?"

"Nothing at the moment, but I'm considering a walking program to get some exercise and relieve my stress."

"That sounds good to me, when do we start?"

"You are really funny," I said, laughing.

"I'm as serious as a heart attack," he answered.

"Ha, ha, bad doctor joke, don't quit your day job."

"Listen to me, no joke, I need to exercise and we can motivate each other. Just tell me when we start, where, and I'm there." His phone vibrated, he looked at it and said, "I've got to go, take this," and then he handed me a small shiny green pill. I looked at him puzzled as he walked away and he mouthed the words, "Trust Me."

That was totally weird, but I've discovered that when you're working in a hospital there's something out of the ordinary happening all day and every day. I struggled through the rest of the afternoon, drove straight home, popped a frozen entrée in the microwave, and prepared to vegetate in front of the television.

I fell asleep on the sofa and woke up in the middle of the night unable to get back to sleep. I started to feel antsy and alone but I couldn't call anybody this late, not even my sister Paula. I laid there awake for two hours and felt like I was going to cry. I didn't want those flood gates opened so I got up and took the pill that I had tucked in my blazer pocket. I got back into bed and turned the TV back on needing the sound to block out the noise in my head.

Fifteen minutes later I felt so peaceful, like I was swinging in a hammock, back and forth in the tropical breezes of the Bahamas. That's where I was when the alarm went off the next morning. When I stood up I felt a little shaky like I had drunk too much but at least I had gotten some rest.

The first thing I did when I got to the office was to go into the employee directory and find David Tucker's name. I shot him an e-mail that said, "Meet me in front of the Parthenon with your running shoes on at 6:00 today. Your walking partner."

It was around 4:00 before he responded with a message that said, "I'll be there."

I had come prepared and changed into my royal blue TSU

Chapter Six

warm-up suit before I left for the park. I got there a couple of minutes early so I took a few swigs of water and got out to warm up. Then David pulled up in a huge white Escalade, not at all what I expected him to drive. He jumped out in brand new sneaks and sweats with the stickers and tags still on them.

"My fault for not giving advance notice but you seemed anxious to get started," I said.

"I'm here aren't I?" he said, shrugging his shoulders with his arms stretched out.

"Indeed you are and since this is our first day why don't we start with two miles."

"Two miles sounds ambitious but I'm game."

"You are not telling me that you're a cardiologist who doesn't work out regularly."

"Let me stretch and loosen up first and then I'm going to answer all those questions that are stirring around in your head."

We made our way to one-mile walking path that circled by the duck pond and the edges of the park, and then David started to tell me about himself.

"I was born in Atlanta, Georgia, went to Morehouse College and Morehouse School of Medicine. I married my college sweetheart from undergrad and we had two daughters who are now in college, one here at Belmont and the other at Tuskegee. We divorced ten years ago, my fault, I was unfaithful. I married again five years ago and we have a three year old son."

"That was a mouthful," I said as I absorbed all of his personal information.

"I just wanted to save you the time of asking me one question at a time."

"That was so thoughtful of you," I replied, being facetious.

"I aim to please."

"Since infidelity ended your first marriage, are you a faithful husband now?"

"No, I'm not, it's not in me to be with just one woman," he said matter-of-factly.

"Then why do you keep getting married?" I asked him.

"I love women, and I need a wife," he answered bluntly.

"Does your current wife have any problems with you going outside of your marriage?" I asked, eager to hear his response.

"I don't disrespect her, and if she knows she hasn't said anything about it."

"Now that's interesting," I said, thinking about the crazy lives we all lead.

We finished our two miles in about forty-five minutes. I had barely broken a sweat at that pace but the outside of David's jogging suit was soaked. We did a cool down stretch and then I asked him the question I really wanted answered.

"What was that pill you gave me yesterday?"

"Did you take it?" he asked with a half-smile on his face.

"Yeah, I did. I couldn't sleep last night and I was curious if it might help."

"Did it help?"

"It did help somewhat, but I don't think it was a sleeping pill."

"Did you like it?" he asked, still wearing his smirk.

"It was nice when I first took it but it gave me a hangover in the morning."

"I'll have to give you something else," he said nonchalantly.

I didn't want to seem too anxious so I let that opportunity for my proposal go by.

"When are we going to walk again?" I asked him.

"This felt good, thanks for getting me out here. Why don't we walk every Tuesday and Thursday?"

"Sounds like a plan to me," I said, feeling optimistic.

From then on David and I walked twice a week after work and eventually he started stopping by the house for a few hours on the weekends too. I would order a pizza or fix us some snacks while we watched a DVD or a boxing match. We became confidants or even what you would call close friends. One Friday night we were eating hot wings and drinking beer, having a good time, and then his mood changed.

"You know my wife is just a few years older than my eldest daughter."

"Wow, I didn't know you had gone that far back down the road," I remarked, a little surprised.

"I wasn't looking for a younger woman per se; I met her in a club and was very attracted to her. We started dating and it went on from there."

"Excuse me while I get a box of Kleenex this is breaking my heart, it's so sad," I said with much sarcasm.

"Stop, it's not all that, she's my trophy wife, yes, but we don't have anything else besides my son in common. I can't even carry on a conversation with her unless it has something to do with buying something."

"So you're raising your wife, what's the problem with that? I'm sure you're not the only one," I added jokingly.

"Big problems," he said seriously, "Her age has really come between me and my girls and that tears me up, I love my babies and I miss the time we used to spend together."

"I'm sorry about that but they'll come around eventually. After forty, none of them will want to talk about their ages anymore." Then we both got a good laugh.

David's sharing of that personal predicament with me made me feel like I could open up some and reveal what I was going through.

"I haven't shared this with anyone at the hospital, but almost four years ago I lost my son Nicholas. He was only seventeen years old, playing varsity football in high school when he had sudden cardiac arrest."

"Portia, that really is heartbreaking, I don't know if I could survive something like that."

"It is devastating, and I'm still struggling to come to terms with the reality of it. It was really hard on my family and it was at the root of the break-up in my marriage."

"That's tough," he said, shaking his head.

"Things just fell apart afterward. That's why I have problems sleeping."

"I'm going to write you a prescription for some anti-depressants, you don't have to bear all this with no help," he said, and it was music to my ears.

I tried the meds during the day that David had prescribed but I didn't feel like they made a difference. I didn't have a problem functioning during the day hours. The problem was at night when I turned off the TV, the radio, and shut down all the noise around me, the void inside my heart and soul threatened to swallow me up. Thoughts of Nick and all the things I wished I could have done differently screamed in my head and I couldn't sleep. It was torture and my only hope was the propofol and the instant glorious sleep it promised.

***

"Do you mind if I add some liquor to your bar?" David asked on the next Friday when he came over, "Yours lacks a certain quality and variety."

"Knock yourself out," I said, when I saw all the expensive cognac he pulled out of the box he was carrying.

David liked to drink and he liked good liquor. He cracked open one of the bottles and I grabbed two snifters.

"How about listening to some jazz?" he asked before I sat down.

"Do you like Gerald Albright or do you want to go old school with some Coltrane?"

"Albright sounds good, anything but some rap."

"That's right, you went hip hop," I said, kidding with him as I turned on the stereo.

We sipped and talked about music, about writers we like to read, and artists whose work we admire. After a couple of hours of talking and half of bottle of cognac he kissed me. There wasn't any real chemistry between us, at least on my part, but one thing led to another. The whole thing only made me wish I would have taken George up on his offer.

The sex wasn't that great with David, but he was a man after my heart; he was always putting some kind of pill in his mouth, vitamins, Diazepam, oxycontin, or Viagra. He didn't see anything wrong with leaning on a crutch if you needed one, "that's what they are there for," he would tell me. He was definitely the one for me; he understood pain, dependence, inadequacy, and weakness in people and he didn't mind self-medicating. It wasn't a sex thing between us; our relationship was more friends than anything. He said he enjoyed talking to a classy mature woman who could carry on an intelligent conversation.

We seldom went out to restaurants or bars, he preferred to stay at my home and look at movies or talk, and he liked to cook for me. We talked about politics, religion, sports, and we even compared our bucket lists.

One evening we were kicked back on the sofa drinking and talking about fantasies and David said, "I have a fantasy about you dressing up and spanking me."

"That's unexpected but not impossible," I said with a chuckle.

"What's yours?" he asked.

"It may surprise you."

"Nothing surprises me."

"Okay, I would like to experiment with propofol, I want to experience the euphoric deep sleep and wake up feeling exhilarated."

"That's also unexpected but not impossible," he said.

Did I hear him correctly or was it wishful thinking? "Is this just a conversation or will we really fulfill the other's fantasy?"

"That's up to you, Portia, tell me when you're ready," he said as he stood up to leave.

"I'll do that," I said, walking him to the door. I shut it behind him and threw my hands up in jubilation, my plan was within reach.

Chapter Seven

It was on Friday, the evening before the 4th of July, when David showed up with a red and black shopping bag from Performance Studio Costumes.

"What better day to set off our fireworks," he said, all smiles when I opened the door. He handed me the bag and I took a look inside, it was a cowgirl costume, not at all what I expected.

"Put it on," he said.

"Don't you want something to eat, something to drink, or even a minute to sit down and relax?" I asked, feeling nervous and flustered by the sight of the outfit.

"No, I'm fine, go on, put it on," he said, motioning me towards the stairs.

"All right but I'm having my doubts," I said as I walked slowly up the stairs to my bedroom to change.

"Portia, what are you doing?" I asked as I looked at myself in the full length mirror. The outfit was complete with fringes on the tight jacket and mini-skirt, boots, and a horse crop. I was forty-five years old but this was totally new to me.

When I walked down into the den it took all of my reserve to keep from screaming, David was standing in the middle of the floor naked except for a brown thong and a riding bit with reigns that hung from his mouth. It was official, we're both crazy. He got down on all fours and I was at a loss. I poured myself a glass of liquid courage at the bar and tried to get into character. The best I could do was pretend he was Raymond, because that was the only man I felt like spanking. When I lifted up the reigns from the floor David reared back so fast it scared me and by reflex I gave him his first lash and I panicked as the welt rose on his bare behind.

"Bad horse," I scolded as I pick up the reigns again and popped him on the ass again. "I'm running this damn rodeo show," I shouted and popped him again on the other side afraid to hit him in the same spot.

He pranced around the room bucking like a bull and I held the reigns playing the game of a sexy cowgirl trying to train her wild horse. After a while I got tired and climbed on his back, yelled giddy up and spanked his behind until it looked like two tender pork roasts ready to be cooked.

Twenty minutes later David laid on the floor physical drained and fell asleep. I was thankful for the spacious lot around my house that separated it from the houses of my neighbors or surely the police would have come knocking. I took the opportunity to shower and change into some pajamas. In the shower I felt the water pressure drop off and that let me know that David was in the guest bathroom getting cleaned up. I made it back to the den before he came out of the guestroom.

"How do you feel?" I asked, afraid to look him in the eye when he came back into the room totally dressed.

"I feel great, fantastic, like I've purged all the tension and frustration of the last five years."

"Come on," I said, looking him in the face and doubting his reaction.

"Really," he said, "All that bad energy that I suppress builds up and weighs me down, now it's gone. I feel lighter and younger. It was everything I hoped it would be."

All I could say in response was, "Wow," I was speechless.

"Are you ready to take your trip to lullaby-land?" he asked.

"I'm nervous but I'm ready," I answered.

"Now, where do you want to sleep?" he asked.

"Upstairs in my bedroom."

David followed me up the stairs and I got comfortable on the bed.

"I'm going to give you a smaller dose because you may not have metabolized all of the alcohol that you drank earlier. I'll stay for a while and check your vital signs to make sure you're not having a reaction and then I'll let myself out."

He opened up his attaché case and pulled out a vial of what looked like milk, alcohol pads, another tube of cream and two syringes. When I saw all the paraphernalia I got second and third thoughts, what if something went wrong, what about Pam?

"I'm getting scared," I said, hoping he would talk me out of it.

"Trust me, I trusted you," David said, looking in my eyes.

I laid back on the pillow and watched David use an alcohol pad to sterilize the area on my arm and then apply the lidocaine cream. He filled the syringe with a small amount of the milky solution and then I felt a slight burn before he faded away.

I'm floating in another atmosphere of nothingness and I start to wonder if I'm having an out of body experience. Beams of light are circling around me and I feel like I'm moving faster and faster until I'm spinning. I can see faint images rotating within the light around me and then they begin to sharpen but they are speeding so fast my eyes don't have time to focus. I start to see flashes of my life, as a young child with Paula and Mama, my high school graduation, an image of my wedding flies by, and then I catch a glimpse of Nicholas smiling at me and my eyes latch onto the vision and then I'm unconscious.

"I just had déjà vu," I say to Nick.

"Really, Mom, like you've been in here shopping for a tuxedo before."

"Whatever, boy, what color is Tasha wearing again?"

"She said get light turquoise, that's all I know."

"Excuse me," I say to the attendant, "Can you help us get him outfitted?"

"Yes, ma'am, what is the occasion?"

"Junior prom," Nick answered.

"Okay, what color for the tux, black or white, and the color of the ladies dress?" the attendant asks, appearing very professional.

"Black for the tux and light turquoise for the dress," I say as I take one of the seats in the center area to wait.

"What's wrong with me?" I ask myself in a low whisper. I'm feeling over emotional and I don't know why. It's only a prom, the boy isn't getting married. When Nick comes out of the dressing room looking so grown-up and handsome it overwhelms me and I want to cry. I hold it all in except for one tear that escapes and rolls down my cheek.

Chapter Seven

"Mom, stop, that is embarrassing."

"I'm sorry but you look so nice."

I stand up and he walks over towards me and gives me a hug and I just don't want to let him go. I feel him pull away and I scratch the back of his head as he walks back into the dressing room.

"It'll be ready for pick-up on Thursday at 3:00," the attendant says.

"Thank you," I say as we leave the shop.

"Mom, if I had known you were going to trip I would've come with Dad," Nick says, teasing me. Why don't you give me the keys so I can drive since you acting crazy?"

I reach in my pocket and when I hand them over I grip his hand in mine and say, "I love you and I'm proud of you, that's never gonna change."

I don't like to close my eyes while this boy is driving but I feel like I need to rest for just a minute. The breeze through the window is so relaxing it almost feels like the wind above the waves at the beach.

***

I wake up and look at the clock and it reads 4:00. I feel so refreshed and peaceful but I haven't even slept through the night.

"Raymond, what are you doing?" I yelled out towards the bathroom.

I didn't get an answer so I got up to make sure he was okay. I looked into the empty bathroom and then it all came back to me, it was the propofol. Nick was gone and Raymond didn't live here anymore. I sat down in my lay-z-boy to reflect on what happened. I don't think I was dreaming. It didn't feel like a dream. It was too vivid in sight and sound, besides it was something that actually happened, except it wasn't a memory, it was real-time. How could that be? It was strange. Something had happened, it wasn't a drug induced dream or hallucination, it was something supernatural.

My first impulse was to call my sister, then call my Dad at his assisted-living home in St. Louis, and tell them about my experience, but my instincts said to wait. Dad wouldn't even know what I was talking about, Paula wouldn't approve of what I had done, and there was no question I was going to do it again. Next, I began to feel grateful that Pam had gotten an internship in Virginia and would be out of the house for the whole summer.

Later that morning, I felt like I could eat a big breakfast but I hadn't been grocery shopping in a while. I went to the kitchen and opened the refrigerator to see if I had a taste for anything in there and that's when I saw the vial with the milk colored mixture inside. I felt like a miner who had just discovered a very large diamond. That vial had given me my son back if only for a brief moment and for me it was more valuable than anything else I could think of. I took the vial and hid in it in the small compartment for the butter.

My thoughts were all jumbled up in my mind. I needed to get out of the house so I could think clearly. I dressed quickly in jeans and a t-shirt and drove to the Starbucks on Metrocenter to get a cup of coffee.

I watched the foam bubbles burst on the surface of my cappuccino while I re-organized my plan. The propofol lived up to my every expectation even in a small dose. I had been able to re-visit my past and see, hear, and touch Nick again. My prayers had been answered. What had me sitting here straining my brain was the feeling that I had transcended some type of dimension and I couldn't even explain it to myself much less anyone else. The sensation I had was not of sleep but a different level of consciousness. I wanted to go there again but I had to contain my enthusiasm. It was a drug and I knew that it was addictive. By the time the last bubble of foam has disappeared I had resolved to only take my milk dose on Friday nights, everything in moderation. Living for the weekend took on a hold new connotation for me.

Chapter Eight

"Good morning, Ms. Roberts, you look nice today, you must have had a good weekend," Keisha said sweetly with a look of suspicion.

"Thank you, Keisha, good morning to you too, I did have a good weekend," I said, graciously. "Did you enjoy your extended weekend?"

Keisha was famous for taking off Fridays and Mondays.

"I was sick for two days but I started feeling better yesterday," she said, remembering her cover story for her absence.

"I'm glad to hear that, you've been sick a lot lately, I was concerned. I might need to set an appointment for you to get a full check-up," I said, toying with her.

"It's nothing serious, mostly allergies," she said, turning back to her computer screen.

I proceeded into my office and looked at my scheduled appointments and my to-do list. It looked like it would be a light week. I was about to call my sister when David walked in the door.

"It's good to see you in the land of the living; I was a little worried about you," he said, coming around my desk and rubbing my shoulder.

"I couldn't be better; the patient has made a miraculous recovery. How about yourself? Is that booty still tender?" I asked, unable to keep the smile off my face as I got an outrageous flashback of the two of us.

"I think it needs a bit more time to heal but no complaints," he said.

"By the way, where did you get the milk from?" I asked, wanting to get a year's supply.

"If I tell you then I'll have to kill you."

"Don't start that comedy routine, it's too early in the week."

"Really, the less you know the better."

"That's fine, agent 007. I was just wondering because I accidently dropped the bottle on the floor and it broke."

"We'll talk when we walk tomorrow," he said as he left my office.

"I need to settle down," I said to myself, "I'm already lying like a drug addict after only one dose."

I picked up the phone and called my sister, Paula, she always calmed me down.

"Look who has time to make a personal call during the day," she answered jovially.

"Yes, it's a different world for me now, I don't have to watch the stock market every minute."

"You should have made the switch a long time ago."

"I know, sometimes it takes some incentive before you can make a change."

"So what else is going on?"

"I had a dream about Nick the other night and it was like I went back and shared a special time with him and it was so comforting."

Chapter Eight

"That's good, Portia, you have to focus on the good times and not dwell so much on what happened."

"You're right, I'm going to try and do that more, anyway, I just wanted to call and see what you and Charles are up to."

"You know Charles, he's moved on to his next get rich quick scheme, flipping houses. The harder he tries to make us money the less we have."

"Tell him I said keep up the good work."

"I'll do that, all the way to bankruptcy court," she laughed. "I'll call you next week if my phone is still on."

***

The sun was beaming like it was noon and it was still over ninety degrees even though it was after 6:00 on our scheduled walking time on Tuesday.

"It's too hot to walk," David said, getting out of his car in gym shorts and a t-shirt.

"If you're not feeling it we can sit it out, one day missed shouldn't hurt," I said, more than agreeable to pass on a trek in the stifling heat.

I spotted a swing in the shade and we walked across the grass to sit down relax and talk.

"You doing okay?" he asked.

"Yeah, I'm fine," I said, feeling a little awkward after our night of fantasies.

"I want to know what your trip was like?" he asked.

"It was idyllic; everything I hoped it would be and I woke up feeling so tranquil and well-rested. It was like a revelation to me."

I hesitated to tell him about my experience with Nick because it was so personal.

"Did you feel like you were high?" he asked.

"No, it wasn't like a high; it was a sense of peace."

"To each his own," he said, shaking his head, "I crave intensity, high stimulation, everything turned up two notches above normal. I operate on auto-pilot so much I need feelings that remind me that I'm alive even if it's pain."

"Why aren't your fantasies something that you can share with your wife? Surrendering to someone is over the top intimacy. You two don't have that type of bond?"

"I have to command a certain respect in my house, I have to maintain control, so I can't allow her to know that I have feelings like that. She hasn't lived enough life to understand the complexities of human nature."

"That's deep, but I have to admit it's true," I said, "Things only get more complicated from the time you leave your mama's womb."

"She did get suspicious though, so I'm going to have to walk the line for a while."

"Does that mean I don't get any more milk?"

"I've got you, but after this time I'm done, I don't want you getting hooked on that stuff."

"You're my hero," I said, giving him a kiss on the cheek.

We walked back to the cars and he said, "Don't look for me to walk until the temp drops under eighty degrees. I'm not trying to have a heat stroke out here."

"I hear you," I said, smiling as I drove off.

Chapter Eight

***

Thank God it was Friday at last, the week had started off fast and then it slowed to a crawl by hump day. Thursday felt like 48 hours. I was so keyed up I could barely focus. The door bell rang about seven-thirty and I was elated that David had finally arrived.

"You got a Heineken?" he asked.

"Sure," I said going into the kitchen. David followed and sat in a chair at the bar.

"I can't stay so I'm going to show you how to inject yourself. You clean your arm with alcohol and then apply the lidocaine first. The most accessible vein in your arm is here," he said, pulling my arm towards him to show me. "I'll fill the syringe for you. You need to inject steadily and quickly because you'll be out in less than thirty seconds. If you're uncomfortable with it you don't have to do this today, you can wait until next week and I'll do it for you."

This was even better news, I was more than happy to be by myself, I didn't feel like going through anymore freaky scenes. David and I were searching for very different things; there was a complete contrast between our desires that went from the sublime to the bizarre.

I took the vial and all the stuff David left and carried it to my bedroom. I searched in my closet for an old make-up case that would be a perfect size to hold the items I needed for the injection. If only this drug was a pill it would be so much easier. I could definitely understand why someone would pay someone else to handle the whole process.

I got comfortable in the middle of the bed, glad I was wearing my short sleeved silk pajamas. I cleaned my arm, smoothed on the lidocaine and found the vein David had shown me. My right hand shook from nervousness but I stuck the vein and quickly injected the contents of the syringe. I pulled it out and barely had time to lay it on the night stand before the sensation of weightlessness and floating overtakes me. The bright beams of light appear and I'm moving so fast I can't tell if I'm spinning or if the atmosphere is spinning around me. Once again the beams of light break into colors and the speed slows and I can see the flashing images. I see Pam and Nick running on the beach and I can't look away and then I lose consciousness.

"Don't run to close to the water," Raymond yells to the kids while he lies across my lap.

There are less than two years between Pam and Nick but she's tall and lean. She's wearing the yellow two-piece she begged me to buy and you can't tell her anything. I love the beach, watching the waves is like a mother rocking her baby, it's so soothing. It's the first time we've been on a real vacation since Nick was born. I take off my shades and lay them on the blanket next to me so I can film the kids with the camcorder.

"He's not going to give up until he catches her," I say.

"Unless she gets tired that's not going to be today, her legs are almost twice as long as his," he says, "But you got to love his determination."

I watch them running with the waves lapping at their bare

feet and I'm so glad we decided to come to Hilton Head. We're usually so busy working that we don't take time to enjoy each other as a family.

"Thanks for rearranging your schedule so we could all go," I say, rubbing Ray on the head.

"No problem, I love you guys and I realize that sometimes you have to stop and value what's important to you in this life."

Nicky looks to see where we are and it must seem too far to him because he just stops and starts running back to us.

"No fair," Pam protests when she realizes he's not chasing her anymore. "Wait for me," she yells, trying to catch him.

She's so competitive even with her little brother. He starts laughing because he knows she won't beat him back under the umbrella. When he gets close he dives on top of us like he's sliding into home plate and it's so funny.

"Mama, I beat Pam, I'm faster than her."

"No you're not, you cheated," she argues with her hands on her little hips.

"You both are the fastest runners I've ever seen," I tell them as I brush the sand off of Nicky's short legs.

"Mama I wish we could live here," he says.

"Me too," I say, giving him a kiss on his round cheek.

He squeezes in between Raymond and me and sits in my lap and I love it. His brown skin is moist from running by the water and it's still soft like a baby's even though he's almost five years old. On the ride back to the hotel I can hear them in the back seat singing with Aaliyah on the radio and they sound so sweet. It's been a perfect day. I lean back on the headrest and fall asleep.

The next morning when I woke up I felt like I had received the best gift of my life and I could not have been happier. I couldn't stop smiling. My mission was accomplished; the propofol had done what I hoped it would. I had found the way to see my son whenever I wanted to at any age I wanted. I could touch him and hear his voice. I could just catch the image or time in his life that I wanted to relive.

It changed everything; the emptiness I had felt wasn't a permanent part of my life as long as I had a supply of the propofol. I felt like I had discovered a well kept secret, one that Michael Jackson had shared. I understood his obsession so clearly now. The propofol allowed him to escape from the media frenzy that was his life. He could go to any part of his life that he desired. His yearning to be Peter Pan and never grow old was fulfilled whenever he could breach this level of consciousness. I had to resist the temptation to give myself another injection. Once a week I reminded myself.

It's hard for me to behave normally, difficult not to share the information with the people I love, but who would believe me. Most of the family and friends that I'm close to have watched me teetering on the edge of sanity for some years now, they would probably assume that I finally crossed the line. I would have to keep it to myself at least for now. The pain had ebbed some; I could get back to living again.

I considered calling George, I missed him. He was a quality man and he had brought that quality to my life when we were

Chapter Eight

seeing each other, but I wasn't ready to be in a relationship with anybody. I was still struggling with how to live with myself. I spent the rest of the day walking around in daze wondering about what was really happening when was I unconscious and my curiosity was building.

It was still Saturday, so unlike Rip Van Winkle, I hadn't lost time sleeping. From what I could ascertain I had reached a level of my consciousness where there was an opening to transcend to another dimension without my body even leaving the room. I needed to talk and sort out my feelings so I called Paula.

"Get up and get a move on," I said, joking when she answered. That was the way our Mom charged into our room every morning to wake us up for school.

I couldn't believe that it had been thirty years since she passed away from complications of her diabetes. My Dad slowly retreated in his own world after that, so I missed them both.

"Stop it, girl, not today, I was out late last night, Charles wanted to go see that new movie playing, Avatar."

"I haven't seen it, how did you like it?" I asked.

"It was too far out there for me, you know I don't like sci-fi."

"You never know what's out there in the universe."

"Good, that's the way I want to keep it. Every time I watch that stuff it gives me nightmares, anyway, how are you doing?"

"I can't complain, Pam's doing her thing in Virginia and I haven't heard from Raymond in months."

"That's a shame; I thought y'all would have pulled it together by now."

"Its fine, I'm all right with it. I even stepped out for a few dates."

"Are you kidding?"

"No, I'm for real."

"Did you meet anybody special?"

"I think I did, but I'm not ready to get serious just yet."

"Why not, it's not like you have a whole lot of time to waste. You probably only have about twelve months of good looks left so you better get somebody on lockdown, we're not getting younger, baby."

"Speaking of younger, I went cougar and dated one of the doctors from work."

"Stop, hold on, I've got to get some popcorn to chew while I listen, this is better than the movie last night."

"His name is Keith and he has a thing for older women. If all I wanted was hot sex on the regular he would have been the one for me."

"Portia, I can't believe you, are you finally breaking out of your prudish shell."

"Let's just say the shell disintegrated."

"I'm stunned, you've got to give me Keith's number, I want to write it in my little black book just in case."

"See, I called you to have an intelligent conversation and we got way off track." I decided not to tell her about George or David yet, I don't think she could take it all at one time. "Do you remember that movie where the guy travels back to the past in a time machine?"

Chapter Eight

"Yeah, I saw it but I don't' remember much about it."

"What do you think about that theory that all time exists simultaneously?"

"I have no idea; living in the here and now is more than I can deal with."

"If you could go back and visit your past would you do it?"

"I'm not sure; I already have my memories, what would be the point, I might be interested in the future though, definitely in next week's Mega millions number. Are you thinking you want to go back to your past?"

"I definitely do, to me it would be like having another taste of something delicious, what's wrong with that?"

"It would seem like torture to me because you can't change anything, and you don't just relive the good, the bad comes with it. I know it's hard, Portia, but if you could find an interest or something you are passionate about I believe you'll find your life again."

"I'm working on it, sis, and its coming together, I just wanted to call and say hello and check on my family."

"You need to come and check on us in person, I miss you."

"I will, I promise, I'm doing what T.D. Jakes says we need to do, I'm preparing for a breakthrough."

Chapter Nine

David called to chat whenever he could to see what I was up to, given that his wife was on high alert and all of his time had to be accounted for. It was a relief for me because the path I was traveling along was a personal one that I couldn't share with anyone else right now. David required a lot of attention and I had too many of my own unanswered questions to entertain those of somebody else. Not to mention, an idea had been circulating in my head all week. What if I increased the dosage by ten percent? My trips were so short I wondered if more propofol would extend my time in the past. I wasn't under that long with the amount I was taking. I usually woke up after four hours, so I figured if I took a larger dose it might help me sleep longer and I could have more time with Nick. The experiences I'd had weren't long enough for me. I had gotten what I wanted, I was more at peace, but I was greedy.

On Friday night I climbed into bed with my kit and increased the dose in the syringe by ten percent and found the vein in my left arm. Its different this time, I'm falling at a higher rate of speed, I feel disconcerted like I'm losing connection with myself and I'm afraid of the nothingness. Then the beams of light shoot out from the darkness towards me like rockets and they are spinning around me. Colors blend into the white rays and images are moving fast and mixing into one. I can feel heat engulfing me and the colors are like fire. I see people running with fear in their eyes all around me, I want to scream but I have no voice, and then I hear her calling.

"Jed, Jed, wake up."

I focus on the sound of my name and I open my eyes to the ceiling of our house and my eyes trail down the side of the wall made of clay and straw. It wasn't real; it was just a dream. I'm safe in our village in the mountains many miles east of the city. I can't believe I'm still having nightmares about the invasion; it's been three years since King Nebuchadnezzar of Babylon returned to Jerusalem with his army to destroy the second of Solomon's Temples and burn down the palace. The soldiers showed no mercy, killing Hebrews for sport, crushing the white limestone blocks, breaking down the walls, and setting off blazes in a path of destruction. It was a ghastly scene and the horror replays in my mind even when I'm awake.

Now I can see that those who died escaped a worse fate, the suffering of those who were spared has seen no end. The heat of the fires created a hell all through Jerusalem. Mama says that God was angered that his laws handed down to the people of Israel had been disobeyed and they were worshipping idols. I have been haunted by the sight of the blood that ran in the streets from men, women, children and even animals. We barely escaped with our lives, saved by my Papa who hid my mother and me in piles of straw behind our home while the soldiers ravaged the city slicing everything in sight with their long swords.

"Jed," she calls again with more urgency.

Chapter Nine

"Yes, mother," I say, turning and rubbing the sleep from my eyes, "I'm awake."

"Is that so, I've only been calling you for ten minutes."

The sun is still rising but I can see her across the room preparing the bread in the dim light. "She's always working," I say to myself, from the moment she wakes up and long after I lay down. She deserves more than this, why should a person be born with nothing, work so hard all their lives and still have so little. Once I had dreamed that I could learn a valuable trade where I could provide her with more, but with all the skilled craftsmen and blacksmiths living in exile in Babylon who's left to teach me. I'm stuck here without hope of anything more than a life of breaking my back and having nothing to show for it.

"Son, what is troubling you this morning," she fusses, "You're behind time and the flocks are waiting. If your father were home he would be very angry with you."

It was true and I was glad he wasn't. It was my time as the youngest son to feed the sheep. He and my brother Uriah had gone on a journey to Jerusalem to pay tithes from the crops to the priests. It didn't make much sense to me. The priests in the old Temples had been corrupted with the money and riches from the people, how would these new priests be able to resist the same temptations?

"Keep up, son, get your head out of the clouds," my Papa would say over and over when my feet would slow to take in the beauty of the Temples and the opulence of the palace.

"It has to be like heaven to live inside those buildings, Papa," I would tell him, "Surely God would want to dwell in their glory."

Except, they were gone now, brought down to the ground as dust.

My Papa is never happy with what I do, he thinks I'm lazy, but it's not true. No matter how hard I worked in the fields he thinks I'm worthless. It seems I can't do enough to please him and I don't want to see any more disappointment in his eyes. I had seen enough when my two older brothers were taken into the Babylonian army after the walls of Jerusalem were torn down. The strong and the well-trained were taken away and the poor like us were left behind to farm the land. I don't know why we're being punished with the evil ones who reveled in sin; my Mama and Papa never turned away from the one God of Israel.

I stretch out my long legs and stand up and roll up the mat of skins where I slept on the clay floor. I pull the tangles out of my hair with my hand and wrap my head in my cloth, and put on my sandals.

"Come drink your milk," Mama says, "Time is wasting.

"I don't see why we have to work from sun up to sun down to give away the little we have," I say to her.

"Shut up that selfish talk, we must offer the first grain harvest as a sacrifice to the priests at the Temple so our family will be blessed."

"This isn't what I want for me, being a shepherd or a farmer. I want to study and learn things, Mama. I was thinking that maybe I could do better in Babylon with my brothers, there's nothing to do out here. We're only one step from being in the wilderness."

"Jed, if you don't learn to be grateful you will surely bring

Chapter Nine

God's punishment on yourself, we are blessed. There are some who only have tents to cover them and no food to eat. God has provided our family with fruitful land to farm and feed ourselves."

"Yes, Mama, forgive me" I say, eating a bite of bread and swallowing the milk. I could hear my father's words echoing in my head as I grabbed my shepherd's bag, my sling, my flute, and my rod, "Get your head out of the clouds, lest we have no flock."

The air had fewer chills on it lately so I put my mantle on over my tunic with the wool side out. I walk down to the pen to tend to the sheep just as my older brothers Joel, Zuriel, and Uriah had done before me. I need to show Father I am responsible, I won't lose a single sheep while they are gone into Jerusalem.

"Asher," I yell out towards the valley, taking my staff that leaned against the side of our house. That dog of mine was always wondering around down there looking for rabbits or something to chase. He is the most faithful of friends, working at my side come rain, cold, or the hot sun. He runs past me to the sheepfold and I follow him to open the gate.

"Come on, my ready army, we need to eat to stay strong," I say above the sheep as they move out of the gate.

Forty-one is the count when the last one saunters out under the rod. I lead the flock to a green pasture on high ground four miles to the east where they can graze. I sit down in the grass near the herd and reach in my scrip where my mother has packed me a meal of bread, cheese, fruit, and olives. I eat while I watch the sheep get their fill.

The air smells so fresh and unspoiled compared to the city

and I take off my sandals to feel the deep carpet of grass around my feet. Asher sits at my side and I share some of the food that I have left and he opens his mouth in a smile. Boredom is the hardest thing to overcome out in the pasture so I reach for my flute and start to play the tunes I have taught myself in these hours of solitude. When the sheep begin to listen and come close to me I know they are done feeding and want water.

"Asher, to the stream," I call out and he starts barking and heading down the mountain to the stream below. I look around for strays but the flock has stayed tight. At the stream I kneel down to refill my water pouch while the sheep drink and cool their feet.

That's when I see it, a lion at the entrance of the forest beyond the clearing. He has the advantage of the trees and the darkness of a cave to his left while I am without a shield at the edge of the water. My eyes lock to the animal's and I try to anticipate his next move. Was he a man-eater or would he drag off one of my sheep? Our eyes stay locked as I slowly reach for my sling and the lion begins to pace and his mouth drops open. I can see the sharpness of his teeth that rip flesh as easy as my knife.

I scrape over the ground with the bottom of my sandal hoping to feel a rock close to the surface. Yet I know that if he charges I won't have time to retrieve the stone under foot and throw it. Then Asher catches sight of him and starts barking, the lion is distracted, and the sheep are alarmed and start to scatter. In that moment of confusion I snatch up the rock from the dirt. I place it in the sling, swing it in a circle twice and then let it fly praying

Chapter Nine

it will hit its mark. Wounded and dazed the lion skirts back into the cover of the trees. I round up the flock as quickly as I can and rush them up the side of the mountain to safety. Asher dashes to the front and I guard them from the rear.

Back in the safety of the sheepfold I count them again. Thank goodness the number is still forty-one, Papa would be proud of me, but I still have a problem. I have to get rid of the lion. The herd would have to eat again tomorrow and the next day. What if it ventures close to the house and attacks my Mama? There was only one thing I can do; I have to return to the cave. I fill my scrip with heavy sharp rocks for my sling and feel in my pocket for my knife.

"Come, Asher, we have to get that lion out of our territory," I say as he trots beside me to the other side of the mountain.

In the clearing of the stream I see it in the shadows of the trees waiting for some thirsty animal to drink.

"Quiet, Asher," I say as I put a heavy rock in my sling.

I swing it high over my head until it begins to whirr and then I release it. I follow it to the point between the eyes of the lion. He roars with pain, looks in our direction, and then he charges toward us.

"Run, Asher," I shout as I start running toward the forest hoping to find a tree I can climb. The lion is hurt and is running slower, thank God. There's an opening on the other side of the trees and I keep running through it. I turn around to look back to see if the lion has given up the chase and that's when I stumble over a branch on the edge of a cliff. I'm falling faster and then faster until I can't see what's around me. I reach my arms out to grab hold of anything to break my fall and then I pass out. When I open my eyes I'm lying in the ruffled sheets of my bed and I feel like I've been sleep for at least a week. I turn the TV on to CNN just to make sure it was still Saturday and that I hadn't been asleep for days.

"What the hell was that all about?" I asked as I stood in the mirror making sure that I have the same face I had last night. That episode was mind-boggling; that excerpt wasn't from my life. That experience had to be from another life in another era. Yet, it was as vivid as my other experiences and I felt that I was actually present in the life. When I was there it was me, I'm sure of that, but what's up with the shepherd boy? I didn't get the impression that we were two individuals. I was acting on my own volition. This was so confusing; I wasn't sure what had gone wrong. I had to get some coffee and something to eat. I took a quick shower and changed since I hate to cook in pajamas.

I took my time and made myself some French toast while I went over everything that had happened. The difference was the increase in the dosage. Could it have put my conscious mind or my spirit in a deeper state where it separated from my life and went to another? The whole thing was getting more spacey by the minute. I went into my home office and turned on the computer. I googled the date that King Solomon's Temples were destroyed and read that it occurred five centuries before Jesus Christ was born. Then I googled time travel, but I couldn't understand much of what I read and most of it didn't seem to apply.

Chapter Nine

It wasn't my tangible body that had done the traveling; it was the essence of me or my spirit that was transported to my body at another space and time. I started to wonder if the spirit was some type of trinity that might exist in three parts, the past, present, and the future. What if I had gone from my present life to another life thousands of years before? The notion fascinated me; I had been a male, a Jew. Without this experience I never would have thought I could have been anything other than a black female.

Then there's another possibility, maybe I'm spending too much time by myself and insanity is setting in. Yet, I couldn't help but recognize a shared problem. It was the fear of nightmares and the dreams of a traumatic event. Being Jed I saw how ridiculous it was to be afraid of dreams when the daily challenges of life are much more daunting. After that experience I needed some company from my present. I called George to see if he wanted to go out to dinner.

***

The hostess sat us in a quiet private booth at Jim Kelley's and George ordered us a couple glasses of wine.

"I was surprised to hear from you, it's been a while. How have you been?" he asked.

"I'm doing well," I said, "I've been getting a lot more rest and it's been good for me."

"How about your marital status, have there been any changes that might interest me?"

"You didn't waste any time getting to the point. I haven't filed any papers as of yet but I'm ready to move on."

"That's encouraging," he said as he lifted his glass for me to toast.

"What about you, have you been dating anyone?" I asked curiously.

"I have met a few women and I've been out several times but not with anyone who appeals to me like you do."

"I see you still know how to make a woman feel good."

"I'm here whenever you're ready to take the next step; I've told you where I stand."

"I know that, and I think about it more than you know."

"Well then what are we waiting for?" he asked just as the waitress came over to the table.

"I think we need to order," I said, changing the subject.

"Do you need a few more minutes?" the waitress asked.

"Just a few," George answered. "Do you want an appetizer?" he asked, looking at the menu.

"No, the shrimp with pasta is enough for me."

When the waitress came back George ordered the baked chicken and the shrimp for me.

"So if you're not ready to be my woman, to what do I owe this invitation?"

"I missed your company and I wanted to see you."

"I'm not interested in hanging out, Portia; I'm looking for someone to share my life with."

"You're way ahead of me and I'm trying to catch up. I've just gotten to the point where I can relax, allow myself to be happy, and have a good time."

Chapter Nine

What I couldn't say was that the pressure and anxiety about getting propofol was gone but I was doing something he wouldn't understand or condone, and I wasn't ready to stop.

"This looks delicious," George said when the server brought our food out, "I just remembered that I didn't have lunch today."

For George it was all or nothing and I was still being pulled in several directions. I ate slowly to extend the time that I could have his attention.

"Thanks for joining me," I said at the end at of the evening.

"It was my pleasure," he said, walking me to my car.

"I'll be in touch," I said as he closed the car door.

He nodded and walked away.

Chapter Ten

Pam was coming home for a couple of weeks before the fall semester started and I wanted to spend some quality time with her. It was obvious to me now that I had checked out on her trying to retrieve what I lost. Strange as it may seem, now that I knew I could see Nick whenever I wanted I was able to let go a little more. It began to dawn on me that Nicholas' life was continual and that his spirit lived in another dimension and that he was probably happy. On my way to the airport I made up my mind to try to treasure the child I had in the present.

"She looks so grownup," I thought to myself as I saw Pam coming down on the escalator. It was as if I closed my eyes for a minute and she went from being a little girl to a woman.

"I really missed you, girl," I said as I hugged her tight feeling her hair and smooth skin against my face.

"You look good, Mom, what have you been doing?" she asked as we walked to join the crowd at the luggage conveyor.

"Sweetie, I've been busy, that's all I can say."

"You must really like your new job. I didn't think you would enjoy working in a hospital, it seemed like too much drama for you."

"You're right about that but it has its perks," I said as the baggage belt began to rotate, "Forget me, what's going on with you, how was the job?"

"It was good even though I didn't learn that much. At least I got to hang out at the beach for the whole summer."

"I don't guess there's anything wrong with that, downtime is good now and then. What do you want to do in the time you have before the fall semester starts?"

"Daddy wants me to spend a week with him," she said, cutting off my air supply for a second.

"Wow, that sounds nice, but I didn't know you two were communicating," I said, hiding my astonishment with my eyes on the suitcases revolving in front of me.

"Yeah, he called me about four months ago and we've been talking on a regular basis. He came out to Virginia to see me for a weekend."

Now I'm really shocked. I hadn't even considered Raymond, I hadn't seen or heard from him in so long I assumed he'd left both of our lives. Pam grabbed her bags when they circled in front of us and we each took one and rolled them to the car.

I can't explain it, but I was feeling jealous that Raymond would have gone out to Virginia to see Pam and I hadn't. I couldn't help but feel guilty because of the precious years I had wasted with her while I was absorbed in my sorrow over Nick. Just when I thought I could make it up to her Raymond beat me to it. It was my own fault; I couldn't expect her life to be on hold while I tried to pull myself back together.

We rode in silence until Pam said, "Dad was thinking that we all might go out to eat together before I go back to school."

All of us together, going out, what was this about? I had enough things going on right now.

"It doesn't sound like a bad idea, after all we're family," I said, trying to sound casual. "How's he doing?"

"He's doing real good, Mom, he said he's been in counseling and would like all of us to go together with him one day."

Okay, now I've reached my limit, that's all the new information I can comprehend in one hour. I took a deep breath to steady my emotions since I was behind the wheel.

"It's something we'll have to talk about when we go out," I said, refusing to be the bad guy by saying no outright.

"Anyway you never told me what you've been doing all summer?" she said.

"Not much, just taking some time for some much needed introspection."

I wanted Pam and me to spend as much time together as possible so I took a week of vacation from work. I also texted David and told him my daughter was home just in case he thought about dropping by. It was good to have Pam home, the house seemed normal again. We cooked out on the grill just for ouselves, shopped until we dropped, and rented a bunch of Redbox movies that we watched late into the night hours.

One night I asked, "Did you date anybody in Virginia?"

"We don't really go out one-on-one like that, Mom; we just meet up at a club or restaurant, or go to a set at somebody's house."

"So that's how it's done now, no wonder your generation can't hook up. What would you think about me dating again?"

"I think you should go out for fun but not to get serious. I think you and Daddy will probably get back together again."

"I don't know about that, however, my mind has been opened up to a whole world of possibilities."

***

At the end of the week Pam packed up some things to take to Raymond's place. He rang the door bell around 7:30. I stood in the foyer frozen in my tracks; I hadn't seen my husband in two years and I didn't know what to expect. Pam walked around me and opened the door. Time had stood still for him; he looked the same as he did the day he walked out on us.

"Hey, sweetheart," he said, giving her a hug.

"Hey, Daddy," she said, "Let me go upstairs and get my bag."

"Hello, Portia," he said warmly, "How are you?"

"I'm good and how are you?" I asked formally, trying not to stare.

"I'm better," he said, acting as if he had only been gone a week or two.

"That's good, Pam seems happy about seeing you."

"It's taken me a while to get my head straight but she's my heart and I want to be here for her. I'm hoping that you and I can talk soon and clear the air between us."

"Sure, I think we should," I replied as Pam ran down the steps with her small suitcase.

She gave me a hug and kiss and they went out the door. I could hear their voices and then laughter through the door before the car doors shut and then I felt left out. It was unnerving for me to see him standing in our house again. He was so casual,

Chapter Ten

disregarding all the hurt he added when he walked out. I couldn't deal with it, I needed to get away. I headed straight in the kitchen to the refrigerator, reached behind the sticks of Land O' Lakes in the butter compartment, grabbed one of the vials of the milk that took me places, went up the stairs to my room, pulled the kit from under the bed, and injected the higher dose.

I close my eyes and I feel the weight of my body lessening and the next moment I'm floating like air within a fog. I'm floating in a circle and I'm moving faster and faster. I have the sensation of spinning and then I'm falling. Streaks of brilliant lights are flying past me. The white light divides and I can see motionless images like the negatives from a roll of film. Colors bleed into the light and I focus on the most beautiful vision I've ever seen.

A drum beat reverberates in my chest quickening my heartbeat. The sound of horns blaring pierces my ears. My feet hit the stucco platform hard and my necklace of turquoise bounces up and hits me in the teeth. On the ground I can see that I have lost several of the most colorful plumes from my headdress in the jump down from the royal seating area. I crouch down and move closer to the stairs that lead the way out of the theater. The scraped skin on the side of my foot starts to burn and chafe under my sandal, but all of it was a small price to pay for my escape out of the Great Plaza.

I refuse to sit through another sickening and brutal display of the ballgame. I don't know why they even go through the pretense, just cut the man's head off and be done with it. From what I've seen it's not the gods who are the bloodthirsty ones.

I move quickly along the left side of the Temple Pyramid running my hands along the intricate carvings that embellish the limestone with my servant, Star, following close behind me to get back to the royal house.

We first stop at the Queen's place where the noble women like to gather but my mother wasn't there. I want to find her because I know she's feeling downhearted today. It is the first time Father has been seen publicly with his second wife. I'm upset for her; to me it is an insult to my mother. Why should a man take another wife just because the first bore him two daughters and he wants a son. I get to my room and I can still hear the roaring of the crowd through my open window.

"Star, help me change out of this huipil," I say, disgusted with the events of the day.

I remove the ornately decorated headdress that weighs heavily on my head with its gold and jade stones. I love it, it is my favorite one, so beautiful with all the feathers that reach out high above the top, and it always makes me feel as splendid as the multihued birds that live in the rain forests. I change into a brightly woven skirt and tie the belt firm around my waist.

"Lady, your hair is mussed, I need to fix it," Star says, she is my friend as well as my maidservant.

I sit there fuming while Star takes down my ponytail and plaites the long ribbons of color in my hair. In the chair my eyes drift down to my arms and I follow the intricate patterns and swirls that had taken hours to be painted on my skin and it calms me down. Soon they'll be permanently carved and my skin will always be adorned. When Star is done with my hair I continue the search to find my mother.

"Mother, where are you," I shout, trying to locate her in the royal residence quarters. "Mother," I call again, entering into her private sleeping room, and then I see her seated with her back to me by the window.

"Bird, does your father know that you have left the ceremony?" she asks.

"He just wanted me there for his imperial promenade in the Plaza. He doesn't care about us anymore, Mother; we've been tossed aside so he can replace us with a new family."

"That's not true, Bird, we won't be replaced, you must understand the ways of our people, and taking another wife doesn't diminish his love for us."

"I still can't understand why it's necessary to dress in the finest robes and the most exquisite jewelry just to watch another man meet his demise."

"The people want to see their king adorned with supreme garments and headdress whenever he's appears to the public. You're the princess, Bird, the next in line to the throne; you're going to have to learn to accept the responsibility that comes along with it."

"I sat there for the spiritual dance, the music of the drums and the horns, I enjoy that portion of the festivity very much," I say in my defense.

"All the rituals of the Mayan people of Mutul are important; sacrifices must be made to the Sun, Moon, and the planets."

"Mother, it's backward and barbaric. What's the sense in so much studying and learning if we won't rely on rational thinking? If we're not going to behave as civilized human beings then why don't we just go back into the jungle?"

"You're being obstinate, my child, you need to go and speak with the priests for more understanding."

"You're right, Mother, I should go for more lessons in the Teachers quarters."

I give her a kiss and head over to the far annex of the palace with Star following close behind me. As far as Mother is concerned Father is her god, she doesn't see any wrong in anything he does. It is so frustrating; no one wants to take heed to the warnings that are all around us.

"Greeting my Priest," I say, bowing my head with respect.

"Come in, Lady Nine, why aren't you at the King's right hand?"

"We aren't seeing eye to eye at this time."

"A father's love is never in doubt, Bird."

"My teacher, you are the only father I have ever known, to him I'm merely a prized possession, not a confidant. I love him dearly but he is misguided and I fear his pride will weaken his leadership, constant warfare will only bring our own destruction."

"Such strong words to be spoken by such a gentle creature, what stirs all this furor?"

"Teacher, I have been to the top of Temple V and have taken note of the changes in the alignments of the planets and sun. If the wars and fighting don't cease they will surely lead to our end. We only make more enemies when we resolve our conflicts

Chapter Ten

by cutting off the heads of captured warriors? When the caged panther breaks loose, we can expect to be eaten."

"You worry too much for a young girl; it must be time for you to marry soon."

That comment lets me know he's not taking me seriously, another male who doesn't respect the intelligence of a female.

"Excuse me, teacher, I must not be late to the evening meal," I say, choosing to return to the royal quarters of the palace.

"I missed you, daughter, at the final of the game?" father says at the table.

"I'm sorry, Father; I was feeling ill for a moment and needed to lie down."

"Did you call for the priests?" he asks Mother.

"She's fine now," she answers.

"Very good, I can't have my princess getting sick."

I watch him rush through the meal, rolling all of his food into the tortilla to eat and then washing it down with the corn liquor.

"By the way, I have a meeting with the noble elders this evening, there is more trouble brewing," he says to Mother as he leaves the dining room.

I sip on my hot chocolate for a few minutes before I say, "No good will come from that meeting, Mother, they all think alike. You can't have a rational conversation with only one point of view."

"Daughter, men are like animals, very territorial with the philosophy of 'kill or be killed.'"

"It makes no sense, Mother; you can't truly control another

human being that has free will. Why can't they be happy? Nature has given us the rainforests, and we have wealth and culture. Why throw it all away for what they think is more power? It's only a concept, it's not real."

"This is the way it's always been since the beginning of time, Bird."

"The priests say men are better rulers because females are emotional beings that allow their hearts to lead them, but it isn't true, Mother. Females make decisions after considering the consequences in their minds while men move on impulse and rule with emotion, why else would there be so much killing?"

"Bird, I'm not sure if you were born too early or too late," she said, rising from the table.

***

I go to the top of the Temples over the next week to chart the orientation of the planets and the moon and the signs don't change.

Then over the morning meal, Father says to Mother, "The priests tell me that Venus is in the ideal position for our victory, it is time for us to join our military forces with the King of Caracol and deliver a humiliating defeat to the Calakmul."

I wait until the servants have left the room before I speak.

"Father, please don't accompany the army, I'm worried, the positions of Venus are not favorable to us right now."

"Daughter, I'm a warrior king, I have always led my military and I always will. The priests have advised us well and I have no fear in my heart," he says before he leaves us alone at the table.

Chapter Ten

I push away my cup of chocolate, it tastes bitter to me.

"Mother, the pattern of the heavens are shifting daily, I don't see what the priests see. I don't think the timing is good."

"They are more experienced than you, Bird; they have guided your father for many years before you were born. He trusts them."

The sun is at its highest point of the day; the time for the army to gather has arrived. The drums have already begun to beat a slow steady rhythm and I watch as my mother adjusts Father's jaguar cape and places his helmet on his head. He looks strong and impressive but it doesn't soothe my worries.

"Come back to us with your head held high," she says to him.

"That is my intention," he says as he gives her an affectionate hug.

He reaches for his spear and walks out of the royal quarters with his attendants at his sides. I hear the trumpets ring out to signal the march out into the jungle. The paint on my skin begins to itch with my perspiration and I hear the jingle of my jewelry in the background as I shake with trepidation.

I go for a bath before I retreat into the private space of my room without Star. I take off my sandals and remove the ribbons of color from my plaits. I get my bloodletting bowl and place it on the floor in the center of my room. I kneel over it and pierce the underside of my tongue with a blade of obsidian and drip my blood into the bowl.

"Speak to me," I plead to my ancestors, "Tell me what to do, what to say to protect my Father the King. I fear great danger is upon us. I've seen the signs in the heavens. I fear there is a traitor, one or many among us. Reveal to me the identities of those who would betray us for the security of the city is at stake."

All of a sudden I feel a rumbling under the ground, it grows stronger until I feel the whole structure shake and then my bowl is turned over and my blood is spilled. I crawl across the room to my bed despondent, it's too late, and nothing can be done.

There were agonizing days before I am summoned to the central room of the palace.

I stand before the expressionless faces of the priests and elders and listen as my mother says, "Bird, there is terrible news, your father has been captured, and he will most certainly be executed or forced into a brutal ballgame before he is sacrificed. You will be Queen, my daughter. You will have to rule, Bird."

I was too dazed by her words to cry for my father, and I wouldn't dare shed a tear in the presence of these men who think me unworthy.

I walk over and whisper to my teacher and confidant, "Meet me at the top of the central pyramid, there the gods will give me guidance."

I return to my quarters and sit down on my hands in a futile attempt to stop them from shaking. What should I do, should I send warriors to hunt for their King, should I plot revenge, or should I take the unheard of approach and negotiate peace.

At the top of the pyramid I'm humbled by the majesty of the Temple and the beauty of the sea of green trees below me. I look into the sky in search of answers and then I raise my arms up in prayer. Suddenly I feel a heavy force in my back and then my

Chapter Ten

body jolts forward. Someone pushed me, who and why? I am the Queen now, who would dare to commit a crime against me. I lose my footing and tumble forward. I'm falling. It feels like I'm moving in slow motion and then I'm falling so fast I can't see, I can only feel the leaves of trees against my skin. I reach out my arms to catch myself but I don't' feel anything. I close my eyes and I lose consciousness.

When I wake up I'm laying on the floor beside my bed. What is going on? The only thing I was convinced of was that I wasn't going to worry myself to death, like Lady Nine, we don't have the power to change the inescapable and doing so only causes us more aggravation.

Chapter Eleven

My mind is blown even more with the possibility that the spirit can live in so many dimensions, crossing thousands of years in opposite parts of the world. Trying to understand what is actually happening is way above my head. I've never thought this deeply about the essence of life. A few months ago I wouldn't have even thought this was possible. I'm a Christian and I believe in eternal life but now I'm not sure what that means. Where does heaven and hell fit in. This is all too deep, my perception of the boundaries of life is expanding but my view of the world seems to contract. I still have so many questions. Am I getting visions of the past or is this happening in real-time. I couldn't hold all of this to myself; I needed to talk to David. On Monday morning I texted him and asked him to bring his walking shoes to the park after work.

The summer wasn't over, it was still quite warm, but the sky was overcast shielding the landscape from the sun, David shouldn't complain too badly about the heat. I got out of the car to stretch and clear my head some; I had too much going on. There was the change in Raymond, my feelings for George, Pam starting her senior year, and me traveling to what I think are my past lives.

"More time at home with the wife certainly has its side effects I see," I said to David when he pulled in beside me and got out of his car.

"Don't start with me, Portia, I know I've put on a few pounds, my lady has been trying to keep me happy by cooking me gourmet meals every day."

"A heart doctor should know better, it's time for you to get back out here with me and burn some of those calories you're packing."

"You're right, so what's up, how have you been?"

"I've been good but I wanted to talk to you about the propofol."

"Uh-huh, what about it?" he asked suspiciously, "You know I'm not comfortable with you doing that when I'm not around."

"I haven't had any problems, it's just that I've had some truly bizarre experiences that I didn't tell you about and now I've got to tell somebody about it and you're the only person who I can be open with and discuss it."

"That sounds mysterious, is this something physical or mental?"

I decided then not to tell him about the shepherd boy or the Mayan princess, he would think I'm certifiably insane. I kept the conversation limited to my present life.

"I don't know how to categorize it so I'll just cut to the chase. When I'm under it I flash back to memories of my past."

"It's probably just a dream. Whenever I eat marinara sauce I have crazy dreams."

"David it's more than that, it's like being in a scene of my life that's been re-winded and played out for me again. They're occurrences and conversations that actually happened."

Chapter Eleven

"I don't think that's abnormal or unusual, they're your memories and they're in your subconscious."

"That makes sense, but have you ever talked to any of the residents who have taken it?"

"Ethically speaking, it's not the kind of thing that we'd want to sit around and talk about."

"You're right, I'm probably making too much out of it."

"Anyway, you've had your fantasy and that's the end of it, but it wouldn't hurt you to talk to a professional."

"On that note, time for more walking and less talking."

We put in two miles and broke a good sweat, but I hadn't gotten any clarity.

"See you on Thursday," David said before he pulled off.

Now who else could I talk to? I knew it wasn't simply a dream; I've been having dreams my whole life, it was phenomenal and I needed to figure out what was happening. I was going to have to do my own research. On the drive home from the park I was much more aware of the world around me. The complexity of the sun hanging in the sky, the gravity that holds us attached to the earth, the miracle of night and day, and the freedom of the wind and rain. There are surely more mysteries we have yet to unfold.

When I got inside I grabbed an Arizona tea and sat down at the computer before I even showered. First I googled time travel and when Albert Einstein's name popped up I knew I was in trouble. I read a little about his theory of relativity but when I got to quantum physics and the speed of light I knew that I had really gone into another dimension. My next google was to find a physics professor at TSU. I selected Dr. Olivia Myers; her research interests included quantum field theory and philosophy of science. I wrote down her number and e-mail and put it in my messenger bag on my way to get cleaned up.

***

"Hello Keisha," I said, not pausing for any pleasantries when I got to work.

"You have two appointments this morning," she said offhandedly to my back.

"Thank you," I answered, but my first order of business was to call the professor.

"Good morning, Dr. Myers," I said, surprised to hear an actual person answer their phone on the first attempt, but nevertheless another lie makes its way to my lips.

"My name is Portia Roberts and I'm preparing a speech for my Toastmaster's meeting about time travel. I read on the TSU Physics Department website that you are interested in quantum theory. I'm an alumnus and I was wondering if I could buy you a cup of coffee and pick your brain for a few minutes."

"That sounds intriguing, it just so happens that I have space in my office hours this afternoon around 3:00 if you can make it on short notice."

"No problem, my schedule is flexible, I'll see you then."

"Good, my office is in the engineering building in room 322, and black with two sugars."

I left the hospital at around 2:15, swung by Starbucks and got

Chapter Eleven

to the office suite at the top of the hour. The door was open but no one was there so I took a seat by the door to wait. Dr. Myers' office was not at all what I expected. I thought it would be dark and dusty and piled high with text books and papers, but it was very neat with plants and decorated with pictures and drawings from her family, not to mention the candy dish filled with cinnamon jaw breakers.

"Excuse me for being late; I had to use the little girls' room," Dr .Myers said with a smile when she saw me.

I smiled back at her surprised again, her skin was nearly translucent like she never got any sun and her hair was completely white, she looked like a grandmother who spent most of her time baking cookies. I stood up and we shook hands and I handed her the cup of coffee.

"Oh, that's so good," she said after taking a sip. "Now Ms. Roberts, what would you like to know?"

"Well, to start with, are there any new scientific theories on traveling through time?"

"A ton of research has been done but most of the theories are just extensions of Einstein's quantum theory. There is some support for the far-fetched theory of wormholes, where by incredibly an opening can be created when a mass presses on two dimensions of the universe and they are brought together forming a tunnel that allows passage from one to another."

"So the scientific theory of time travel is based on actual transport of something physical to another time, like a machine or an aircraft?"

"That would be their dream approach but so far it's still science fiction, we haven't figured out how Scotty can beam us up."

"Well, what do you think about Einstein's theory that the past, present, and future exist simultaneously?"

"I believe time is relative, and within ten seconds of time there is the past, present, and future, they are so close."

"I never thought about it in that way, but it's true," I said.

"In my opinion, we'll never find a way to travel into the past, however there is some remote possibility that we will be able to travel into the future but the only thing I'm sure about is that it won't be in my lifetime."

"You never know what can happen these days," I said, thinking about my mystical travels over centuries. "One last question, we have been speaking about mass or a person traveling through time, what about something weightless, like the human spirit, traveling like the speed of light?"

"That's the point where science and religion collide or more so crash, the reference point depends on what you believe about the nature of human beings."

"I see, well, I really appreciate you taking the time to talk with me," I said, standing and shaking her hand across the desk.

"I hope I gave you something to put in your speech," she said, smiling.

"Yes, you certainly did, thanks," I said, shaking her hand again before I exited out of the door.

That was definitely a dry run. I didn't learn anymore than I did on the internet, although her reference to religion might be on

Chapter Eleven

point, science hasn't been able to explain a tenth of the mysteries of life on earth. The ring of the cell phone brings me back to reality.

"Hey, Mom, what're you doing?" Pam said through the receiver.

"Hey, girl, I'm driving home, what are you doing?"

"Dad and I are going to the mall."

"That's amazing, how did you accomplish that?"

"Stop, it wasn't that hard, I'm calling because we want you to come to dinner with us tomorrow since I'm moving into the dorm this weekend."

"Dinner with you two and I don't have to cook, let me ink that in."

"Very cute, Mom, it's your choice where we eat so call me back and let me know where you want to go."

"Now I'm truly amazed, I get to choose the restaurant, things have really changed."

"Bye, Mom."

***

I had a taste for seafood but I didn't feel like getting my hands dirty at the crab shack so we met at Red Lobster. I got there first, unsurprisingly; those two are always late wherever they go. As they made their way over to the table they both looked comfortable and happy and I couldn't help but wonder how I looked to them. They both seemed to be moving on and adjusting well, why couldn't I get my shit together? Raymond really looked good, what was he doing with himself? From all appearances he had found a way to reverse time, he hadn't age one day. His face was so relaxed and he smiled so easily, I considered that maybe there was another woman in his life.

"Hello, you two, late as usual," I said.

"It was Dad, not me; I was dressed and ready before he even got in the shower," Pam said, sliding into the booth.

"The defense can rest, my dear, I know who the guilty party is, and I'm very familiar with your daddy's routine."

"No fair, I haven't even stated my case yet," Raymond said, laughing as he sat beside Pam.

"There's no need and the punishment is dinner is on you," I said with a chuckle.

The waiter brought over two more menus and took our drink orders.

"I'll be having the lobster," Pam chimed in.

"That sounds good, I think I'll join you on that. What about you, Portia?" he asked.

I could feel his eyes on me but I kept my gaze pasted on the menu, "I want some type of sampler or platter where I can get a taste of everything."

"All right, Mom, you want some seafood for real," Pam joked.

"That's what I said didn't I?"

"Yes you did and that's why we're here," Raymond said.

The waiter came back with our drinks and we ordered our entrees. Dinner conversation was casual; we talked about the food, the classes Pam would take, and what movie they wanted to see after dinner. Raymond helped me eat the large platter I'd ordered like he had always done and Pam tugged on the lobsters until the shells were empty.

"Ooo, I am so full and I need to wash my hands," she said, rising up from the table.

Raymond shifted his legs to the side to let her get by and when she was out of earshot he said, "I've missed you, Portia."

"It's been a long time," I responded.

"I missed you during all of that time."

"Why, you didn't have to, I never asked you to leave, I really needed you back then."

"Baby, I couldn't hold myself up much less anyone else. I was walking around like a zombie, and there were days that I considered taking myself out of my misery. Nothing in my life had torn me down like that before, I was empty inside."

Raymond's words felt like a punch in the gut and my stomach started to gurgle on all the fish I had eaten.

"I had no idea what you were going through, Ray, we never talked about it," I said with regret, "Remember I was drowning in my own grief."

"I just want to say how sorry I am for not being there for you," he said earnestly.

"You don't have to apologize, I don't blame you; none of it was your fault. Besides, you seem like you have things under control now."

"I'm in a good place."

"What did you do, how did you get over, through, or around everything? You seem so different."

"It's nothing but Jesus."

"It took a minute to get that lobster smell off my hands," Pam said, sliding back in the booth next to her Dad.

Seeing them side-by-side again made me want to pull out my phone camera, but being together was awkward for me, I took a mental picture of them instead.

"Thanks, you two, for the invite, I really enjoyed the company and the dinner," I said after the waiter brought the check and started to clear the table. "We have to do it again sometime."

"Yeah, that sounds good," Pam added.

"We'll have to reward ourselves after we get this child moved back on campus," Raymond said, bumping his shoulder against hers.

***

It took all day to get Pam moved in and settled in the campus apartments and I was tired. I was emotionally drained; I wanted to escape from the confusion of my life for a while. It seemed like Raymond wanted us to get close again after all this time, but I still thought about George quite often, and I didn't know what was going on with David and me. The only thing that I was sure of was that I wanted another shot of propofol. I wanted to know who I was at another time. It was more interesting and less stressful than my life was right now. I had refrained from even thinking about it while Pam was in the house. I couldn't take a chance on her coming into my room with all my drug paraphernalia exposed. That would have taken more explaining than I could do even if I had ten tongues and till the end of time.

I took a long shower and got comfortable in the bed. I prepared

Chapter Eleven

the syringe just like I did the last time and then I pushed the milky fluid into my arm. The room faded into black and I was falling away from myself and then I had the feeling of weightlessness. I started floating and then I began to spin like water going down a drain. Then three spinning beams of light appeared and I watched as color began to blend into them. Images began to flash quickly within one of the beams. I was drawn to point of fiery orange brightness that felt hot when I focused on it. I closed my eyes to shield them from the direct light and that's when I heard the clumping sound and felt the rumbling of the earth beneath me.

I open my eyes after the noon prayer and I rise to my feet hoping Allah hasn't turned his face away from us today. Each time the pounding hoofs of horses and camels shake the dust from the sands surrounding the Mosques I fear the next civil war or invasion from the outside. I look out of the window hoping the danger has passed and see my group of students reassembling in the fog-filled courtyard for the afternoon lesson. I know in my heart that this university, this beacon of knowledge and spirituality won't survive much longer in the midst of such debauchery. You can only swim with the crocodile for so long before you feel his bite and he swallows you up.

We're supposed to be spreading the great teachings of Islam at this oasis in the desert, except now Timbuktu has become a willing participant in the trading of slaves and not all in accordance with the laws of the Qur'an. It's as if rivalries and conflicts are being created to instigate fighting where the spoils of war are claimed along with men, women, and children who are sold like cattle. It provides us with a comfortable living while others do our dirty work. Needless to say, no one cares what I think about it.

Anyway, the direction of the sun tells me it's time to return to my class and finish the morning lesson. I walk outside the Mosque to the area where most of my students are sitting and talking among themselves under the shade of an acacia tree. Many of them have traveled great distances only to find themselves in the midst of a war zone.

Interestingly, there is one particular student who I feel I've met before and when he returns I ask him, "Have you attended the Sankore University previously, you seem so familiar to me?"

"No I haven't," he answers, "This is my first time coming to Timbuktu."

"Do you have any other family members here in the city?"

"No, sir, I don't."

"Well, I hope it fills all of your expectations," I say as he takes a seat.

During the class I still can't shake the sense that I've known him before today, however, that shouldn't surprise me with the thousands of students that I have met over the years, but it's like we met a long time ago. No matter, he probably reminds me of my younger self despite the fact it's only been a few years since I graduated and received my turban.

"Attention class, this afternoon we'll have an informal debate on the basis of Islamic law or Sharia. Can anyone tell me the core philosophy of law?"

I take notice of the hand of the student I just spoke with and

Chapter Eleven

nod for him to answer.

"Justice is the central element of all law and has been from the beginning of time," he says.

"Correct, the Qur'an says *'A moment of justice is better than seventy years of worship in which you keep fasts and pass the nights in offering prayers and worship to Allah.'*"

A lively debate begins and the students discuss the merits of social justice and moral thinking. I'm satisfied that this first day of learning has been a good one and from the discourse I can see that I have several exceptional students enrolled in my class.

I wait for my wife, Amina, outside of the Mosque after the evening prayer for our walk home. The students studying medicine have many questions and she's usually delayed long after the class session has ended.

"Hello, Mohammad, how was your day?" she asks with a smile that belies the exhaustion she must feel.

I take the manuscripts from her arms and place them with my own under my arm.

"It was encouraging, and how are you feeling since you insist on teaching another class before the baby is born."

"No one is even aware that I'm pregnant and the class will end before they realize it."

"I worry about you wearing yourself out."

"You worry about everything; Fatima cooks, cleans, and goes to the market. I'm not helpless."

"That's another thing that worries me, I teach all day that we are equal and I have a slave in my home."

"Fatima has been with me since I was a young girl."

"That was in your father's house not mine; it's a contradiction of my beliefs. I want you to be comfortable and taken care of but not at the expense of someone else."

Amina is quiet as we walk past the bustling marketplace where women are selling corn, milk, butter, and pottery, she doesn't understand my misgivings, she is the third generation of scholars in her family and she's always had servants around her. I come from a family that worked the fields, hunted, and sacrificed to send me to school.

"It's been easy for you, Amina, so it's hard for you to understand."

"Easy for a woman in a man's world, that's nonsense, and you say I'm detached from reality."

I have to laugh in my defense because I can't argue the point. "I'm sorry; I get so worked up in class. I know I needed to relax and enjoy my life and my wife but I'm one of those people who get worried when everything is going great."

Close to home I shake my head in dismay when another caravan of camels passes us on their way to the market to trade cloth, tea, spices, and kola nuts for salt, gold, and slaves. After dinner I prepare my lesson for tomorrow and I think about the lines of camels and ships that are constantly coming into the city and it worries me. The salt mines around us are as valuable as the gold and that prosperity attracts enemies as well as friends. The Moroccans are too close for comfort and their interest is not in intellectual or spiritual knowledge. One thing I have learned

Chapter Eleven

in my studies is that when the opportunity for financial gain increases the moral standard decreases. In my last prayer I ask for strength and wisdom for the Askia Empire which has been compromised and corrupted by the lucrative slave trade and I wonder if Allah will continue to protect us when we have gone against his laws. I close my books to see if Amina has completed her reading but when I go into our room she is already asleep.

***

On our morning walk to the mosque I can detect a change in the atmosphere; there is uneasiness among the men and women in the marketplace. It's as if a massive sandstorm has been predicted. On one hand I wanted to know what the murmurs are about and then on the other I preferred to stay ignorant to them. There have been many civil wars and I pray we are not about to see another one. I take Amina's hand and move quickly to get to the University. We are met with even more confusion, crowds of students are moving in all directions, and the head instructors seem to be troubled.

"What's going on?" I ask a fellow scholar.

"Word has come that the Moroccan Army has taken over Songai and is advancing towards Timbuktu," he answers.

It was the very thing I had dreaded over the last few years. The higher you rise the more you become a clear target.

I go into the courtyard to give a lesson to the students who have chosen to remain. We are all distracted and the subject of family law is the last thing on any of their minds. The end of the day was a welcome relief as I was anxious to get Amina and hurry back to our home. Soldiers are guarding the Mosque and the market is vacant when we pass it.

Over dinner I ask, "Do you think we should try to leave before the Moroccans get to the city?"

"I don't believe we have anything to fear, Mohammad, it would be a miracle for an army to make it across the desert."

"You have no idea how great a motivator that greed can be."

"Mohammad, stop your worrying, you'll ruin your digestion."

"You're right," I say, "There's nothing that can be done about it now anyway."

The next morning I'm awakened by a terrible ruckus. I peer over the edge of the window and the village is immersed in clouds of dust and sand. Through the billows I can see the Moroccan soldiers suited in their armor wielding spears and swords, but the clamoring sound I hear is from their hand weapons that sound like cannons.

"Come out," a voice commands and there's beating against the door.

"Sit in the chair," I tell Amina just before the door bursts open.

Two men push me aside and another holds my arms.

Two more grab Amina and she yells, "Get your hands off me, I'm a member of the Haidara family."

"Good for you," one of them laughs.

They drag us out into the violent swirls of sand whipped up by the melee and we are shuffled with a horde of professors to the Mosques. They take us to the front of the libraries and I'm horrified when they set fire to it. A fellow teacher lurches

Chapter Eleven

forward to fight the flames and he is shot by one of the soldiers with the hand weapon. I hear Amina scream but my mouth hangs open and I can't form words. The huge group of scholars are taken into the Mosque individually and questioned and that's when Amina and I are separated.

A tall imposing man dressed in red and blue asks, "Where are you from?"

"I'm from Songhai," I answer.

"What do your people do?"

"They're farmers," I answer.

"What are you doing here?"

"I'm a teacher; I earned my turban as a scholar at the University."

"What is it that you teach?"

"I teach Islamic law and philosophy."

"You have wasted your mind on useless subjects; maybe you can accomplish something with your physical strength. Join the others back outside."

I breathe a sigh of relief assured that I would be re-united with Amina in a matter of time. Before nightfall we are escorted to the central marketplace where we are kept in tents. Before dawn I hear whispers, Songhai forces have come to our rescue.

"Move quickly, you can find refuge on our islands on the Niger River," they say.

We rush to the shore with only the moon for light and climb into the long boats.

"Where are the rest of the teachers, will they be liberated later," I ask.

"Much later, my friend, those they haven't killed are in route to be exiled in Morocco."

"Nooo," I shout, I have to find Amina.

I run to the stern of the ship and jump feet first into the river. I fall deep into the darkness and the ripples of water circle around me.

I wake up and I'm damp with perspiration. I forgot to turn on the ceiling fan when I turned the air conditioner down. I lie there trying to take in the experience. Somehow again I was able to cross dimensions. Was I in a self-induced light coma where the spirit can roam while the body is held in suspension? What was going on? It was over the top, an African professor with a wife expecting a baby in Timbuktu. This was beyond my comprehension; I believe that God is a supreme entity above gender, but it seemed to me that who we are as humans and the essence of our being can't be separated from our sexual characteristics. However, if we can be a different race and nationality must the gender remain the same? I'm usually invigorated from the propofol induced sleep but the countless questions about what's really happening to me are exhausting. The phone rings and it startles me. "Hello," I whisper into the receiver.

"Good morning, sleepy head, get dressed, I want to take you to church with me this morning. I'll pick you up in about an hour," Raymond said pleasantly.

Chapter Twelve

Raymond had always been a CME worshipper, going to church on Christmas, Mother's Day, and Easter, and that was with much encouragement. Him inviting me to church was incredible, an opportunity I couldn't turn down. He beeped the horn when he pulled up and I swallowed the last bite of toast with a mouthful of orange juice before I dashed out. I opened the door to the car and he looked handsome, well-groomed and suited up in my favorite color of navy blue.

"You look nice," he said as he got in and shut the door.

"Praise the Lord," I answered and we both laughed like we used to before our lives fell apart.

The service was uplifting and it soothed and quieted my mind. The scripture reading said that we were promised an eternal life and now I was truly a firm believer in that fact.

"Can we go to lunch before I take you home?" Raymond asked.

"I'm not that hungry but I could use the company," I answered.

"I know just what the doctor ordered," he said, driving out of the church parking lot.

"Do you now?" I said, thinking that if he only knew, he probably wouldn't be here right now.

"Mind if I open the sun roof?" he asked as he pushed the button.

"No, I need to breathe some fresh air," I said.

Raymond pulled onto the interstate behind a Fedex truck

and the gaseous fumes circulated inside the car and all at once I remembered how fresh the air was in the valley outside of Jerusalem and in the rainforests of South America.

"Raymond, do you believe that we've lived other lives besides the one we're living now?"

"What do mean, like reincarnation?"

"Yeah, something like that."

"I believe there's a heaven and a hell and as far as the rest of it in between, I'm not sure, but I believe that anything is possible in this world.

Raymond exited the interstate at the Opryland Hotel and drove up to the valet.

"Let's walk around for a while and build up an appetite, I know you always wanted to come here for the Sunday Brunch."

"I did but I never thought it was worth the money."

"I think you're worth splurging on and it's a special occasion."

"Really, what's the occasion?"

"We're celebrating you and me spending the whole Sunday together, just us."

"You're right, that's something we've never done before," I said, thinking back.

We walked through the hotel, looked in the windows of the shops, and read the menus outside of several restaurants on our way to the atrium.

"It's really pretty inside here with all the tropical plants and trees growing and the goldfish swimming in the ponds," I said.

"Let's sit over there near the waterfalls," he said, taking my hand.

Chapter Twelve

"Okay, now you're making me feel very special, what's really going on?" I asked, sitting at a table for two.

"Portia, I can't make up to you for all that has gone down, and I know I added to the terrible hurt that you were feeling, but I just want to say I'm sorry, sincerely."

"Thank you for saying that again but it's not necessary. You don't have to convince me of that. None of us are perfect; we all just do the best we can. Now where's the food?" I asked, wanting to maintain my good mood.

He signaled for the waitress to come over and she took our order for champagne and we went to help ourselves to the huge buffet set up in the atrium. The food was so good that we just ate and enjoyed the flavor in silence. After I got my stomach to where it was somewhat satisfied I couldn't hold the questions back any longer.

"Raymond, it's been over two-and-a-half years since we've seen each other, what have you been up to?"

"I've been working mostly and trying to get my mind, body, and soul together again."

"It seems like you've accomplished it all, what's your secret?"

"I've told you, there's no secret, I work out at the gym, I've gotten back in church, and I'm seeing a therapist."

"I can't believe it, after all the times that I asked you to go into counseling with me."

"I wasn't ready then; it would have been a big waste of time. I had to want to do it for myself, not just for you and Pam."

"Wow, I'm blown away," I said, shrugging my shoulders.

"Don't feel like that about it, I loved you both, I still do, and you better than anyone else should know what I was going through."

"Yeah, I did, but I didn't have the luxury of checking out like you did, somebody had to be there for Pam."

"We've had this argument before and I don't see any reason for us to have it again, we've both come along way."

"You're right; we can let it be. So, have you been going out or dating?" I asked, completely changing the subject.

"That's kind of a difficult thing to discuss with my wife," he said, appearing a bit flustered and embarrassed with the question.

"We've been separated for close to three years I wouldn't expect you to live your life without some companionship."

"Portia, I still think of myself as a married man even though we've been apart. I have to be honest with you though, I have gone out a few times."

For some reason that hurt me even though my own record was tarnished.

"Are you back here to finally go through with the divorce?" I asked, probing deeper.

"The only thing that I know for sure is that I missed my family and I wanted to see you. I'm still healing but I want you and Pam back in my life."

"I can't argue with that, it was hard losing my husband and my best friend at the same time, I was a mess."

"See, you can't say nice things like that to me, you almost made me tear up out here in public," he said, and we shared a deep and

Chapter Twelve

cleansing laugh that purged all of the tension between us.

I raised my glass and said, "To friendship," and he tapped it with his.

It was late in the afternoon when he finally drove me back to the house and even after these past two and a half years it felt unnatural for him to drop me off and leave what used to be our home together for almost twenty years. Nevertheless, it had been a good day. I was really happy that Raymond and I had reconnected, in spite of everything; we had a daughter we both loved. I could never completely close the door to that part of my life. The things that attracted me to him so many years ago are still there and that's why we'll always be friends. The sad part is that even now we probably share too much grief to make each other happy as a couple.

***

The alarm went off the next morning and all I could do was shake my head and get out of bed. I didn't even feel like I had a weekend. I had spent the last two hours watching my bedroom get brighter as the moon shifted and the sun rose signaling Monday morning. Spending time with Raymond yesterday and seeing the peace that he had gained started me thinking again. I was strongly considering finding a therapist for myself. I had made some progress in moving forward without Nick and I had learned that our lives are continuous, but Raymond seemed to have made peace with everything and I hadn't. He had a serenity about him and that I craved. I'd been chasing the answer to my melancholy for more than a year, even taken the propofol, and I still wasn't satisfied.

"Good morning, Keisha," I said when I walked into my office suite.

"Good morning, Ms. Roberts," she answered, looking like she'd brought an attitude in with her. "Your husband called and would like you to call him back," she said with a twisted emphasis on the word husband.

"Thanks," I told her without changing my expression.

That was the disadvantage of having an administrative assistant; they were always in your business as if they knew what was going on, except I never discussed my personal life with her so she could think whatever she liked. I closed my door behind me and turned on my computer to search for a therapist.

I googled therapists in Nashville and clicked on a website for Psychologists Today. They had pages of therapists and social workers that practiced in town with their pictures and some information about their education and the area of their practices. Looking at their photos I tried to decide which one I thought would be less judgmental, a woman or a man. I couldn't make up my mind so I decided to make the decision based on their written introductions. So many of them specialized in trauma or healing, quite a few in addictions and sexual abuse, less in personality disorders, and then I saw a male psychologist who focused on sleep disorders and other anxiety issues. I wrote the number down to his office and dialed it on my cell phone.

"Hello, this is Dr. Hollis Lanier's office," the voice on the other end answered.

"Hello, I'm looking for a therapist and I saw Dr. Lanier's profile online, is he accepting new patients?"

"Yes, ma'am, he is, how soon would you be interested in setting up an appointment?"

"As soon as I can," I said.

"What is the nature of the problem you would like to focus on?" the voice inquired.

"Uh, I'm having problems with sleeping," I answered vaguely.

"Okay, Dr. Lanier has an opening next week on Thursday afternoon at 4:00, could you make that one?"

"That'll be perfect," I replied.

"All right, may I have your name and insurance company?"

"Yes, my name is Portia Roberts and I'm insured under HealthShield at Metro General."

I had done it. I called and made an appointment. I was actually going to have someone I could trust to talk to about everything. I felt like some of the weight on me had already been lifted just by making the call. Then I called Raymond.

"What's up?" I asked when he picked up.

"I just wanted to tell you how much I enjoyed your company yesterday," he said.

"I had a good time too, thanks for the invitation."

"When can we do it again?"

"So soon?" I asked.

"Portia, I haven't had a chance to talk to you for almost three years, I need a little more time to catch up."

"Okay, what do you have in mind?"

"I was thinking we could go to J. Alexander's, you always used to like their food."

"I still do."

"What about Friday night around 7:00, I know you like to eat early."

"All right, let's do it."

"Good, I'll pick you up."

I leaned back in my chair and spun around to look at the picture of the empty boat sitting on the lake that hung on the wall. That's where I needed to be, drifting alone in that boat on still waters. I had been in a whirlwind for the last year and I was getting overwhelmed.

Then the phone vibrated, it was a text from David saying, "Meet me at the park tomorrow ready to walk."

***

David beat me to the park and that was unusual for him to be early. He was the most unpredictable man I had ever met. I had no idea of what had motivated him to get out and walk.

"Wow, look who's raring to get their workout going today," I said as I stepped out of the car to join him.

"Very funny, it's the only way I get to talk to you nowadays; you don't call or e-mail a brother anymore," he said as he began stretching out his legs.

"I'm just trying to give you some space so you don't mess up your happy home," I said, twisting my arms to loosen up my back.

"Come on now, you know what's up. It's not the ideal situation and I'm not perfect but I'm gonna make it work.

"That's sounds honorable," I said, clapping my hands in approval.

"It's not easy, Portia. While you're joking she's been acting like my warden and I'm about to break out."

"She knows your history, so she's just a woman trying to protect what's hers and I don't blame her."

"I know I kind of left you hanging, but I've been thinking about you a lot lately. I need to spend some time with you ASAP or I'm going to explode."

I started walking towards the one-mile trail searching for a way to keep the conversation from going in the direction I feared it was headed. We'd walked about a half mile when David pulled me off the trail to talk under a magnolia tree. I looked up at the lovely blossoms and dreaded the words that were coming.

"What we did, the fantasy thing, I can't tell you what it did for me. It was a release that I can't describe and I've been jonesing for that feeling again."

I sympathized with him; I had my own set of demons but couldn't see myself spanking his behind again.

"I hear what you're saying about how good it was for you, but I felt like I was hurting you. You're my friend; I can't abuse you like that."

"You don't understand, it's like I need the pain to release all the mess that builds up inside me."

"And you're the one who told me I need to talk with a professional."

"Baby, I already know what works for me I just need you to say when. I already have a cute policewoman costume for you to wear."

"Come on, we need to keep walking," I said, leading him back onto the park trail.

I upped the pace so he couldn't talk until we had walked another mile-and-a-half back to where our cars were parked. I had gathered my thoughts by then and I was glad I didn't have to tell him a bold-faced lie.

"David, while you were home busy with your wife my husband came back on the scene."

"You're kidding."

"No I'm not; we're going to dinner this weekend, so I won't be available to whip that ass for you."

"I thought you were practically divorced, you haven't seen him for more than two years."

"That's true, but he's been working hard on getting himself together and technically we're still married."

"Portia, our relationship is very important to me, we have a special friendship that I haven't had with another male or female. There are things between us that neither of us can share with anybody else."

"Listen, I feel the same about you, you have no idea what you've done for me. I just think that it will be best for our families if we keep it on the friendship level."

"Look, he just came around; I don't think we need to make any decisions about it right now."

Chapter Twelve

"Okay, let's give it some time," I said as I got into my car.

This was more than I could handle with everything else. Driving home I felt so keyed up I could have walked another three miles. The situations with the men around me made me very nervous and I didn't need that kind of pressure. David and I were like partners in crime with secrets that neither of us wanted revealed. I had started this whole thing trying to find some peace of mind for myself and now I felt like I was enmeshed in a feature film of the Twilight Zone. I had crossed the fence and done some things that I wasn't proud so I don't like to judge people, but David's freaky fantasies were farther that I wanted to go even for the propofol. There was still a full vial in my refrigerator and when that was done I was done. I wouldn't take any more trips into Michael Jackson's Neverland.

Chapter Thirteen

I kept a low-profile for the rest of the week, coming early to work with a packed lunch so I didn't have to go to the cafeteria, and staying in my office until late in the day after most people had already gone home. I had Keisha take all the calls to the office and relay the messages to me. I didn't want to see or talk to anyone if I didn't have to. At this point I didn't know what to say to George even though I missed seeing him, and David wanting somebody to spank him was making me crazy. I could tell I was desperate because I was considering leaving the least stressful job that I had ever had in my life. I really needed some time off to process what was actually was happening when I injected the propofol.

I called Pam's cell phone to check on her and get my mind off of my own problems.

"Hey, Pammy," I said when she answered.

"What's up, mother dear?"

"I haven't talked to you in a while and I wanted to see how you're doing with your classes and everything."

"Things are going good so far; Dad called me and said you two are going out tonight."

"Yeah we are and we'll spend most of the time talking about you."

"I don't know why, y'all have enough to talk about without

even mentioning me, anyway I have a question for you?"

"Oh, is that so?"

"Yes, if Dad wants to come back home would you consider it?"

"All I can tell you is that your dad and I will always be family no matter what."

"That's cool; just don't think you have to do anything for my benefit because I'm grown."

"You may not be as grown as you think."

"Anyway," she said with a little cynicism, "I've got to go."

"All right, but you can call me every now and then."

"I do," she said, whining.

"Well do better, love you."

"Love you too, bye."

I hung up regretting that we weren't as close as we used to be, I knew it was my fault, I had zoned out on her and she didn't have a choice except to find a way to make it on her own.

***

It had been a tough week and I didn't feel like getting dressed up to go out. It wasn't like it was a date, it was Raymond and I hanging out and mending our fences. I looked in the closet and pulled some black jeans off of their hanger; if I put on a blazer I could dress them up some and blend into the crowd at J. Alexander's. I sent him a text to see if we were going to meet at the restaurant or ride together.

"I was thinking that we would ride together just in case you wanted to stop somewhere else," he said, calling me back on the phone.

"Okay, do you want me to come by your place?"

"Stop trying to be nosy about where I'm staying. If you must know, I have a one-bedroom apartment on Metrocenter."

"You mean you've been staying that close to us all this time and we never saw you."

"Come on, Portia, let's not go down that road, we've already turned the corner. I'll pick you up in less than an hour."

Eating at J. Alexander's was just like old times, we ordered an appetizer and one entrée to share.

"So are you still mad at me after all this time?" Raymond asked.

"It wasn't that I was mad at you, I was just upset that we couldn't be there for each other. When you left, I thought it was selfish because I couldn't run out, like I've mentioned before, somebody had to be there for Pam."

"Honestly, part of it was seeing you so miserable and not being able to do anything about it. I felt like I had let you both down."

"Don't worry about it anymore, Raymond, I'm not mad, we were all going through it then and now I'm just glad we came out of it as well as we have."

"I feel better hearing you say that, it really means a lot, but on Sunday we didn't get to talk much about you."

"There's not that much to talk about, except I did change jobs about a year ago."

"You asked me about dating but you didn't say if you had gotten back out there again."

Now he'd finally asked but I wasn't interested in playing truth or dare so I said, "I've been on a few dates, but not a serious relationship."

"Was there anybody special in those dates?" he asked, pushing further.

"What about you?" I asked, deflecting the question.

"I can definitely say nobody who compared to you."

"Now who could compare to me?" I said with a laugh to lighten things up.

Raymond paid the check and we walked to the car.

"Do you feel like going down to B.B. King's? It's Friday and you don't have to get up in the morning."

That reminded me that it was Friday night, the night that I saved to take the propofol injection. I looked at my watch and it wasn't that late.

"Maybe for an hour or so, I haven't been there since the last time we went."

Driving downtown I couldn't help thinking that we had eaten here so many times and driven down West End so many times. It amazed me how people who've shared their lives for a long time can see each other after years and it all seems like yesterday.

The streets and sidewalks of Lower Broadway were filled with a mix of tourists, college students, and us working folks trying to catch a happy hour at the end of the week. We paid to park in a garage on Union Street to save ourselves the time of driving around looking for a parking meter on the streets. It was a great night for walking, the evening temperature was around 70 degrees and a soft breeze blew low to the ground to keep us cool.

Chapter Thirteen

We turned onto Second Avenue two blocks from B.B. King's and the vibe changed from country music and Rock n' Roll on Lower Broadway to the Blues. The street glowed in the darkness lined with the neon signs and lights of stores that stayed open late for the out of town visitors looking for souvenirs. Outside of the club I could hear a band playing and a woman belting out the blues even before we got inside. It was packed wall-to-wall as usual with one seat at the bar near the back.

I gently pushed my way through the maze of people to get to the bar before that last seat was taken. It took Raymond another minute to catch up and find me at the bar.

"How about Long Island Teas?" he asked.

"All right, I guess we can save time if we put all our drinks in one glass."

He laughed and said, "You know they'll probably be watered down."

"We'll see," I said.

Waiting for our drinks my eyes scanned over the room looking at all the outfits, make-up, and shoes that people were wearing these days.

"Okay, time for the taste test," Raymond said, handing me my drink.

I looked down in the cloudy brown mixture and stirred it with the straw before I took a sip and it tasted pretty strong to me.

"I think they left the water out this time," I said.

"Good, we don't want to pay for the water."

I relaxed as the drink warmed my throat and streamed down

to my stomach.

"The band is thumping," Raymond said, rocking his shoulders to the music.

I looked up towards the front to see who was playing and that's when I saw him. It was George sitting at a table in the second row from the stage with an attractive lady. Even though she was sitting I could tell she was tall and slim in her purple cocktail dress. Slightly overdressed for B.B. King's I thought to myself. She was light-skinned and her short hair was styled in spikes on the top that tapered down to her scalp on the sides and the back. She looked like she was at least ten years younger than me. George was his usual debonair self in bleached blue jeans and a polo shirt under a sport coat. They seemed to be enjoying themselves talking back and forth while they nursed their drinks, the dark liquid in his glass was probably an expensive cognac and she was drinking a Heineken from the bottle.

I wasn't prepared for my emotional reaction, I could feel my blood pressure rise as my heart began to beat faster, I was jealous. The dance floor was jammed with people shaking, rolling, and moving their bodies to the rhythm of the music but for me the sound had gone out of the room; I was consumed by the sight of George sitting there with somebody else.

"You wanna dance?" Raymond asked, noticing my attention fixed in the direction of the dance floor.

"No, I'm tired and they're practically on top of each other, I'll just sit here with my drink."

I took a big gulp that rounded into a ball that nearly choked me at the back of my throat. It hurt when I finally swallowed.

"Slow down with that drink, I don't want to have to carry you out of here."

"You just handle yours, I'm cool," I said, but I wasn't, so I took another gulp.

What was my problem? Here I was sitting at the bar with my husband upset about another woman sitting over there with George. I really did need counseling, therapy, and psychoanalysis.

"You look like you're beat, Portia; you must have had a rough week pushing all those papers at work, let's call it a night."

"Sure, Mr. Funny Man."

I could feel Raymond's arms circling around my shoulders and lifting me to my feet, but my legs felt wobbly. I wasn't sure if it was the drink or the shock of seeing George with Miss Whoever.

"It has been a full week," I said, steadying myself.

I looked straight ahead as I walked towards the door hoping that George wouldn't see me on my way out. The wind slapped me in the face when I stepped down on the sidewalk and I was grateful, it seemed to bring my senses back. I could hear clearly again.

"Look who can't hang, you must have been traveling in the slow lane too long," Raymond said with a laugh before grabbing my hand while we walked to the car.

"You'd be surprised," I said, shaking my head.

By the time Raymond pulled the car into the driveway my anxiety was peaking to a new level. I didn't know if I was going or coming. Raymond and I were out like the last three years hadn't happened. One minute it was comforting and the next minute I was totally confused. The greatest part of the confusion was my feelings for George; I hadn't closed the book on that relationship, and obviously I cared more about him than I admitted. I thought he would always be an option for me whenever I got myself on solid footing. I hadn't considered the possibility that he would move on before I got it together.

"Are you okay, you seem out of it tonight?" Raymond said, looking deep into my eyes as if the problem would be written in them.

"I'm just having one of those days I guess, I'm all right."

"I can stay for a while or spend the night if you want to talk."

"I don't really feel like talking, maybe there's a good movie on cable we can watch for a while."

Raymond hung up his jacket and went into the den to surf the channels while I went to change into something to lounge in. I closed the door to my bedroom and all I wanted to do was lay down, take a shot, and get away from all the drama in my life. I had only done it five times but it was something I looked forward to at the end of the week, but Raymond was here and would probably spend the night. I wanted the company but I felt like I needed my privacy at the same time.

"Have you found anything decent to look at?" I asked, walking into the den.

"Not much except for a re-run of 'Shawshank Redemption'."

"You want something to eat or drink?"

"I'll take a beer if you have one."

Chapter Thirteen

I went in the kitchen and opened the fridge and there was a Heineken on the shelf, it reminded me of the woman sitting with George at the club. I grabbed it and stomped back into the den. I sat down and faced the television screen even though my mind had already drifted into another place. I reflected on what I called my trips to other lives in other lands and that's where I wanted to be. My reverie was interrupted by a growl; Raymond was in a deep sleep snoring on the other end of the couch. I covered him with a blanket from the linen closet, took a vial out of the butter compartment and retreated back into my bedroom.

There wasn't a lock on the door so I just closed it behind me. I reached under the bed for my kit and when I felt it I could already feel the tension of the evening begin to recede. I had up to this time promised myself that I wouldn't take the chance of doing this with anyone else in the house except for David, but I felt like I needed a trip and I didn't want to wait. I filled the syringe and I had to contain the nervous excitement I felt about where this trip would take me so I could steady the needle in my vein. I pushed the cloudy fluid in and pulled out the syringe before the weight of my body faded away. I floated in the rainbow of light around me, twirling, almost dancing while the familiar beams became more visible and I spun faster. I focused on the spinning beam to my left following a bright spot that glowed in deep purple and I knew I had made contact when I felt the sensation of falling.

The blade swung low on the ground under me slicing only air as I jumped backward and landed on my feet.

"I've waited to bring you down off that pedestal, Helena, and today is the day," Julia hisses at me from behind her shield.

"I knew it would only be a matter of time before I would collide with your petty jealousies, and this arena is the place I prefer to resolve any grievances against me," I answer.

Springing to the left Julia thrust her sword towards me and it scrapes against the leather of my arm guard.

"So you want to draw blood," I say as we move counter-clockwise in a circle with our eyes locked. "Careful that it's not your own that you see spilled today," I warn as I swing high meeting her blade.

The crowd roars in the dim light of the Roman Colosseum excited to see skilled women competitors and I acknowledge them with a quick smile. Julia charges towards me again, her anger building as the crowd chants my name, "Helena, Helena, Helena!" I dodge the wild diagonal swings of her sword.

"I'll fill that mouth of yours with humiliation," she says, lunging forward in an aggressive jab aimed at my chest.

"I wouldn't make promises of things that you are not sure to deliver," I taunt, challenging her speed as I move my sword from side to side and then high and low.

I follow her eyes as she searches for a weakness or an opening to make her attack. I shift my shield an inch to draw her in and she dives forward sure she will finally pierce my flesh; instead she jars her arm against my shield. I take a step back to encourage her to come forward again and she obliges. I crouch low to my right and slash my blade against her left thigh and blood drips from the lengthy cut. She spits on the ground to show she wasn't

Chapter Thirteen

hurt and follows with a flurry of blows that I counter.

The light from the torch flames flicker on our swords as they clang furiously against each other. I am an elusive target as she jumps towards me again and then again. She was no match for my defense, she couldn't penetrate my shield, I was too good, and I had trained too hard. Who was she to think she could challenge me? Our eyes lock again and I can see the frustration of missing her mark and the malice she has for me mixing and adding to her fatigue and as we move in a ring like animals about to pounce.

She hadn't trained like I had and her weakness wasn't her lack of strength, it was her stamina. I can feel the impending victory. I look for the signal from Junius, my tutor, and he raises his hand. That was it, the time for sport was over; a bored audience gets thirsty for blood and death. I roar like a lioness and then I leap high in the air in her direction and before I land on her left, I whip my sword under hers and rip it out of her hand. She falls to her knees and the ferocious look on her face softens in defenselessness as I stand above her. I remove my helmet and nod to my trainer.

"Finish your speech, Julia, I want to hear what you have to say," I insist in a low voice only she can hear and for the first time since I've know her she is silent. "Call for mercy, foolish girl, I have no desire to do you harm."

"I don't want any favors from you, Helena," she answers with a scowl on her face.

"Julia, raise your finger. There's no shame in wanting to live,

I'm a gladiatrice, not a murderer."

"I have my honor," she answers.

"There's little honor in death," I tell her as I raise my sword to the crowd.

"Helena, Helena, Helena," they continue to shout and I turn to the Emperor's box, to the orchestra and the consul, and then to the crowd where the thumbs facing the heavens give her a reprieve.

It is my stage and my moment as I claim my victory once again.

The bad blood between the Cornelii and Nautia families had been passed down through four generations and I hope this kindness will put an end to the quarrel for once. Julia's father and mine are both members of the Roman Senate with family wealth from agricultural businesses that don't compete against each other; the only basis for the rivalry is historical. It was my recent marriage to Claudius, another senator, and my triumphs in the arena that gall Julia beyond her tolerance level while she remains a single woman in her father's house. She was attractive enough but her brooding keeps most men at a distance. I relish my victory as we both retreat under the stage to the underground passage.

"Do you still bear animosity to me after I spared your life?"

"You and your family think you're superior to us, but you're not," she answers angrily.

"Those are your words not mine, Julia, I've always admired your spirit even if it was misdirected."

Chapter Thirteen

Julia stares hard trying to see into my soul and then she says, "Since we didn't kill each other, let's bury the grudge of our families once and for all."

"Agreed," I say with my arm stretched out to salute her. Our fingers touch and we head in opposite directions.

I leave the games in my chariot to go to my villa to refresh and beautify myself before Claudius returns.

"You were magnificent, my love," Claudius says as he comes into our bedroom.

"No ridicule from the others who always question my femininity."

"Whenever they remark, I just question the manhood of anyone who is put off by the power of a beautiful woman."

"I always want you to be proud of me," I say as I stand up to greet him.

"I am proud of you, Helena, how could I not be when you stand out there, the vision of a goddess, the perfect mix of fitness and flesh," he said, embracing me around my waist.

"Sweet words that I love to taste," I say with a full kiss on his mouth.

"You have the energy to love your husband even after combat?" he asks, teasing me.

"It was an easy match, a mere appetizer for the grand event that will take place in three months time. It will be the contest between me and the renowned Ethiopian gladiatrice, she's the most formidable of all the amazons."

"In that case you need to save your strength my love," he says, lifting me in his arms and carrying me to the bed.

***

Early in the day after breakfast I go to school to train with Junius. He has been my private tutor in the martial arts since I was nine years old starting out as a gymnast and he has served me well.

"Well done, Helena, but your next challenge will be your greatest," he says, greeting me.

"I'm ready, Junius, I have endured your rigorous training and combat lessons for twelve years."

Under his instruction, I had run hundreds of miles with chains around my ankles and my combat training had been done with a wooden sword weighted heavily with lead.

"Never forget to respect the training and preparation of your opponent, Helena; they want to win just as much as you do."

He was right, I've always been confident and I consider it as my strongest weapon, I am still undefeated.

"I've heard that only on rare occasions do her fights fail to end with the death of her challenger," he says.

"I intend to be among those exceptional instances," I reply with self-assurance.

"We'll limit your training to only four hours until the match. You will need to conserve your power."

I change into a shorter tunic for my exercises.

"I want you to jump straight up in the air as high as you can," he directs.

I do a shallow squat and then jump.

Chapter Thirteen

"Again, again, and again," Junius calls out for ten minutes.

"I thought we planned to save my energy," I say between quick breaths.

"We will but your legs need to be strong with the agility of a tiger for this match."

"Now walk in a circle to loosen your muscles and we'll complete another set."

My legs are already aching by the time we begin our sparring session. The wooden sword is heavy in my hand as I swing it against the metal one Junius uses. One hour later my tunic is soaked in perspiration.

"Now you're ready to run," Junius says.

I start out with a slow pace toward the gymnasium; I can chart my distance by circling the outside. I run for over an hour with nothing but my thoughts to keep me company.

"You will win, Helena, you are a master of martial arts; the supreme gladiatrice," I tell myself. "I will not allow myself to sink into complacency; I will stay disciplined and train hard."

***

It is the fifth day of the Emperor's Festival, the day of my event, and Claudius is already at the arena. I will not attend the morning games, Junius advised me to rest and eat lightly throughout the day. The contest between the Ethiopian and I will be the highlight of the afternoon games. It was the reason I prefer not to wrestle, I refuse to make a mockery of myself fighting matches with dwarfs. I am a serious fighter not a circus act.

Coming out into the arena from the underground passage

the crowd welcomes me. I am dressed in nothing more than my helmet, a loin cloth, and my sandals. I look high into the scores of people in the arena and their eyes are all on me. Their attention fills me more than any food or wine. To stand under the huge torches of light and hear the appreciative ovation from the crowd, it is what I hunger for. It is on these rare occasions that I remove myself from the large shadow cast by my husband. It is for the taste of this moment that I willingly suffer the razor sharp pains of the sword.

The entrance of the Ethiopian draws me out of my reverie. It is her dominating appearance that causes my first tinge of doubt. She towers over the men who stand at either side of the door of the passage. Her dark skin is flawless, and her form seems to be carved out of marble. She advances towards me moving with the sleekness and power of a panther. She gives me a nod of respect and raises her sword and I do the same. I make the first strike but her height gives her better leverage against me. The muscles of my arm ache with each strike against her sword pounding against mine. We trade jabs before she moves closer with only the lengths of our swords separating us. I admire her techniques and timing but I stand toe-to-toe with her as our two swords dance. Moving quicker than the wind, she takes a broad step with her left leg and trips me with her right foot. My head hits the ground with a thud and my helmet falls to the side. The cheers of the crowd thunder above my head as if I'm under water and dots of white light flash before my eyes.

"Get up, Helena, get up," voices scream from the orchestra

Chapter Thirteen

where Claudius and my tutor Junius are seated.

Through the lights in my eyes I see the Ethiopian taking deep breaths. I drag myself up from the ground ignoring the sting of the grit and rock pellets that scraped the skin from my bare breasts. Digging deep for the last ounce of strength I feel within me I pull my knees under me climb to my feet with my shield still in my hands. My shin is chafed under the leg guard and I feel drops of blood roll down to my ankle and my loincloth is stuck to my body with sweat. My vision clears just in time for me to see her sleek form charging towards me. I grab the sword that lay inches to the side of my foot and raise it to meet hers. We fight fiercely for what seems like hours and the movement of the swords in the darkness makes me dizzy.

I jump high in the air and yell, "Stop," before I collapse on the ground with all my body's resources spent.

"What the hell is all this shit?" Raymond demanded, jerking me back into consciousness.

I opened my eyes and he's standing above me holding up the needle in his hand. This is exactly what I didn't want to happen. I should have insisted that he go home to his apartment.

"What are you doing?" he asked, shaking the syringe in my face.

"I'm minding my own business, who gave you permission to come into my room?"

"Technically, this house still belongs to both of us."

"So what rights do you think that gives you?" I asked, turning my back on him.

"Portia, you are still my wife."

"Since when? Before three months ago, I hadn't seen you in practically three years."

"I asked you before, what drugs are you taking with this needle?"

"It's not what you think; it's just something to help me sleep, so you can stop all the ranting and raving."

"What is it and who prescribed it too you?"

"Right now you are asking entirely too many questions for somebody who walked out on me. Get out of my room and give me some space and we'll talk about it later."

He puts the syringe down on the night stand.

"I'm not leaving without answers to my many questions," he said, mocking me.

"I should have known better," I said, getting up to shower.

"So what's going on with you?" Raymond asked as soon as I set one foot into the kitchen.

At least I could have some coffee before he gave me the third degree I thought as a poured myself a cup before I sat down.

"There's not that much going on Raymond, you're making too much out of this."

"I walk into the bedroom and you're laid out in the bed with a damn empty syringe next to you and there's nothing to it. I don't think so, Portia, or would you care to explain it to me and Pam at the same time, it's your choice."

He had me backed into a corner. It was all I could do to keep from grinning as I flashed back to my life as a female gladiator.

Chapter Thirteen

"This is the deal, Raymond, I've had a hard time sleeping since we lost Nick and it has been wearing me down. I've tried all kinds of sleeping pills and none of them seemed to help much. One of the doctors at work gave me the medication that I'm taking but it doesn't come in a pill form, it has to be injected."

"What exactly is the medication?"

"It's Diprivan," I said, using the brand name hoping he wouldn't recognize it as the drug Michael Jackson overdosed on.

"Do you do this every night; this doesn't sound right to me?"

"No, I don't, I only use it when I've been up for a few days."

He sat down across from me and mulled over the things I had just said.

"I understand what you're going through, baby, I still have problems maintaining my peace of mind too but this can't be healthy."

"It has changed a lot of things for me, Ray, the first time I took it I went to a place where I saw Nick again and it was healing for me," I said, careful not to say too much.

"How long have you been taking this anyway?" he asked, looking like he wanted to turn me over to the narcotics squad.

"Only for a month or so and it has helped me accept what happened in a different light, and I really don't need to take it anymore."

He looked confused for a second before he said, "Any medication that you have to inject with a needle is a high powered drug and those types of drugs are highly addictive, you're probably already hooked on it."

"I only do it every now and then, how can I be hooked?"

"You may not be hooked on the drug, but you are addicted to the experience. This isn't about Nicholas anymore; you've got to stop it, Portia."

"I will, Ray, don't worry about it, I've got an appointment with a psychologist on Thursday."

"I don't know if I should leave you here by yourself or not. I'm totally blown away, I don't know what to do."

He was showing a little too much upset for someone who had pulled his disappearing act.

"Look, I'm a grown woman, I don't need a babysitter."

"Maybe you do," he said sarcastically.

"You're overreacting and it's stressing me out. There's nothing else to say, I need some space, please."

"All right, I'll go for now, but we're not through talking about this."

I shook my head while I watched him grab his clothes up from the couch and stomp down the hall to the guestroom and slam the door shut. He was probably going to take a shower.

"A little late to respect my privacy now," I said under my breath.

I really had a good time with him last night. I was sorry it ended like this. We had gotten close to the place where we might have been friends again. Except he has a lot of nerve thinking he could judge me. When he walked out on us he didn't care how I survived and now the time for his concerned-husband-routine has run out.

Chapter Thirteen

There was no way I was going to cook breakfast and prolong the time before he was out of here and on his way. When the guestroom door finally opened I could smell the soap. He had his coat in his hand and I walked behind him into the foyer.

"I'll be in touch," he said, looking at me suspiciously like he was my new probation officer and I couldn't blame anyone but myself.

Chapter Fourteen

At last, I thought when the front door was shut; Raymond had totally blown my mellow morning and the exhilaration I usually feel when I wake up after an injection. That was just too much drama for a Saturday, I wished I could push rewind and start all over again. Now he was deep in my business and I knew I hadn't heard the last of his protests. I needed to get outside where I could breathe and get my bearings. I threw on some sweats and sneaks, put a baseball cap on my uncombed hair, and headed out the door walking.

It was a beautiful morning. The sky was a clear blue, birds were singing, squirrels scurried from one tree to another, and a pair of dogs trotted in front of me sniffing along the curb. It was all so carefree; the real turmoil of the world took place behind closed doors. All of sudden I felt like running but my knees started hurting before I made it down two blocks. I knew I couldn't run from my problems so at the end of the street I crossed over and walked as fast as I could back to the house. When I finally made it back to the garage I felt better, the negative energy had been burned off. I could feel it leaving my body in the drops of sweat dripping down my face and the center of my back.

As soon as I walked in the house the phone started ringing.

"Hey, child, what you been up too?" Paula said, sounding upbeat.

"You wouldn't believe me if I told you," I said, wondering if Raymond had the nerve to call my sister about me.

"Well, it's time for us to catch up; I haven't heard from you in a couple of weeks, how are things going with Prince Charming?"

"You are not going to worry me today, Paula," I said, even though I was wondering what was going on with him myself.

"Come on, girl, I don't have all day, let's take inventory?"

"Okay, Ms. Nosey, Pam is finishing up her last year at TSU, I'm enjoying the stress-free environment at work, and I've done a lot more healing over Nick."

"That all sounds good, sister-girl, I'm happy for you, but what about Ray and the new man?"

"Hold on a minute while I get a glass of juice, I've got to sit down on this one," I said, going into the kitchen. I poured myself a cup of grape juice and pulled out a chair. "Raymond and I went out again last night."

"Excuse me; I didn't realize that you all had gone out the first time."

"We're just mending fences and trying to understand what went wrong back then."

"That's deep, is he trying to get back with you?"

"I'm not sure; I think we're trying to be friends again."

"Have you thought about it?"

"I've got a ton of things going on and I can't even think about that right now, but we are family."

"It sounds like your life is a reality show right now."

"Go get your popcorn, P, because it gets better."

Chapter Fourteen

"Are you for real, because if you are, I'm going to have to put you on hold while I make myself a snack?"

"You might need to pour yourself a drink?"

"Stop it, what's going on?" she demanded, sounding like she was coming through the receiver.

"Raymond and I were at B.B's last night and I saw George sitting at the table with a 'Halle Berry wanna be' and it totally freaked me out."

"Did you say something to them?"

"No, I didn't. What could I say? I was out with Raymond."

"What are you going to do?"

"I don't know, my hands are full right now."

"That's the truth, I'm sorry I've got to go, Charles is waiting in the car, but you better call me back with the next episode of this one, love you, sis."

"Love you too," I said, hanging up the phone.

It was killing me to think that George was moving on without me. I wanted to call him, but if he was still with her from last night, I didn't think I could handle it. I decided to wait until Monday to call him just in case. One realization I had come to from being in the same room with him and Raymond; it was George who had my attention.

***

I don't think I have ever been this eager to get to work before, I was actually ten minutes early. Obviously Keisha didn't share my enthusiasm with the sour face she was wearing when I walked into the office suite.

"Good morning Keisha, did you have a nice weekend?" I asked, trying to be congenial.

"It wasn't long enough for me but I'm here," she answered, dryly.

It had been too long as far as I was concerned.

"I already made coffee if you want a cup," she said without taking her eyes away from her computer screen.

I was already wired as I searched for the key to unlock my door but I poured a cup to take into my office. Once I got the door opened, I set the hot mug down on my desk while I hung up my jacket. Then I sat down to count to ten before I called George.

"Well, hello, pretty lady, it's good to hear from you," he said with that sexy accent, sounding happy and refreshed.

"I've been thinking about you day and night."

"Is that right? Are you ready to stop playing hard to get?"

"I believe I am, but are you still available? I saw you out on the town with a date."

"I'm a single man, Portia. I asked you to put me on lockdown but you had some issues to deal with. I was out with a nice young lady and I had a good time, no harm no foul."

"I'm not mad about it or accusing you of anything, I'm just jealous that's all."

"You don't have to be, I told you I wanted you, it was your choice."

"I made a mistake."

"What was that, baby?"

Chapter Fourteen

"I took you for granted and I shouldn't have done that."

"Look, Portia; don't feel pressured to be with me just because you saw me with somebody else. I told you I'll wait for you to make up your mind, at least a little while," he said with a laugh, "Now I've got to get back to work."

I hung up the phone feeling like I had to get my life back on track. I started out on this quest searching for a few answers and all I had done was create a mass of new questions.

***

I was hoping that my appointment with the psychologist would give me the clarity I needed from my trips through time. My initial mission had been to get my head straight and make contact with Nick, and I felt like I had done that, but now I was distracted or even seduced by the fascination with exploring what I believed were my past lives. For me the possibility was a monumental discovery. Not to mention the contact was always at some dramatic moment. Maybe the most significant events of the life are the easiest to reach because they are higher in the subconscious.

Dr. Lanier's office was much different than I expected. It didn't have the ambiance of a clinic or doctor's office. It was a large townhouse that had been converted into a suite of offices. I checked in with the receptionist on the first floor where she copied my insurance card and gave me a large questionnaire to fill out. It was the standard form that all health providers require and I rushed through it and handed it back to her.

"Dr. Lanier's office is on the third floor, the office on the right," she said courteously.

"Thank you," I said, walking around her desk to the winding staircase in the middle of the room.

There were other doctor's names painted on the closed doors on the second floor and as I continued my hike up to the third floor and I could hear a violin playing. I knocked on the door with Dr. Lanier's name plate on it.

"Come on in," a male voice called out.

I opened the door and peered in. There was a man who looked to be in his mid-thirties with dark brown hair putting a violin back into its case. He was average in height with a slim build.

"Hello, I'm Dr. Lanier," he said, extending his hand in greeting.

I reached for it and his handshake felt soft and warm. He looked deep into my eyes like an optometrist and I looked back into his. They were a faded blue color with short eyelashes.

"Hello," I said, "I'm Portia Roberts."

"Welcome, please sit down and make yourself comfortable. Can I get you some coffee, tea, or water?"

"Some hot tea would be nice," I said, sitting down on the fluffy couch.

"Sugar or lemon?" he asked.

"Both please," I answered as I put down my handbag and took off my jacket.

"You mentioned that you were having problems sleeping, when did that begin?" he asked as he brought the cup of tea in a saucer with a spoon over to me in one hand and a notepad in the other.

Chapter Fourteen

I put in two sugars, squeezed the lemons and took a sip of the hot liquid. It soothed me. I sat the tea down on the table and leaned back on the burgundy colored paisley sofa.

"It all began with the death of my son Nicholas four years ago. My grief and thoughts of him kept me awake late into nights."

"That's a normal response under the circumstances."

"Yes, I know that, but it has been a continual problem for me even three years later.

"Have you consulted with a medical doctor?" he asked, writing something on his notepad.

"On several occasions I did seek medical attention to help deal with it without much change. Recently there have been some differences. About three months ago I had a dream where I was able to re-live a particular day that I spent with my son in exact detail."

"It's not uncommon for our subconscious to revert back to our memories while we are sleep."

"I had the experience again and it was another event, as if it was a movie being replayed for me, and I didn't have the sensation of dreaming that I usually have when I'm asleep."

"What do you think is happening, Ms. Roberts?"

"I think that I traveled back in time and was actually living that moment again."

I could see Dr. Lanier shift in his seat out of the side of my eye but I kept looking forward.

"Have you ever taken any psychedelic drugs before?"

"What is a psychedelic drug?" I asked, unsure if I had.

"They would be something like LSD or magic mushrooms, a drug that might induce hallucinations or visions of things that aren't there."

"No, I haven't," I said, leaning up to take another sip of the tea, "I'm sure that it was a paranormal experience.

"Excuse me, while I get a cup of coffee," Dr. Lanier said, rising from his chair and heading over to the counter area. "Why are you so sure that you're not asleep dreaming or awake having hallucinations?" he asked as he sat back down with his mug.

"The first time it happened someone was with me while I slept. During the experience I'm positive that my body was sleep but my consciousness was at another level."

"Have these experiences only included your son and your memories with him?"

"No, they haven't, the third one I had took place in another life before the time of Christ. I was a shepherd boy living outside of Jerusalem. It's not like I'm a spectator during the experience, the thoughts and actions are my own, and I'm totally within a different existence. When I'm there I'm not conscious of any other life."

When I look back at him for a response, he's looking at me like I'm nuttier than last year's fruitcake.

"How often do you have these experiences, are they random, or does something provoke them?"

"They're not random, I have them about once a week," I said, trying not to reveal too much information.

"Ms. Roberts, I want to be sure that I understand what you

Chapter Fourteen

think is happening," he said, leaning towards me with his mug in his hand.

"What I believe is that I reach a level of consciousness where my spirit can detach from the present and journey to a past life that exists simultaneously."

"The imagination is a powerful thing, there is the possibility that you just imagined you were this shepherd boy."

"I have imagined many things in my life and I know the difference between what's real and what's imagined."

I wanted to tell him about the Mayan princess, the African professor, the Roman Gladiatrice and how the propofol induced a level of consciousness that allowed time travel to another dimension but I knew that would probably qualify me for a padded room.

"I'm not saying I don't believe you, Ms. Roberts, I just need to take into account the basis for the events that you are having. Would you consider hypnosis as a method to explore your memories and your subconscious?"

"I don't have any objections to anything that would help me better understand what's happening."

"All right, well, our time is up for today and I would like the chance to confer with a few colleagues before our next appointment. I'm going to ask our receptionist to schedule you back in two weeks. In the meantime, what I'd like you to do is to take notes and write down as much as you can about the events that you are experiencing in as much detail as possible."

"Dr. Lanier, my reason for seeking out a psychologist was to investigate the connection between the mind and the spirit in these events."

"Ms. Roberts, it more probable that your questions are less mental than they are spiritual and the events are more imaginings than actuality, but we'll keep an open mind."

"Thank you, doctor," I said, placing my bag on my shoulder to leave.

I felt disappointed after the appointment; I had hoped it would have given me an insight into something, a way to deal with my grief better, or at least help me figure out what I was doing. I wasn't even sure if I was coming back again. If I wanted a fresh start in my life all I had to do was take it and put the rest behind me. When I got back to the car I reached in my bag for my cell phone and dialed his number.

"Hey, George, I was wondering if you would like to go out tomorrow. I miss you and I want to spend some time with you," I said as soon as he said hello.

"I wish I could, lovely lady, but I've already made plans, can I get a rain check?"

"Sure no problem, whenever you're not busy," I replied, feeling dejected.

"By the way, have you filed for your divorce yet?" he asked.

"I don't really want to talk about it over the phone."

"I see," he said.

"I'm driving so I better get off the phone, I'll be in touch," I said.

I couldn't blame him for holding my feet to the fire, I had

Chapter Fourteen

already wasted too much of his time. I wouldn't call him back unless I was prepared for a relationship. I pulled onto the interstate in a rush to get home.

Chapter Fifteen

"Good morning, Ms. Roberts," Keisha said, twisting her lips to the side of her face in judgment. "Dr. Tucker called about four times after you left yesterday, he says it's an emergency and needs you to call him immediately."

"Thank you, Keisha," I said, digging for my cell phone and walking into my office.

Her dirty little mind was working overtime again and David calling and coming by so often only fed her suspicions about my personal business.

Oops, I had forgotten to take my phone off of silent mode after my head shrinking appointment and there were seven missed calls and three voice messages. Four of the missed calls and two of the voice mails were from David, the rest were from Raymond. I figured I better hurry and call David before he came by the office while Keisha was here.

"Where's the fire?" I asked when he answered.

"Come on, Portia, you know I have been trying to get some time to see you, I've been under a lot of pressure lately and you know what I need."

"David, my life is a mess right now."

"Tell me what you need and I'll take care of it, I just need you to work this out. I don't have anybody else I can ask."

"I'm just guessing, but I'm sure your wife would be glad to whip that ass for you," I said exasperated. "Have you ever thought about picking up the phone book or googling to find a professional who knows what they're doing?"

"You know my position, I can't jeopardize my career or my marriage with somebody I don't know or trust."

"My ex is coming around a lot and what if my daughter comes home," I said, trying to get him to let it go.

"Once more, Portia, and I swear I won't ask you again."

"When do you want to do this, David? You said your wife is keeping close tabs on you."

"I can come over tonight around 7:00, she's hanging out with her girls."

This was not the way I wanted to spend my Friday evening. George had turned me down and now David was pushing me to the edge.

"I can't keep going on like this," I said to myself as I paced back and forth across my office wearing down the carpet.

I still had my cell phone in my hand so I called Raymond; there wasn't any reason to put it off.

"Hello, Ray, I got your message. How's everything?"

"I'm all right, just trying not to worry about you."

"I'm good, there's no need to worry."

"How did your appointment go yesterday?"

"It was okay but I think it's a slow process."

"It is, so give it some time before you give up."

"I will. I'm going back in two weeks."

Chapter Fifteen

"That's good. The reason I called was I wanted you to go to church with me again on Sunday."

"It's hard to say no to that invitation," I said. More to the point, I really needed to talk with him.

It was an unusually busy day in the office. The open enrollment period for benefits at the hospital was beginning next week and Keisha and I had to finish the updates, modifications, and new plan offerings to be sent out by e-mail before the end of the day. Somehow we had gotten everything handled, but next week was going to be even more of a challenge when we were bombarded with employee questions and changes.

Have a good weekend, Ms. Roberts," Keisha said, sticking her head in the door to say goodbye.

"Same to you, Keisha, and please make sure you take care of yourself and get some rest, I don't want you to get sick and be out of the office next week."

"I definitely will, I'm not doing anything. How about you, do you have anything special planned?" she asked, looking at me like she knew all about my undercover life.

"Nothing to write home about," I said, smiling back at her until she closed the door.

I took my time walking to my car and I drove the scenic route home. I stopped at the Sonic drive-thru to pick up a salad for dinner. As soon I got inside the house I took off my shoes and poured myself a glass of wine to help me unwind. I put the salad in the refrigerator and washed a potato to put in the microwave, I didn't feel like I had the energy to chew raw veggies. I sat down fully dressed in my stocking feet with my baked potato and watched two re-runs of "Girlfriends." I thought about the women I had been close to over the years and how we drifted apart losing touch after everything happened. "Why is life so complicated?" I shouted up into air.

Then the doorbell rang, it wasn't the answer I was looking for.

"I didn't know if you were here, I didn't see your car," David said when I opened the door.

"I pulled it in the garage." I said, irritated that he would come by without calling.

"Oh," he said, stepping inside the door and walking past me.

"I brought some things for you," he said, lifting two large shopping bags in his arms.

"Come on in the den and let me see what you got," I said, too tired to put up a fuss.

I sat down and he handed me the bags. In one was the policewoman outfit he had mentioned to me before.

"Do you like it?" he asked, watching me sift through the bag.

"It's different, what's in the other bag?" I asked, not really interested.

"I know how much women like shoes so I bought you some to wear with the outfit."

"It's quite a big box for a pair of shoes."

"Check them out," he said, smiling at me.

I opened the box and inside there was a pair of the most exquisite black over-the-knee boots and elbow-length gloves that I had ever seen. The Italian leather on the boots felt as soft

Chapter Fifteen

as the gloves. They were high quality; he had spent top dollar for them.

"These are gorgeous; I can't believe you went to so much trouble," I said, running my hands over the leather.

"I wanted to get you something to show how much I appreciate you and our friendship; I can't put a price tag on it."

"Even though this is the last time I can help with your fantasy?" I said, giving him a stern look.

"For me it's not conditional," he said.

"Thank you," I said, taking the bags and heading upstairs to change.

I turned on the shower, hoping the hot water would revive me enough to get through the evening. I took my time enjoying the water streams as they massaged my tired body, hoping that he might have to leave by the time I got finished. I dried off and rubbed myself down liberally with lotion, the chill of the autumn air always made my skin feel dry.

I turned the costume shopping bag upside down on the bed and all I could do was shake my head in contempt. Then I stopped, who was I to feel superior to David or anyone else? I thought about the lengths that I had gone to in order to soothe my own demons. Then I slipped on the lace panties and into the tight sexy police dress. I pulled on the luxurious boots and gloves, fastened the handcuffs to my holster, and put on the rhinestone studded police hat. I had to admit this was a helluva outfit and I looked damn good in it. Looking in the mirror it gave me a new attitude. I grabbed my whip and headed down the stairs to find my suspect.

I could hear a Foxy Brown CD playing before I got to the den and I could see a flashing police light in the doorway. The freaky was now bordering on comical, but I had to give him credit, David believed in setting the stage. I walked in the room standing tall in my high-fashion boots with much attitude to find him standing by the window with his pants sagging. Now that was a sight that made me mad enough to whip some ass.

"Nigga, what are you doing around here? This ain't your hood," I hollered, grabbing him by the arm. He opened his mouth to speak, "No, shut up, I don't wanna hear the bullshit. You wanted some trouble, now you got some. You walking around with your pants down, you wanna show your ass, take em off."

"It's not like that," he said.

"Oh, yes, it is, take it all off, strip nigga." I watched him take off his clothes and his whole demeanor changed, he even looked like a different person. "Put your hands behind your back," I shouted while I unhooked the handcuffs from my belt. I snatched his hands, put the handcuffs on his wrists, and tried to get my mind ready for act II.

"Get your black ass on the ground," I said, popping him for the first time.

His skin swelled in a thin red line on his right hip and I could see a grimace on his face.

"You need to be taught a lesson don't you?"

"Yes, officer," he said, kneeling on the floor.

"Do you wanna go to jail, nigga?" I asked as I swung the whip

Chapter Fifteen

across the center of his plump behind.

"No, officer," he said, holding his head down.

"Well, then you need to learn how to obey the goddam law."

I close my eyes and lashed out four more times. I could hear him grunting from the pain and when I opened my eyes his behind was swollen with welts all across it.

"This is what happens when you don't abide by my rules," I yelled, hitting him again. He collapsed onto the floor and then I got worried. I grabbed him by the hair; "You got a problem nigga?" I asked, trying to stay in character.

"No, I don't have a problem," he answered with the bass back in his voice. I raised the whip high over my shoulder and landed it across his lower back.

"Get your ass out of here and don't let me see you back around here again or you might not live to tell about it," I said, taking off the handcuffs.

I gave him one last pop across the back of his thighs not having the heart to hit his wounded butt again and went upstairs.

I changed into some flannel pajamas and sat on the bed to take a breath and give David some time to pull himself back together after our scenario. When I got down to the kitchen he was drinking a cold beer.

"How are you doing?" I asked, pouring some more wine in the glass I had earlier.

"Great, I'm much better than I was. You don't know what that did for me."

"I'm sorry if I got too rough."

"Woman, I wish I had the words to tell you how freeing that was for me, and you are so good."

"I'm sure you'll find someone who's a lot better than I am."

"I wish I didn't have to," he said, looking at me with true sincerity, "Nobody will ever take your place, Portia, you were my first."

"David, you are truly an original," I said, escorting him to the door. "Make sure you don't let Mrs. Tucker see you without some clothes on."

"Don't worry, I'm going to put on some PJ's and sleep like a baby. Thanks again, partner, I know it's not your thing."

"The things we do for a friend," I said, giving him a hug before I shut the door and turned off the lights.

The next morning I was hungry but I couldn't decide what I wanted, not to mention there wasn't much food in the house. I couldn't remember the last time I brought groceries. I put on my royal blue TSU jogging suit to wear to Kroger's since homecoming was getting close. Just as I pulled in to a parking space I saw my nosey neighbor, Cynthia, standing in front of the store waving feverishly at me.

"Not this morning, I am not in the mood," I said under my breath while trying to keep a smile on my face.

"I've been meaning to come and check on you, Portia, honey. There have been so many different cars pulled in front of your house I was getting worried that maybe something was wrong," she said, looking me up and down searching for hints about what was going on.

"Everything's fine, Cynthia, it's just a lot more extra business to handle since I changed jobs."

"Okay, child, I can understand that, we all got to make a living, but those after-hour business associates of yours are looking good and driving good, honey. I wouldn't mind helping out as your assistant. Remember it's good to share the wealth sometimes," she said, giving me a little goodbye wave of her hand as she walked away.

I rolled through every aisle as quickly as I could, picking up fresh fruit and vegetables, bread, rice, and pasta. I grabbed can soups, bottle juices, cookies, crackers, popcorn, fresh meat, frozen fish, ice cream, cheeses, eggs, milk, and butter. I didn't want to take a chance of bumping into Cynthia again for at least another month while I was under unauthorized surveillance. I needed time to reel my life in. First and foremost, there would be no more evening visits from David. I rolled my cart up to the checkout counter and practically threw all of it on the conveyor belt. When the cashier finished scanning and bagging I had rung up a final tab of $237.58.

I stayed in the house all day Saturday laying low and watching movies on the Lifetime Channel. When the phone rang it scared me, I was still jumpy from last night.

"Hello," I said, making a sorry attempt to disguise my voice.

"What's up, sister-girl?" Paula said, full of enthusiasm.

"Nothing much, just hanging around being a couch potato."

"It's the weekend, baby, don't tell me your love life fizzled out already."

"You're the one with a love life; all I've got is drama."

"A husband is not a love life, you had one so you know," and we both had to laugh at that.

"How can I forget, I've still got one and this limbo thing is not working for me anymore."

"What do you mean, Portia?" she asked, getting serious.

"If we're not going to be together we need to make it official, I can't go on with my life if we're still legally married."

"Are you sure you're ready to make that move?"

"He's the one who made it years ago."

"You don't love him anymore?" she asked kindheartedly.

"I'll always love him, P, we shared a life together, but the passion and excitement isn't there. I didn't think about it that much until I met George."

"George, huh, it's nothing wrong with a little excitement, it keeps the blood flowing, at least that's what I hear. I need a cattle prod to get Charles off the couch."

"Leave Charles alone, you've just drained him dry, he deserves some rest."

"Uh-uh, you can't rest until it's over and they throw the last handful of dirt. Anyway, call me after you talk about this to Ray, my popcorn will already be popped and buttered."

"You know you are crazy don't you?"

"Who isn't these days?" she giggled, and she didn't know the half of it.

"Bye, Paula," I said, hanging up the phone.

Raymond picked me up early for church but I had been dressed for a while. We rode in the car without much conversation.

Chapter Fifteen

The distance we had made up the last time we went to church together was back between us again. I didn't know if it was my fault for taking the propofol or if it was his fault for coming into my room. My mind wandered during the service and I didn't get much of the sermon. All I could think about was what I was going to say to Raymond later.

"Do you feel like getting something to eat?" he asked as we walked out of the church.

"Sure, I haven't eaten anything today."

"Me neither, let's go the Garden Brunch Café on Jefferson Street."

"That sounds real good," I said.

"I'm really sorry about coming in your room and invading your privacy," Raymond said after we got in the car. "I know you think I overreacted but it just threw me when I saw the needle on the bed. I thought you were hooked on heroin or something."

"We haven't lived together for a long time and that makes it confusing because the boundaries between us are blurred. We have to define our relationship; we can't live halfway in and halfway out of our marriage," I said.

"What are you suggesting?" Raymond asked, pulling out of the parking lot.

"It's hard to say but I think we should file the legal papers."

"I just lost my appetite," he said, looking straight ahead.

"Raymond, people committed to their marriage live together. We haven't lived together for three years."

"When I lost my son I never thought I would lose my whole

family," he said, apparently not remembering he walked away.

"You'll never lose Pam but things will never be the same between us. You left me at the lowest point in my life."

"I want us to get back together," he said, closing his eyes in frustration.

"When did you decide this, Ray, last year, last month, or last week?"

"I wanted to come back for a lot longer time than I can tell you but I couldn't because I didn't know how to make it up to you, leaving my family alone like that."

"Let it go, Raymond. We're all right and I'm glad you're all right."

"I don't think you're all right, I think you need me."

"I love you and I always will but I don't think we can be happy together. Too much has happened and too much time has passed."

"If you don't mind I'll pass on brunch today," he said, turning in the direction of the house.

"We'll talk some more after you think about it," I said, getting out of the car.

He wouldn't look at me; he just nodded his head and looked out of the front windshield. I walked inside straight to the kitchen and opened the overloaded refrigerator. I didn't see anything I wanted; I had lost my appetite too. I felt bad for Raymond; it wasn't my intention to hurt him but I didn't know what else I could do. My trips to the past had shown me that even if you can go back to the past you can't change anything. It is what it is. I sat on the sofa in the den and pulled off my heels before I picked up the phone to call Pam.

Chapter Fifteen

"Hey, Pammy," I said after she picked up.

"What's up, Mama?" she said, sighing.

"You sound tired or like you just got up. Did you make it to church today?"

"No, I didn't make it; I've got midterm exams to study for before homecoming week."

"I can't believe how fast the semester is flying by. I know you have things to do and I don't want to hold you up long but I need to talk to you for a few minutes. Your daddy and I went to church together and after the service we were talking, to make a long story short, I suggested that we go forward with a divorce and he said he wanted us to get back together."

"Mom, I've got a ton of studying to do, I can't deal with this right now."

"I'm sorry but I needed to let you know what's going on so it won't be a shock to you."

"Okay, and I don't mean to be disrespectful but I don't want to be in the middle of whatever happens between you and Dad. I love you both, but I'm grown, this doesn't have anything to do with me."

"I hear you, Pam, focus on your books and I'll call you on the weekend."

I couldn't blame Pam for not wanting to be involved; Ray and I had been so preoccupied with our issues that we hadn't considered what effect it might have had on her.

Chapter Sixteen

I waited until 9:10 before I called the office. The open enrollment period had ended last week and the flow in the Benefits Department had returned to normal.

"Hello, Keisha, I'm going to be working out of the office for most of the week. I need to do some research on some new funds."

"Would you like me to call you if anything comes up or do you want me to hold all your messages?"

"Go ahead and call me if you need to, it won't be a problem," I said before we hung up.

I had several things I needed to do and I wasn't going to take the chance of Keisha eavesdropping and overhearing any of my business and spreading it through the hospital. I made some coffee and turned on the computer in my home office and looked up a lawyer referral service and called the number.

"May I help you?" the voice on the other end asked.

"Yes, I'm looking for a divorce lawyer."

"Yes, ma'am, we have a number of qualified attorneys who specialize in family law. Do you have preference for working with a male or female?"

I really didn't, but since I had a male psychologist I thought I should support the professional females this time.

"I believe I would prefer a female."

"That's fine. Are there any children or custody issues involved?"

"No, there are not."

"Are there any large assets or property that can be disputed?"

"No, there aren't."

"Has there been any spousal abuse or criminal activity to be considered?"

"No, not at all."

"Would a downtown office be convenient for you?"

"Yes, it would."

"If you have a pen, I have the number for Deirdre Sloan's office. You can give her a call and the initial consultation is free. If after the consultation you don't feel comfortable, call us back and we can give you another referral."

She gave me the number and I thanked her for her time and then I called Ms. Sloan's office and made an appointment for Wednesday afternoon.

I went into the kitchen and made a chef salad for lunch to keep all the fresh vegetables that I bought from going to waste and then I sat down to read a prospectus from the pile of new funds in my messenger bag. The phone rang a couple of times in the afternoon but it wasn't from Keisha or business related, it was David and I didn't feel like talking to him. I sent him a text saying I would be in the office tomorrow.

While I had the phone in my hand I sent a text to Raymond that said, "How are you? Give me a call when you get a chance." I wanted to give him fair warning that I planned to hire a lawyer and file for the divorce before the week was out.

Chapter Sixteen

***

The law office was on the corner of 4th and Union Street in suite 317. The receptionist greeted me and showed me into a small conference room where the dark cherry wood on the walls and desk gave the room a warm antique feel of old money. I sat down in one of the green leather chairs and swiveled around looking at the pictures of magnolia flowers that decorated the walls. The door opened and a young black woman in her early thirties walked in, she was impeccably dressed in a gray Brooks Brothers suit with pink pinstripe that was coordinated with a pink tailored shirt and gray suede pumps. Her hair was cut short and layered to the nape of her neck. She was the picture of style and I wanted to give her a high-five in recognition.

"Good afternoon, Ms. Roberts, I'm Deirdre Sloan, I received your information from the referral agency. Can I get you something to drink, coffee, tea, or water?"

"No, I'm fine thank you."

She took her legal pad out of the burgundy leather case and poised the shiny silver pen to take her notes.

"How long have you been married, Mrs. Roberts?"

"Twenty-three years," I told her.

She raised her eyebrows as she wrote and said, "That's a real accomplishment. What is the number of children born in the marriage?"

"Two," I answered.

"What are their ages?"

"My daughter is twenty-two years old and my son passed away

at seventeen."

"I'm sorry to hear that, how long ago was that?"

"It was four years ago."

"Would you say that was a contributing factor in the break-up of your marriage?"

"Indirectly yes, my husband abandoned the family a year later, he couldn't handle it."

"Have the two of you had any communication over the last three years?"

"About four months ago we reconnected through our daughter."

"Are you on friendly terms?"

"Very much so, until I suggested the divorce. He wants us to get back together."

"Have you given it serious consideration?" she asked.

"I have but I don't think it will work and enough time has passed, our marriage is over."

"So your intentions are to file for divorce?" she asked soberly.

"Absolutely, without any hesitation," I said, looking her in the eye.

"That's fine, I just need you to fill out this retainer and I'll do the necessary paperwork. Do you have an address or place of employment for your husband?"

"Yes, I do," I said, searching for a pen in my bag."

"I have an extra," she said, handing me a slim black pen."

The reality of what I had just done was lost on me. Sitting in that office was more of an out-of-body experience than any of the night trips I had been on. I had never thought I would be

Chapter Sixteen

in this position four years ago. Instead of getting my car and heading home I walked around the corner to Printer's Alley and went inside the Bourbon Street Blues and Boogie Bar to buy myself a stiff drink.

The music inside the bar sounded more country than Blues or Boogie but it didn't matter my mind was on other things.

"What are you having?" the bartender asked when I sat down.

"White Russian," I said, looking around at the thin crowd before happy hour began.

"No chance for a big white country boy?" he said, trying to make a joke.

"None at all," I said, forcing a fake smile.

He made the drink and placed it in front of me before moving to the opposite end of the bar. I took a sip and tasted the cool coffee flavor while the vodka warmed my throat. My eyes drifted along the line of colorfully decorated bottles on the back of the bar while my thoughts drifted back to my life five years ago. A petite older white woman dressed in blue jeans, a matching jacket, and well-broken in cowboy boots climbed on the stool beside me and ordered a Jack Daniels on the rocks.

"How you doing today? You look like you got a lot on your mind," she said with a heavy southern twang while raising her glass in my direction.

"A rough spot right through here," I said, admiring the intricacy of her newly coiffed big hair.

"Well, all I can tell you is that life moves on and it gets better."

"I'm counting on that."

"Take it from me, honey, I've had three husbands and four children, lost a son in the Gulf War, got a granddaughter strung out on meth, but I've got my health and a half-decent roof over my head. I don't want for anything, I enjoy myself some good music and having a drink, and as far as I'm concerned life is good."

"You've got the right attitude," I told her.

"You got to, my friend, you don't have a choice. Roll with the punches or get knocked out."

"I've been fighting a losing battle for a while now and I'm tired."

"Stop fighting, make peace with whatever it is and then you win."

"What's your name?" I asked her.

"I'm Laura," she said with a smile.

"Laura, my name's Portia, can I buy you another drink?"

"If you put some hot wings with it," she said with a chuckle.

"My pleasure," I said, smiling as I motioned for the bartender.

Who knew you could get a revelation in Printer's Alley but I had an epiphany that changed my thinking in a profound way. Taking the propfol in my desperation I had discovered that I could travel back to the past and relive a beautiful moment from my life, but now I was positive that I didn't want to live in the past. Reliving the memories with Nicholas wasn't what I wanted. I already owned that time. I wanted what had been denied to me, a future with him. Reliving those experiences only served to remind me more of what I couldn't have. I took Laura's advice and made peace with it. It still hurt and probably always would but I was determined to live and be happy. My outlook was so much brighter I even considered canceling my appointment with Dr. Lanier but I wanted to get more insight on my journeys to other lives in other lands.

***

I hesitated at the door when I saw a woman already sitting in Dr. Lanier's office. She rose to her feet when she saw me in the doorway.

"Hello, Ms. Roberts, please come in, I'm Dr. Wright. Dr. Lanier and I consult with each other on some of our more interesting cases."

"Hello," I responded, unsure of what her presence was about.

I walked over to the couch where I sat on my previous appointment.

"Make yourself comfortable," Dr. Wright said, sitting in the chair next to the couch. "Dr. Lanier has told me that you've had what you believe are mental transports to your past lives."

"Listening to you say it I know it sounds crazy but that's what I believe."

"Can I get you something to drink?"

"No, I'm fine," I said, slightly uncomfortable at her invading my appointment.

"What I'd like for you to do," she said, leaning back and crossing her legs, "Is describe what happens before and during the whole experience, what you feel and what you see."

"The first thing that happens is I get the feeling that my body loses its weight and I'm floating in the darkness. The floating sensation turns into the feeling that I'm falling and then I'm spinning while I'm falling. Then the darkness begins to break into what looks like rocket streaks of bright light and they are also spinning. After some time I see colors blend into the spiraling beam of light and the images are blurred like an out of focus movie in fast-forward or rewind. They seem different and disconnected."

"From there how do you make contact with a past life or experience?" she asked.

"I just choose an image randomly, I'm usually drawn to colors or warmth or some other sensation that draws my focus and then I have the sensation of falling again and when I come to consciousness I'm in another body in another place and time."

"In most instances research has shown us that whenever patients feel like they are having an out-of-body experience it's actually the memory and the imagination working together and producing hallucinations that give them the sense of being in a different place," Dr. Wright said, uncrossing her legs and moving to the front edge of her chair.

"In all due respect, Dr. Wright, I've done some research of my own and I've read about that theory, what is different is that in these trips I feel myself inside of these other characters in surroundings that are familiar to me, I am them, but I bear no resemblance to them. There is no connection to me or my present life. At that moment in time that I find myself I am living my life and within that life I have a past that I remember. However, when

Chapter Sixteen

I come back to this present life I'm no longer connected to it in any way and the only thing I can remember is what I experienced and the thoughts that I had during that specific time."

"Ms. Roberts, I find it all fascinating, and I do believe there are things that cannot be explained in this world and most of them will remain mysteries to us, however, I would be doing you a disservice if I encouraged you to believe that these experiences were more than the most elaborate of dreams."

"I have considered that myself, and I have thought about all the dreams I could remember that I have had in my life. In all of them I was myself within the dream. I may have been in a different role or character of myself but I recognized myself, I looked like me and there was no doubt in who I was. What happens to me in these recent instances is that I leave my physical body, I'm not sure if it is mental or spiritual, and I'm able to transcend to my existence in another place and time. I have no effect on it and I'm not conscious of any other life at that time. The only correlation that I see is that the images that I'm drawn to are usually around a significant incident or occasion in that particular life."

"What do you attribute that to?" she asked as if I had all the answers that I came there to get from them.

"Maybe because the traumatic events in our lives are higher in our subconscious, easier to grasp, I don't know."

"Your case is a unique one, and I'm convinced, as is Dr. Lanier, that the experiences you describe are very real to you, I'm just not able to relate them to reality as we know it. The next step would be to recreate the conditions that provoke the onset of the mental travels. Would you be open to doing a sleep study of that nature?"

The last thing I could do was go into a room where I would be observed and inject myself with a controlled substance. I knew I wasn't going to get any information from these two. They were searching for a new subject to put in their next research article. I bowed out as gracefully as I could under the circumstances.

"Most of the distress and problems sleeping that brought me here were related to my son more so than the consequence of time travel. Things have improved lately but I will consider doing the sleep study and give you a call seeing that my time today has ended."

I couldn't wait to get out of the office, I regretted opening my mouth and revealing things I should have kept to myself. If anybody else had experienced this under the propofol they had the sense to keep their mouths shut. I knew I wasn't coming back and I was thankful that civil commitment laws had been changed or they probably would have come with a straitjacket to pick me up and put me under lock and key. If these were just fantasies or figments of my imagination why couldn't I control what I see and just conjure up Michael Jackson himself so that we could talk about it. I moved my hand firmly along the banister as I stepped quickly down the winding staircase and out of the door.

***

"Good morning, Keisha," I said cheerily when I walked in the door the next morning surprising her in the middle of a spider solitaire game.

Chapter Sixteen

"Good morning, Ms. Roberts," she said, clicking her mouse over to her e-mails. "I didn't expect you to come in today since it was Friday."

"I know but I want to get the new funds I've selected added into the Banner system before Monday."

That was only half the truth; I was ready to get my life back to normal and that included going to work. It had been a draining week away from the office between filing for divorce and spilling my guts in Dr, Lanier's office. Being at work was the most serene place I could think of where I didn't feel like I was out of my mind.

I worked steadily throughout the day and got a lot accomplished. The new funds were in the system and links to the prospectuses were in place. At the end of the day I packed up my things satisfied with my productive week and locked the door behind me.

I had barely taken three steps out of the building when I heard, "Portia, what kind of bullshit is this? I thought we meant more to each other than for you to serve me these damn divorce papers on my job," Raymond bellowed angrily.

He had caught me completely by surprise. I kept walking to my car conscious of everything around me even the sound of my heels pounding against the sidewalk. I wondered how long he had been waiting there, but more than anything I wanted to get out of earshot of my co-workers before I responded. Raymond followed close behind me and after I put my bags inside the car I turned around to face him.

"I tried to talk to you about this but you didn't return my phone calls," I said in a low voice, trying to encourage him to do the same.

"I expected more from you than this," he said, holding the large envelope up in his hands.

"You're the one who walked away, Ray, it was just as hard for me, probably harder and now you want me to make things easy for you."

"I did what I had to do to survive, Portia."

"I understand that, believe me I do, but those same rules apply to me also, it's not all about you."

"So this is your way of punishing me for that?"

"I'm not trying to punish anybody. We've both suffered enough."

"So that's it, we just throw away the rest?"

"I don't get this reaction, Ray. What's changed for you all of a sudden, would you have objected a year ago when I hadn't seen or heard from you? I couldn't keep my life on hold forever."

"I'm back now. Doesn't that count for something?"

I looked around at the steady flow of people growing in the parking lot and I didn't want to be the weekend's feature movie so I said, "Do you want to come by the house so we can sit down and talk about this?"

"I'll follow you home," he said, walking away.

I didn't want it to be like this but how else could it be? I ran through every yellow light, eased through stop signs, and beat Raymond to the house, thank God. I rushed inside the door and

Chapter Sixteen

straight up the steps to get out of my business suit and slipped into a t-shirt and yoga pants hoping they will add some zen to the evening. My feet felt cold so I grabbed a thick pair of socks before I hurried back down the steps to the kitchen. At that moment I was so thankful again for all the groceries I'd bought when I looked in the refrigerator. I heard the door open and realized that I must not have locked it when I came in. I'm also taken aback that Raymond walked in without ringing the bell.

"I'm in the kitchen," I yelled out to him. He took his time walking in and I started to feel nervous. I froze for a moment wondering where I had left my cell phone. "Sit down, I'll fry us some fish while we talk. Do you mind peeling some potatoes?"

"I can do that," he said, taking off his jacket and I can sense he has calmed down some.

I get him the potatoes out of the pantry, a paring knife, and some newspaper for the peelings. I stand with my back to him, the dressed catfish sliding through my fingers under the running water, and I can feel his eyes on me. For a second I think maybe I shouldn't have given him anything sharp but I put it out of my mind, he's not homicidal, he's just hurt.

I pour oil in my cast iron skillet and pour some milk in a shallow pan and catch a glimpse of Raymond meticulously peeling a small potato.

We both worked in silence until I heard him say, "We've been through some bad times and our marriage has suffered a lot of damage, but I think it can be salvaged."

I rolled three large catfish in a bag of fish seasoning and

meal before I placed them in the hot grease. I closed my eyes for a second and the sound of the frying reminds me a winter rainstorm. He placed the peeled potatoes on the counter next to me.

"I don't want us to settle for something salvaged, we both deserve something better," I told him as I sliced the peeled potatoes and put them in a pot of water to boil.

"I still love you, Portia."

"I still love you too, Ray, and I always will, but we've got to have more than just history going for us," I said, turning the fish over in the skillet and watching the hot oil react loudly to the coolness of the other side of the fish.

"What else do you want?" he asked, rolling up the peelings in the newspaper.

"I want what most women want; I want romance, passion, someone I know I can depend on, someone who won't leave me."

I took a bag of mixed vegetables out of the freezer and put them in the microwave before I turned the fish over again.

"We can go to counseling and we can work on that, give us a chance before you let it go so easily."

"What makes you think it's easy?" I said, draining the fish on paper towels and turning off the boiled potatoes.

It was hard as hell. Then again, I didn't want to work on it or try to build a fire in the same place that one burned out. I wanted a fresh start. I set the table for us to eat.

Chapter Seventeen

I lay in the bed wide awake that night thinking about the talk Ray and I had over dinner. I had spent the bulk of my life making sacrifices for other people and now I was selfish, I only wanted to think about me. I pulled my kit out from under the bed and went down to the butter compartment of the refrigerator. I came back up into my room and crawled into bed. I prepared the syringe, sterilized my arm, smoothed on the lidocaine, and plunged the needle into my vein. Within a few moments I feel my consciousness drifting into another place and then I feel the now familiar sensation of the weight of my body falling away from me as I drop down. I relax into the spin wanting to escape from my present existence and all its complications. The dazzling beams of light spin around me in the darkness and when the colors bleed in I'm pulled into an image that exudes a brilliant color of red.

"Oooo, ouch, that hurts," I say to the man working steadily behind me and lean my head back to release the strain on my neck.

The pulls and tugs give me a headache while my hair is being straightened and styled into katsuyama style. I can smell the wax in the pomade and I know that I will get little sleep with my head suspended in air on the neck support.

"Beauty has its price, Naomi, my sweet, you pay and then they pay," my Momi says.

"I know, Okasan, but it seems that sometimes I'm on the short end of the bargain."

"I don't know how your lips can say such a thing when you are the most excellent Geisha in all of Kyoto and daughter of the most renowned in over 100 years. Prominent men pay for the privilege of sharing the very air you breathe."

What I couldn't tell her was that I only wanted to share myself with one. That I had done the unthinkable for a business woman, I had fallen in love.

"It is immaculate as usual," she tells the hairdresser after examining his handiwork; "You are still a true artist."

When we are alone she sits beside me and says, "Tonight will be your greatest triumph, all the seats have been sold."

"Momi, if only I didn't feel naked up there with everyone staring at me, I prefer the private appointments," I said, thinking of Takashi.

"They aren't staring; they're mesmerized, my sweet, and the company of many is much more profitable than the company of one, and more efficient I might add. That is your privilege as a woman to use your talent for your benefit, not to be locked away unadmired."

"I know, yet the lasting adoration of one can be more valuable than the fleeting infatuation of a hundred," I say to her.

"Would you like me to lend a hand in putting on your make-up, Naomi?" she asks with a warm caress to my shoulder, ignoring what I just said.

Chapter Seventeen

"No, Okasan, it helps me to see myself transform into character."

I stare at the reflection in the looking glass and I see my mother's face, I inherited her beauty and grace but I can still see the silhouette of the four year old sitting at her knee. That was where my training began.

"Carry your body as if you are the Empress of Japan, every movement is regal from the blink of an eye to the twirl of a finger," she would say as she taught me how to serve tea. "In the dance become one with nature," she would tell me as she glided across the floor like a boat on smooth water. "You must believe the sun rises for you, the wind blows for you, the raindrops search for you, because you are the most beautiful flower."

She talked to me incessantly about everything, literature, science, business, and she taught me many games to entertain when I came home from school. She would instruct me saying, "With your clients speak with just enough knowledge to allow him to expound more of his own." For ten years I shadowed her and mirrored all she did.

My mother had been the most sought after Geishas in the "flower and willow world" for more than thirty years. A shrewd woman of finance, she worked off the debts she owed and worked independently until she purchased her own tea house. She had a Danna, the man who was also my father, he provided support for her for many years, but she always continued to work.

She repeated her promise to me each night when she put me to bed, "You will never have to beg for anything, men will throw their riches at your feet."

True to her word, she taught me everything she knew and saw to it that I had the best dance and music teachers.

"To be magnificent there are hours of preparation for mere moments of glory," she would say whenever I grew weary, "Natural beauty is plentiful in nature, here in Kyoto beauty is created."

When I am done dressing, I can no longer see myself behind the stark white make up and ruby red lips. I tip down the stairs in my sandals with the hope that Takashi will be there in the front to see me.

"You are the 'Maiden Lily,' my sweet," Momi says, complimenting me in my opulent new kimono before she leaves me alone on the stage.

I crouch motionless in the center while the gas lights in the room are dimmed and I can hear the music of the shamisen begin to play. Slowly I rise to my feet stretching each limb upward as a flower in bloom. I move forward to my audience with deliberate and exaggerated movements, lifting my arms like wings in flight and barely touching the floor. I'm surrounded within a mist of smoke and then I start to sing. That's when I have them under my power as the 'Maiden Lily.'

I keep my distance in the fog, an almost invisible barrier that separates me from them; it heightens the yearning for that which is so close yet unattainable. Some think it is some type of magic trick, but my performance is carefully and methodically staged to affect my audience in that way. My secret weapon is in my song, I sing with all the depth of my emotions pouring out my soul, sometimes a high pitch at the top of lungs, other times barely audible, but always without words. The interpretation is left to the listener to hear and feel the words they most desire. That which is within the mind is more powerful and meaningful than anything I could express. Then the room goes dark and I leave the stage. The gas lights are then turned up and I come back to intense applause.

"Well done, my flower," Takashi says to me as the crowd dissipates.

"Others see me, but it is all for you," I tell him in a whisper.

As I turn to speak to another I brush against him with the full length of my right side for a secret caress before he leaves.

Takashi, my true love, is one of the wealthiest of my clients. It was in my second year as a Maiki when I noticed him across the room at a banquet. Above the quiet rumblings of numerous conversations and porcelain clinging against glass our eyes spoke to each other. We met formally when he appeared at the tea house the following week with his father.

"Lily, this is Nakamura-san and his son," Momi announces. I bow my head low and Takashi does the same. I show them to the table for tea.

I pour the sake and ask, "Are you men of business, politics, or learning?"

"We operate in the business world," Nakamura answers, "We trade rice futures and silk."

"The most challenging of all professions, it requires ingenuity and great stamina," I say.

"Assuredly, there is no respite in the race to make money," Takashi says, looking at his father and then turning to me again.

"I offer you a moment of relaxing for the length of my song," I say, reaching for the shamisen to play.

I hum as I play moving my lips and tasting the sugar water that makes them shine, but never opening my mouth. My eyes convey the understanding of a child whose parent never stops pushing them to succeed and our bond is sealed. The fifth day of the week has been reserved for him by contract from that very day. His father paid the price for him as the patron of my mizuage.

"No other man will ever touch me," I tell him before he leaves, he is the only man I have made love to and only for him would I give up my life as a geisha.

***

"Naomi, I need you to buy some things at the market and you must hurry back, you have a client coming soon."

"I won't be long, Okasan," I say, happy to take a morning walk in the warm sun.

On the street I hear a voice calling, "Naomi, hello, how are you?"

It was a friendly rival in the Gion district stopping to talk.

"Hello, I'm good, and yourself?"

Without even answering my greeting she says, "I hear that Takashi Nakamura is soon to be married."

She looks close in my eyes for a reaction knowing of his

loyalty to me.

Refusing to give her any, I lie and say, "What difference should that be to me; I have no desire to be a man's wife."

"It's possible that he won't have time to spend with Geisha once he has a family."

"I have no shortage of clients, if he's absent, the appointment will be filled by another."

"You must share your secret with me, I still have debts to pay," she says as she inspects my kimono with her eyes.

"It is their curiosity from rumors that others spread that bring them to me," I say slyly, "It's my unique skills that keep them returning."

"Interesting, I should not take up any more of your valuable time," she says, stomping off with sound of the wood of her geta clicking in my head making me forget the errands that brought me out today.

"Suzuki-san is here and waiting," my Okasan says as soon as I walk in.

The man is fat and smells bad. I hate serving the old politician tea and rice wine, but I am ever the consummate Geisha, I amuse him with games, my banter filled with innuendo, and I play him a happy song on my shamisen smiling at the same time I hold back my tears.

"I don't want to see any more clients," I tell her after he leaves.

"Naomi, your schedule is filled with appointments and invitations."

"I don't care; I only want to see Takashi."

"Why would you throw away all the work we have done, a lifetime of training, and give yourself to one man when there is a host of gentlemen who compete and bid for the chance to have your undivided attention?"

"I love him, Okasan. Have you never loved a man, what about my father?"

"If not for you that relationship would have brought me nothing but heartache."

"I don't care what happened to you, a life with Takashi is worth the gamble."

***

I hang in limbo waiting for the fifth day of the week and Takashi's standing appointment. I fill the room with lit candles that smell of lavender.

"This is the best part of my week," he says when the door is closed behind us and he kisses my neck.

"I have been dying to see you; the time passes so slowly between our visits," I say.

He starts peeling my clothes off like I am a ripe piece of fruit that he can't wait to enjoy and it thrills me so much I forget about everything else. The passion between us removes my doubts that he could ever love another.

"I love you, Takashi," I tell him, although our love had been largely felt but unspoken before today.

"Naomi, I care for you very much but I am to be married soon. Your place in my heart will not be replaced but I must consider my family now."

Chapter Seventeen

"I would gladly be your wife, don't you love me?" I ask over the lump of emotions rising in my throat.

"I will be your faithful Danna always and my time with you each week will never change, that I can promise you."

"That is not a promise of love, Takashi, if you marry another it will never be the same between us."

"Nothing has to change, why are you upsetting yourself?" he says, becoming frustrated.

"I want to love you and take care of you every day, I want to be your wife, and I want to have your children."

"That can never be, Naomi, I have the reputation of my family and other obligations to consider but that doesn't diminish my love for you."

"All that I am is for you and you say that isn't good enough for your family."

"Don't spoil what we have," he says, standing up.

"Me spoil it, you have broken my heart like cheap glass."

"Nothing will change, I swear."

"Everything has changed; I lived for you and a future I thought we would share."

"I have to go, Naomi," he says, moving to the door.

"So you have told me. Goodbye Takashi," I say, blowing out the candle sitting near the mat.

Momi comes into my room after seeing a client leave abruptly.

"What is wrong, Nakamura-san seemed upset?"

"This is your life, Okasan, not mine, I can't do it anymore."

"It is your life, Naomi; it's what you were born to do."

"That's what you say, not me, I have a right to live my life the way I want to and I have a right to love one man if I choose to."

"If that man loved you he would not have left. I've invested everything I have in you and your future."

"I wish you hadn't," I say, moving quickly to the window. I snatch it open and look down at the ground.

"Don't jump, Naomi," she yells as she rushes over to grab me.

"I wouldn't do that, Momi, I wouldn't hurt you after all you've sacrificed. The Maiden Lily just needed a breath of fresh air."

Fatigued by the drama of the day we collapse to the floor in an embrace.

In the morning I woke up feeling ready to live life on my own terms with no more regrets. I reached over on the nightstand and grabbed the phone.

"I did it Paula," I said as soon as I heard her say hello.

"What did you do?" she asked with worry rising up in her voice.

"I haven't committed a crime so calm down," I answered, even though I wasn't so sure about that after my excursion to another life last night. "I got a lawyer and filed for divorce and Raymond got served yesterday."

"Oh my God, have you talked to him yet?"

"Yeah, he was waiting for me when I got off, pissed as hell, but he came over and we ate and talked and he had mellowed out some by the time he left."

"Sister, I am scared of you and I'm proud of you too, you are taking your life back and it is about time."

Chapter Seventeen

"It is, I'm finally getting it, life is all about choices, and I'm not going to throw my life away. I choose to be happy in spite of whatever gets thrown at me."

"Girl, you are going to make me throw this phone down and shout this morning and when I get to church tomorrow I'll just sit and hold my peace."

"You are too silly but I love you."

"I love you too, and you made my day today, keep me updated; I have got to throw my hands up."

"Good bye, Paula, I'll call you next week."

I felt good this morning, it was like I had finally been lifted out of my rut, and my breakthrough was here at last. I sat down at my computer to plan myself a getaway to celebrate. I perused the internet for hours looking for the perfect place where I could relax and kickback for a weekend before the hustle of the fast approaching holiday season took over and Pam came home for the winter break. I found it just as the sun went down, the ideal place for rest and romance, a cabin in Gatlinburg.

Now all I had to do was convince George to go with me. I hesitated calling him; I just couldn't make myself pick up the phone. What if he was busy, what if he'd met someone else? I couldn't take the rejection right now. I had come so far in picking myself up that I didn't want to take the chance of being knocked down so soon. I just wanted to enjoy the scenery from the first step I'd taken to being whole again.

Chapter Eighteen

I skipped church the next day. I picked up the phone to call Pam and put it down again. I got the sense from our last conversation that she didn't want the updated details of her mom and dad working out their marital problems. I spent the day watching old movies in bed and eating like a junk food junky. After watching two Joan Crawford movies, "The Godfather Part I," and a re-run of "Waiting to Exhale," I had found my courage to call George.

I phoned his office the next morning as soon as I got to work and asked him to meet me for a late lunch at Friday's at 1:00. My eyes bounced between my watch and the clock on my computer and each minute seemed like an hour. I prayed that he wouldn't have an emergency or anything else that would keep me from seeing him. At 12:30, I headed out of the office so fast I forgot my coat and had to double back.

"I'm glad you could come," I said after watching George saunter over to my table in the back of the restaurant.

He looked so good, smart, strong and sexy, and I was even more sure that he was the man I wanted to be with.

"A chance to have lunch with a beautiful woman, I couldn't turn that down," he said, sitting across from me.

"I must admit you had me worried," I said.

"What do you mean?" he asked, putting on his glasses and

picking up the menu.

"I know I was the one reluctant to make our relationship exclusive but the reality of you dating other women was a bit much for me."

"So what are you saying, Portia?" he asked, taking his glasses off and placing them on the table.

"I'm saying that I want us to date exclusively, I mean if that's still something you would be interested in."

"Tell me what's changed; have you filed those papers yet?" he asked, still looking at the menu.

"As a matter of fact I have."

He looked at me puzzled for a few seconds before shaking his head.

"You have succeeded in surprising me today."

"George, I'd like you to take a trip with me this weekend if you can get away," I said, praying he didn't have other plans.

"Let's talk about it over this lunch you're buying me."

The waitress came back and took our orders.

"I just want to show you how special you are to me and I don't want to lose you before I even get a chance to get to know you better."

"I've already told you that you're everything I'm looking for in a woman. I'm crazy about you, but I've also had my share of emotional changes. If you want to do this I'm all for it, but you had some worries, maybe you need to give it some more time."

"That sounds like you're the one backing up, are you involved with someone else?"

Chapter Eighteen

"Not really, I'm not out here to hurt anybody but I'm also not going to be the fool for anybody."

"That's fair, I can understand your hesitation, and I know I flipped the script in Vegas, but my head is on straight now."

"I need you to be honest with me," he said just as the server brought the food to the table.

It gave me a reprieve to think of a response. I had been deceiving so many people lately I wasn't sure if I knew what the truth was.

"What do you want to know?" I asked, spreading my arms wide trying my best to look like an open book.

"I want to know what went down and what I'm dealing with."

"I've told you about it before," I said, taking a bite of my burger to get my mouth too full to talk.

"I want you to put it all out there; I don't want the short version. I want the long sordid story, uncut and uncensored."

"I promise you I will," I said, swallowing enough to talk, "It will take a while and I know you've got patients waiting. If you come with me this weekend I'll put it all out there."

"You have a deal," he said, reaching his hand across the table to seal it. I put my hand in his and it felt warm and safe and I didn't want to let go.

"Where do you plan on taking me?" he asked, biting into his burrito.

"A road trip, I rented a cabin in Gatlinburg."

"Interesting, do you mind if I drive?"

"I can drive you know."

"I'm sure you can but I want you rested when we get there," he said, flashing me that sexy smile.

When we finished lunch, George put his arm around my waist and walked me to my car. I hadn't realized how much I missed his touch. I didn't want to be like Naomi pining over the love of one I couldn't have and miss out on the love in my future.

***

I put my exercise clothes in the car the next morning, it was forecasted to be a warm day and I wanted to go walking after work. I was feeling good, on cloud nine, a new woman, not the beleaguered soul I was a year ago. A faint taste of happiness was forming in my mouth and I wanted to savor it, I had almost forgotten what it was like.

I got a text just before lunch that said, "Thinking about you today," and that further sealed it. I sailed through the afternoon and headed to the park for my workout. I loved the fall when the seasons were changing and the leaves donned their autumn colors before they fell off the trees for the winter. I had been around the mile path once and I was so energized I decided to jog out the next one. I had gone about a quarter of a mile when I heard somebody calling my name.

"Portia, Portia, wait up."

I turned around and it was David staggering up the path to catch me.

"Did you down a Five Hour or a Red Bull? I've been trailing you for a half mile waiting for you to slow up."

"No, David, this is how I roll when you're not around to slow me up," I said, dropping my pace to a walk.

Chapter Eighteen

"Excuse me, Miss Olympic trainee, some of us have real jobs and work all day."

"I know you're not going to tell me the sob story of the poor overworked doctor."

"I won't go there today, but that's real."

"That's why you make the big dollars, my friend."

"I wasn't sure if you'd be out here today so I just took a chance and here you are."

"Lucky you, I've been hitting and missing my walking lately but I'm going to do better."

"I've been kind of busy myself and I've been missing you. Did you get my text earlier?"

"Yeah, I did," I said in an attempt to hide the disappointment in my voice that it wasn't from George; I hadn't bothered to check the number.

"I miss the times when we just kicked back and talked, you know you're my best friend."

"Now I know you want something. What is it?" I said, impatient and upset that he was blowing my mood.

"I need you to do that for me one more time, a third strike and then I'm out."

"Let's finish up this mile and then we'll talk," I said.

When we got around to my car, I got two bottles of water out of the trunk and we walked over to sit on the steps of the Parthenon. I looked up in the evening clouds as if the words would be written there for a polite way to tell him again that I'm done with the freaky role play game.

"Do you remember what I told you about my husband and how he left after our tragedy?"

"Yes, he's been out of the picture for some years now."

"Well, I mentioned to you before that he came back, things didn't work out and now I've filed for a divorce. I need to be real cool, I don't want any problems."

"I hear you, you know I've been there myself," he said, taking a gulp of water.

"I don't think it would be a good idea for you to be around right now, my next-door neighbor is good friends with him and she's watching every move I make."

"So what, this is a free country. You have a right to do whatever you want on your property. He's the one who walked off," he said angrily, kicking an invisible rock with his sneaker.

"It's a real tender spot between him and I right now and I don't want to aggravate things. Besides the semester will be over soon and my daughter will be around."

"So what are you saying?" he asked, standing up and brushing off his sweats.

"What I'm saying is that I was understanding in your family situation and now it's your turn to show me the same courtesy."

"That's cool," he said, but I could tell he was hot under the collar by the way he stormed off without even saying bye.

I kept a low profile for the rest of the week I didn't need any more confrontations. I was thankful to David for taking the risk that opened up my world for me. He played a large part in my healing progress over Nicholas and my whole view of life, but I

Chapter Eighteen

had paid him my dues for that, and now he was becoming a huge pain in my ass. I hoped he wouldn't put pressure on me and turn into a stalker or resort to blackmail. The only consolation I had was that we both needed complete confidentiality or our jobs were in jeopardy. The person who said "beware of the unintended consequences of our actions" should receive a Humanitarian Award, a Nobel Prize, and teach a Master's Class on the Oprah show.

Chapter Nineteen

The weekend couldn't get here fast enough for me and on Friday I called in sick. This was going to be a mental health day for sure. Last night I'd pulled out all the things I wanted to take with me for a cozy mini-vacation in Gatlinburg. I was too excited to eat so I drank some orange juice while I packed my clothes. When I was done I showered and put on my purple Ralph Lauren velour jogging suit, it wasn't sexy but you couldn't beat it for comfort on a road trip. It was just before noon when George pulled up in a pearl-colored Lexus 570, the man believed in going first-class. He loaded up my bags in the back while I got us some Snapples to drink and some nuts and fruit to munch on during the drive before I set the house alarm.

I climbed in the passenger seat and leaned back absorbing all the luxury and I had a handsome driver to boot. In less than five minutes we were on Briley Parkway heading toward the 40 East interstate leading to Knoxville.

I popped the top of a bottle of peach flavored tea and before I got it to my lips George said, "Start talking."

"We just got on the road; we've got plenty of time to talk," I said, hoping to put him off.

"I don't want to spend the whole weekend talking about it. I want to be done with it by the time we get to Knoxville."

I looked out of my window at the white line that ran along the side of the highway, and then I looked over at his profile. I could hear Stevie Wonder singing "Super Woman" on the radio faintly in the background, *"Where were you when I needed you last winter?"*

I didn't think he could deal with everything going on in my head but there was no way around it so I relented, "Where do you want me to start?"

"Start at the beginning and don't stop until you get to the day you met me."

"You've heard most of it before," I said, not wanting to go through this and spoil our trip.

"I like reruns; you always find something you missed the first time."

"Okay, you asked for it."

I looked out of the front windshield as he zoomed past the slower cars in the center and right lane. When he switched back to the far right lane out of the passing lane all I could see was the mountains rising out of the road ahead of us. I put down the bottle and started my story.

"I grew up in St. Louis, my daddy worked at the phone company and my mama was a teacher. There was me and my sister, Paula, we were all really close. When I was in my last year of junior high school Mama got real sick, her diabetes was causing all kinds of problems. Eventually one of her legs was amputated and her kidneys failed. Mama got really depressed and she didn't make it long after that, she died while I was in the tenth grade before Paula graduated from high school. Daddy

Chapter Nineteen

was never the same. Gradually he left us too, a little more every year.

After high school I came to Nashville to go to TSU while Paula stayed home and went to the University of Missouri so she could look after Daddy. Raymond was my college sweetheart, we met in our sophomore year, and we got married after graduation. We bought a house. We had a daughter and a son. Life and love was good for a long time. I think we were happy even with the tough struggles of making a marriage work over the years. The bottom fell out when our teenage son Nicholas passed away suddenly four years ago. Raymond was too hurt to care for me or Pam so he walked away."

I paused for a few minutes to contain the emotions that had welled up inside of me, one more word and I would have choked. George pulled the car over at the next rest stop. He got out of the car without saying anything, walked over to my door, took my hand and pulled me out of my seat. He wrapped me up tight in the warmest heartfelt hug I had ever experienced.

"I'm so sorry, Portia. I'm so sorry you had to go through that," he said as he embraced me and my pain.

That was something Raymond had not been able to do. I held onto him, let my emotions go and cried, not just from the hurt but from the relief. Tears filled with sadness drifted down my face and I flicked them to the ground glad to be rid of them. I got a comfort from George that I had needed for so long, a shoulder to lean on. I rested my head there and breathed in the scent of pine and grass in the cool mountain air.

"Let's stretch our legs," George said after a while, "There's a path that circles around the building."

We walked around the path and then I used the restroom and washed my face. Back in the car, we had gone about three miles down the interstate when I leaned forward to turn up the radio.

"I haven't heard my name yet and we're twenty-five miles from Knoxville," George said without taking his eyes off the road.

I found the button that let my seat back and this was where my honest rendition got a little shady. "A little over a year ago I decided to try and pull myself together and get my life back on track. I changed jobs and went on a few dates." My motivation in these decisions was deliberately omitted along with my dealings with David. "I dated another doctor at the hospital. We went out a couple of times but he was younger and we had different interests. Then you walked into my office and the rest is history."

"Not quite, what about your problems sleeping and your husband coming back on the scene?"

"I did see another doctor about my sleeping issues and a psychologist, and that situation is much better. As far as my relationship with Raymond is concerned, he resurfaced and started communicating with Pam right after we started dating. He seemed like a new man, free from all of his demons. I was stunned; I didn't know what to make of it. After we came back from Vegas he invited me to church and we talked. There weren't any hard feelings on my part and he seemed to think we could pick up where we left off. I felt confused until I saw you at B.B. King's sitting with another woman. I was there with him but all I

Chapter Nineteen

cared about was you. That's when I knew it was over and I filed for the divorce."

"Is he cooperating?"

"Not yet, but he doesn't have a choice, it's all over between us."

Then George turned up the radio and I exhaled.

The traffic was heavy when we got close to Pigeon Forge outside of Gatlinburg. It was so close to the holiday that I hadn't realized so many people would be on the road already. Driving into Gatlinburg was like going into another country. It was a cross between a miniature Las Vegas without the gambling and a miniature Disney World, but when you turned off the main drag it reminded me of the Pocono Mountains in Pennsylvania. We registered at the Smoky Mountain Chalet office and got the keys and garage opener to our cabin.

"Are you sure it's only going to be you and me staying here?" George asked when we pulled up to our log cabin.

"I reserved a two-bedroom to give us some extra space but I don't think I needed to, it's huge."

George opened the door and it was amazing. It was wood everywhere, the walls and the floors, and layered in intricate patterns on the ceiling.

"A weekend here and we'll be too spoiled to go back home," I said.

He put down our bags and gave me a hug and said, "Thanks for the invite."

"Thanks for coming," I said, giving him a welcome kiss.

George and I walked through the cabin; there was a wood

burning fireplace, a deck on the back with a hot tub, a spectacular view with rocking chairs, a theatre room, and an entertainment room complete with a pool table. I opened the kitchen cabinets and refrigerator and there was a nice set of china. The only thing missing was food.

"We need to go out and do some shopping and get this place stocked before we take our coats off," George said, "We may not get back out before the weekend is over."

"That sounds like a plan," I said, following him back out to the car.

We found a Publix grocery store about twenty minutes away.

"You know this is the most mundane thing we've done together," I said, pushing the grocery cart through the bakery section.

"Is that right?" he asked, mulling it over. "I guess I've already received my share of the ordinary, at my age I want it all over the top."

"Not a bad philosophy," I said, reaching for a small pound cake, "Then again, I don't know if they have anything in here to excite your first-class taste buds."

"As a matter of fact, these oatmeal raisin and walnut cookies are calling my name," he said, placing them in the top of the cart.

Further down the aisle I watched him choose some gourmet cheeses and crackers and then four bottles of wine.

"You know we're only going to be here a few days."

"And you said that to say what exactly?" he asked with half of a smile.

Chapter Nineteen

"Nothing at all, the man loves his wine, no problem with that."

The fruit was priced at a small fortune because it was out of season but I picked up some strawberries, blueberries, and grapes.

"You know I like my breakfast," George said, grabbing milk, eggs, bacon, and bread.

We threw a whole chicken and some t-bone steaks into the cart along with some pre-made salads and frozen veggies. George picked up a giant bag of rice and I had to laugh.

"You know we can come back to the store if we need to."

"Baby, I'm from the islands, I don't play. I'm not about to get snowed in these mountains and be hungry."

"Calm down, boy scout, there's no snow in the forecast," I joked, trailing him to the shortest line of the cashiers.

We checked out and George paid the $173 tab.

"This weekend is my treat," I reminded him.

"I know and I expect to be treated very well," he said, loading the groceries in the back.

"I'll cook tonight since you did all the driving," I said on the way back to the cabin, "You know I'm not handicapped."

"You take care of yourself quite nicely but allow me the pleasure to take care of you, I enjoy it."

"Now that's a page out a book I've never read before."

"What do you mean?" he asked, pulling into the cabin garage.

"I guess I've always had the role of taking care of everyone else."

"Is that the role you enjoy?" he asked from behind an armful of bags.

"No, I've done it long enough; I'd trade it in a heartbeat."

"Then relax and let me do for you."

Daylight started to dim once we had put the food away and the colors across the sky reminded me of the beams of light I saw when I took the propofol trips.

I took George by the hand and led him outside on the deck, "Let's watch the sunset before you get started cooking."

There was a plaid flannel blanket in the double rocking chair and we wrapped up in it and watched the blue sky mix with the red and yellow of the sun making a rainbow with purple hues.

"It doesn't get any better than this," I said.

"Always the pessimist," he said, giving me a kiss on the top of my head.

George went in the kitchen to start dinner and I tried to figure out how to start a fire in the fireplace. There was some kindling in a metal tin on the hearth so I sprinkled some over the logs and lit them with the lighter on the mantle. I sat down on the sofa and a feeling of peacefulness began to engulf me like the small spark on the broken branch growing into a flame. It had been such a long time since I could enjoy silence, aside from the crackling of the wood as it slowly burned. I don't remember falling asleep before George came over and woke me. The clean smell of soap wafted around him like an aura and he looked like he stepped off of a magazine cover in a navy cashmere sweater and tan slacks.

"Do you want to freshen up before dinner?" he asked thoughtfully.

Chapter Nineteen

"Yeah, I do," I said, standing up and stretching, "Looks like I have to catch up."

"Take your time, I'm not in a hurry, I sampled a little while I was working."

"Is there any left for me?" I asked with a chuckle as I walked into the master bedroom.

"I made some extra rice," he yelled behind me."

That man's mama surely raised him right, all of his toiletries were neatly arranged and his dirty clothes were in a hamper in the closet. I undressed, put on a shower bonnet and climbed into the glass shower. I took George's advice and took my time enjoying the light massage of the water on my back. I dried off with one of the oversized bath towels and moisturized my skin with my favorite, Coco Chanel lotion. I put on matching red bra and panties and pulled out a navy velour dress to coordinate with George's sweater, and slid on a pair of snake skin mules. I combed my hair down and put on some lip gloss. Walking out to the living area I felt a butterfly flutter in my stomach and it surprised me. Even though I was comfortable with George, the thought of spending the night with him again had me excited.

"You look so beautiful I have to hug you," he said when I walked into the living room.

The smooth jazz he liked was playing and it felt so good to be in his arms that I didn't even want to stop to eat.

He had worked hard preparing the meal so I pulled myself away and said, "So chef, what's for dinner?"

"We're having chicken and rice, Virgin Island style."

"In that case let me set the table."

"It's already done; all you have to do is come into the dining room and sit down and eat."

"I think I can handle that," I said.

George opened up a bottle of wine while I spooned the food on my plate. I said a quick blessing and put a fork full in my mouth. All I could do was shake my head, I loved this man. He was fine, accomplished, the sex was good, and he could cook. After dinner, we sat at the table finishing the bottle of wine and talking.

"This was a good idea; it feels good to get a break from the grind," he said.

"You do so much for me, I was wondering what your expectations are from me?"

"I just want you to look beautiful like you do tonight and love me, the same as most men," he said before quoting Ludacris, "Be a lady in the streets and a freak in the sheets."

"Seriously, I want to know," I said, bursting out in laughter.

"It's the truth, I'm a successful independent man and the things that I want in a woman are very simple, someone who makes me happy, interests me, and excites me. I think you are a fascinating woman and I love it that you are still a mystery to me. I like mysteries. Every day that I'm with you I learn something new about you."

"I could say the same thing about you," I said.

"Now that I'm thinking about it I could use a massage, my neck and back are tight from the drive and working for you all day."

"That's the least I could do after the delicious meal you prepared. Come on over by the fireplace and take off your shirt," I said, rising up from the table and turning up the volume of the music playing on the stereo.

I went in the bedroom, kicked off my mules and got the cocoa butter oil I use on my knees and ankles. There was a comfortable rug on the floor but the blanket was softer so I laid it on top of the rug and kneeled down.

"Take off your shoes and come lay down by the fire it'll relax you." George pulled off his shoes and slid down on the blanket in front of me. "Lie down and get comfortable," I said, pouring some of the oil in my hands to warm it.

This was such a fine specimen in front of me, I just wanted to look and admire it for a minute. I started at his neck rubbing in a downward motion to release the tension. My hands moved down from the neck to the shoulders squeezing the muscles along the slope and above the shoulder blades. I was captivated by the feel of his flesh under my hands as I rubbed and kneaded down his spine and across his back. The light shine from the oil on his skin caught the light of the fire. I thought how intimate it is to touch another person, not for just a moment here and there but to linger and become familiar. I felt like his body belonged to me for my pleasure. I rubbed in a circular motion to his lower back and then I hear him let out a deep moan.

"Why don't you turn over?" I whispered into his ear.

Watching him shift his positions I pulled my dress off over my head.

"Very sexy," he said, looking me in the eyes after taking an extended gaze at my Victoria Secrets.

"Let me help you," I said, unbuckling his belt and unfastening his pants and keeping my eyes locked into his.

He put his hand behind my head and kissed me and I wished I could freeze that moment in time. It was hot in every sense of the word. I had never made love in front of a fireplace before, and as many times as I had seen it done in movies there wasn't one scene that could hold a candle to the one we created that night.

George always made me feel special. He was passionate and meticulous about everything he did and sex was no different. The man handled his business and I showed him all the appreciation that he was due.

Forty-five minutes later he said, "This floor is hard as hell. That soft and warm bed is in there for a reason, let's get in it."

We left the fire dying down and I followed him to the bedroom. He pulled back the covers and laid down and I curled in next to him and fell asleep.

***

I woke up first, eased out of the bed, and put on a robe. The shower would have woken him up and I wanted to make him breakfast first. I washed my hands, wet a paper towel to wipe the skin on my face, and loaded the dishwasher with the dinner dishes. I found some skillets in the cabinets under the sink and I took out the eggs. In twenty minutes I had prepared him a large omelet with some of his cheese, crisp bacon, toast, and fresh coffee. I even washed up some of the berries and put them in a bowl on the side. I discovered a tray on a shelf above the counter, loaded it up with the food and coffee, and poured some juice for myself.

In the bedroom he was sleeping so good that I didn't want to wake him, but in his own words, "I don't like to miss breakfast."

I set the tray down on the chest at the foot of the bed. I sat down on the side of the bed and leaned over and gave him a kiss on the lips until he stirred. He put his arms around me and starting kissing me back.

I could feel him pulling me down in the bed so I said, "George, wake up."

"I'm awake, take off the robe."

"I made you some breakfast and it's getting cold."

"I thought I smelled food," he said, sitting up in the bed.

I got the tray and set it down in the middle of the bed.

"Thank you, baby, this looks wonderful," he said, taking a sip of the coffee.

"I thought this part of my life was over," I commented, watching him eat.

"What part is that?" he inquired, giving me a questioning look.

"The romance and the extra attention from someone," I answered.

"Why would you think that?" he asked, eating a fork of the eggs and then biting the toast.

"It was over already," I said, popping some of the berries in my mouth, "I guess when people have been together a long time they forget to show the love and affection like they did when they first met."

"That's just laziness; it doesn't have to be that way."

"They say familiarity breeds discontent," I remarked with a smile.

"Portia, the odds of finding someone you can be happy with are not in our favor, so if you find it, it's a precious thing. I would never take you for granted and you can believe that, you make a mean omelet," he said, finishing his plate.

"I'll take this in the kitchen," I said, lifting the empty tray, "You can go back to sleep, shower, or whatever you want."

A few minutes later I heard the water of the shower running. I finished cleaning the kitchen and took a few minutes to enjoy the majestic view of the mountains. I wasn't one who likes to travel to places where the weather is cold but the wintery landscape was beautiful. When the water stopped I went to take my turn in the bathroom. Once we were dressed, we put on our coats and hats and headed out the front door.

"Do you want to go for a hike in the woods?" he asked.

"No sir, I don't care to be the accidental target of some crazed hunter out here in the wilderness, keep me on the beaten path," I said, looking down into the terrain.

"Wise decision," he said, and we headed down the hill to Parkway.

I could see my breath in the cool air in front of as we walked and my hands were getting cold. I put the right one in my pocket and reached for George's with the other. He squeezed my hand in his and my whole body warmed up. We walked for several miles looking into gallery windows and the quaint shops that lined the street. Most were filled with Christmas decorations even though Thanksgiving was still ahead of us. It suddenly occurred to me after the hint of my growling stomach that I was starving. I noticed an old-fashioned café on the next corner.

"Could we stop over there and get something to eat?" I asked.

"After the nice breakfast you made for me this morning I can't let you go hungry," he said, teasing me.

We sat down at a metal table with vinyl chairs by the window and ordered two bowls of chili from a waitress who looked like she had stepped out of the 1950s complete with the beehive hairdo. The food was good and I started to wish we had a week instead of just the weekend.

We walked a little further and stopped at an old-fashioned candy store. I felt like I was ten years old again when I saw the jars of red hot dollars and jawbreakers, boxes of Good and Plenty, and Bit O' Honey. I bought a pound of the mixed chocolate-covered nuts.

"We probably need to turn around here or we'll need to catch a cab to get back to the cabin," George said.

"You're right, but I can't promise you we won't need that cab."

We walked into the cold wind and my eyes watered. We braved the blustery weather and made it back to the cabin but the warmth of the chili had cooled and I felt like a Popsicle. I hung up our coats and sat on the sofa to rest.

"I've got some things to check on and a few calls to make," George said, getting his laptop and phone out of his messenger bag.

I eased my shoes off and snuggled under the blanket.

"Help yourself, I'm going to la-la land," I said, closing my eyes.

When I opened my eyes I looked at my watch, it said 5:00. I had been sleep for close to two hours. I sat up and saw George out on the deck taking in the view. I went into the bathroom to brush my teeth and wash my face before I started on dinner.

"What's on your mind?" I asked him when he came in.

"I would ask you the same thing."

"I'm thinking that it's time to start dinner."

"Two heads together can do twice as much in half the time."

"That's good to know," I said with a smile.

"I've got the steaks, you can make the fixings," he said, looking in the fridge.

"Would that be the pre-made salads and frozen veggies?"

"Sounds about right to me."

I set the table while he broiled the steaks and opened a bottle of red wine. When the smell of beef filled the room I tossed the salad in a bowl and the frozen veggies in the microwave. It barely took thirty minutes to prepare but the dinner looked appetizing and the steaks were juicy and well-seasoned.

"How about a game of pool?" George asked after we finished eating.

"I haven't played in a while but I have to warn you that I have skills," I said, following him into the entertainment room.

"Is that right? In that case I think we can make this even more interesting."

"Oh, do you want to put money on it?" I said, choosing a pool cue.

"No, I don't want to take your money," he said self-assured as he chalked his stick. "You know about strip poker, but I'm going to teach you about strip pool."

"Okay, teacher, I'll rack them and you can break them," I said, arranging the balls in the triangle and lifting it off.

He took aim for his first shot and hit the cue ball with such a jolt of force that they clacked hard against each other. The balls split off in various directions and angles on the table and one with a stripe rolled quickly into the right corner pocket. Then it hit me, I hadn't been honest enough with him. Seeing the balls so carefully set, so neat and orderly, be broken apart so quickly and completely, I had the urge to tell him everything, or close to it. I didn't want to take the chance of my secret destroying our relationship or the trust between us.

"There was something I wanted to tell you yesterday but I didn't think it was a good idea while you were driving," I said cautiously.

"Go ahead and talk, I'm not easily distracted," he said. "Ten in the corner pocket."

The ball rolled straight and dropped into the pocket.

"Now you take something off," he said, grinning.

I took off my shoes and put them to the side.

"Do you remember when we were on the plane to Vegas and I told you about my problems sleeping?"

"Yeah, I do," he answered, "Twelve in the side pocket."

The ball rolled in and he said, "Take something else off."

I took off my socks and put them inside my shoes.

"I told you that I wanted to experiment with Diprivan and you advised me not to do it."

"Thirteen in the corner," he said, pointing the stick to the left corner. He leaned over the table as he aimed, pulled the cue back and took the shot, and the orange ball rolled in a smooth path into the pocket. "Now this is starting to get interesting," he said as I took off my shirt and laid it across the back of a barstool.

He walked around the table and called his shot, "Fifteen in the side."

He took aim just as I said the words, "I tried it anyway."

He shot the ball hard and missed and the cue ball rolled into the pocket.

"I hope you're just trying to mess with my game," he griped with the tone of his voice rising in exasperation.

"No, I'm not," I answered with a straight face.

"What are you telling me?" he demanded, standing still on the other side of the table.

"I'm saying that I was having a rough time and I was feeling desperate and I thought it could help."

"Are you out of your mind?" he roared.

"Sometimes I thought I was. I knew it was dangerous, I just wanted some relief."

"Who gave it to you?" he shouted at me.

"One of the doctors at the hospital, but it was my decision, there's no one else to blame."

"Are you addicted to it?" he asked, walking over to me and standing where I could feel his breath on my face.

"No, I only used it a few times and I'm done with it."

"Why didn't you tell me about this before?" he asked sternly.

"I didn't want you to get upset. I'm telling you now because I want to be honest with you and I want to be able to talk about it with you."

"I can't believe you would do something so crazy," he said, shaking his head and sitting down on a barstool.

"That's because you've never been where I've been. I was so consumed with sadness and heartache that I didn't know if I was going or coming, that's why I backed away from you in Vegas. I wanted to be with you but I was a mess inside."

"Why couldn't you just talk to me?"

"It's not easy to expose your open wounds to people; I didn't want to seem weak."

"I don't know what to say."

"You don't have to fix it for me, it's done, and believe it or not, it changed so many things for me."

"You've lost me again."

"Some strange things happened to me when I took the drug. I flashed back to some special moments I had with my son and it helped me to see him again. I was able to let go some, enough where I could move on and not be afraid to be happy again. I know I went too far with it, but it made all the difference to me and I want to share that with you."

"Baby, I had no idea what you were going through or the things that you were dealing with and I'm sorry that I didn't realize you were that serious when you mentioned it to me."

"George, there was no way for you to know, I lived through it, and it's in the past," I said, thinking about the other time trips I had taken.

"It's a good thing you didn't tell me all that while I was driving," he said, putting his arms around me and giving me a tight hug.

"You want to finish the game?" he asked with his sexy smile.

"My nerves are shot," I said, handing him my cue stick.

"Mine are too," he said, putting the sticks in the rack. "Let's get in the hot tub with a bottle of wine and let it go."

"Sounds like a plan," I said, wrapping my arm around his waist and kissing him on the cheek, "Thanks for understanding."

"You're my lady, Portia. What else am I going to do?"

In the Jacuzzi I did my best to make George believe there was not another woman in this world who could make him feel the way I could. Opening up and talking to him had been liberating for me. I was more at peace than I had been in years. I could see that my grief and unhappiness had been magnified by the loneliness and rejection I felt when Raymond left. I already had a broken heart and then he stomped on it. My heart still had a hole in it but at least it was functioning again, and thanks to George, I had a man I could love who wanted to love me back.

"I'm not ready to go back," I said when George pulled me

Chapter Nineteen

close to his chest the next morning.

"I've enjoyed it, but I'm ready to go, it's too country for me."

"I thought it was about you and me being together," I said, laughing and turning around to face him.

"We don't have to be in the Great Smoky Mountains to be together; when we get back home you can come and stay with me."

"Do you realize that I have never been to your home?"

"I just invited you to make it our home."

"You always say things so casually I don't know when you're joking or serious," I said, getting out of the bed.

"Know this," he said, getting up and grabbing my hand, "I'm always serious about you."

We showered, dressed, and packed up our things in the quiet. I liked that we could spend time with each other without feeling we had to talk constantly.

"Can you believe we haven't watched any TV for two days?"

"I don't think we missed anything," he said, winking his eye.

"Is it too late to do that morning thing?" I asked, winking back at him.

"Yeah, it is, it's time to get something to eat and get out of here and seeing as you've got all that energy you can start the drive."

I made some coffee and some sandwiches out of the eggs and bacon and we ate them pretty quickly. There was a lot of food left from our grocery shopping. I bagged up the stuff that wouldn't spoil including the big bag of rice and I washed the fruit to eat on the way back.

We loaded up the car and I climbed into the driver's seat. George slid in the passenger and leaned his seat all the way back to rest. I turned the radio down as I backed out of the garage and whispered a goodbye to my log cabin. It had been a good trip, short, but it had accomplished all the things I hoped it would. I drove for an hour with my mind shifting back and forth between the beauty of the clear blue sky and the calmness of the cows standing out in the fields, then I couldn't help reminiscing about the hot touches and kisses George and I shared in the Jacuzzi last night. Glancing in the rearview mirror I could see the mountains growing smaller behind me and reflected on how my life was so much simpler when I was out of town.

"I'll take us on in," George said, reaching for the keys at a rest stop on the other side of Knoxville.

"Oh, so you've got your strength back," I asked, teasing him.

"Some," he said with a smile, "You never know how tired you are until you slow down for a minute."

"I don't know if this classifies as slowing down, not to mention, I've got a busy week ahead of me with Pam coming home for Thanksgiving next week."

George took the wheel and I was happy to take his leaned back seat. I followed the lines of his profile and then closed my eyes content.

"Wake up sleepyhead you're home," George said, nudging me.
I stretched in the seat while he took my bags out of the back.
"You want me to bring the food in too?" he asked.
"No, I wouldn't feel right about keeping your rice."

Chapter Nineteen

"Very funny," he said, putting my bags at the bottom of the stairs.

"I'm gonna miss you tonight," I said, holding his hand and walking beside him to the door.

"My offer still stands," he said, giving me a soft kiss on the lips. I followed him to the door and waved as his car pulled away.

The honeymoon feeling didn't last long. All of the problems and worries that I left at the door when I left were waiting for me. I barely had time to unpack and put a load of clothes in the washing machine before there was a knock on the door. I opened the door and it was Raymond looking at me like he was an officer of the law with a warrant for my arrest.

Chapter Twenty

"I've been over here several times and you weren't here," he fussed.

"I was out of town, what's going on?" I asked, standing in the door aggravated.

"Do I have to talk to you in the doorway or can I come in?" he asked indignantly.

"Let's make it quick, I'm really tired," I said, walking into the kitchen.

"Is that right, I thought you had problems sleeping?" he said sarcastically as he took off his jacket and put it on the back of the chair.

"Not sleeping doesn't necessarily mean you're not tired." I poured myself a cup of ice tea and sat down in front of him, "So what's up?"

"I looked up Diprivan and I know that it's the same thing as propofol, the anesthesia drug that killed Michael Jackson," he stated with a smug look that said he had solved the crime mystery of the year.

"If it is, so what? It's not illegal," I answered, losing patience with him.

He couldn't even get his shit right for how many years and now he's back to put me in check. He had a lot of nerve.

"I'm sure it's unethical however you got it."

"What difference does that make to you?" I said, getting tired of the inquisition.

"I'm concerned that you might be dependent on it and it's very dangerous."

"I thank you for your concern but I am not a child, I can make my own decisions whether or not you agree with them, but you can relax because I am not dependent, addicted, or whatever other term you might have on the drug. I'm trying to move on with my life and I think you should do the same instead of worrying about me."

"Portia, I just don't believe you're thinking clearly," he said, standing up from the table.

"Why, because I want a divorce?" I asked, wishing he would leave.

"Maybe."

"Don't fight me on this Ray and spoil our friendship."

"I don't need a friend, I want my wife back," he said, towering over me.

"It doesn't matter either way and if you haven't got a lawyer I suggest you get one before the thirty days are up," I said, standing up to look him in the face.

He grabbed his jacket off the chair and charged out the front door, leaving it open. I shut it behind him and locked it.

"What a welcome home," I said out loud.

That was only the beginning.

I woke up Monday with my face feeling like I was wearing one of those theater masks with joy on one side and sorrow on

Chapter Twenty

the other.

"Good morning, Keisha," I said, entering the office, relieved she hadn't pulled another Monday-no-show on me.

"Good morning, Ms. Roberts. I hope you had a restful weekend because you said you wanted to start preparation for the year-end statements this week."

"One more day wouldn't have hurt," I said with trepidation, remembering what was on the schedule. What the hell, I was under siege at home and at work.

Halfway through a hectic day during a moment of respite the phone rang.

"Put your hands up and move away from the computer," Paula said after I picked up.

"I wish I could. It feels like everybody in the building is changing their plans or allotments. How are you guys doing?" I asked with apprehension, she rarely called me at work.

"We're fine, but we miss you guys. We want to come down for Thanksgiving next week if that's okay."

"Sure, I could use some good company as long as you get here on Wednesday to help with the cooking."

"No problem, sis, I'm there."

"Till next week," I said, seeing my office line blink. The momentary pause had ended.

I opened up a can of soup for dinner when I finally got home, showered and went straight to bed. I reached for my cell phone so I could text George, with his schedule and patient load I didn't like to bother him during the day, "Missing you, call me when u can."

The phone rang in less than a minute.

"Hey, pretty lady," he said.

"What do you have planned for the holiday?" I asked, hoping he could come to my family dinner.

"I'm booked up tight. I was going to call you and let you know I've got to go to D.C. for a conference and then it's the holiday for me to have my son. I'm going to take him to St. Maarten for a few days."

"Wow, you are booked; I guess I'll see you sometime before Christmas," I said, feeling let down.

"You know how it is, if you want to see me every day you've got to come live with me."

"Very funny," I said with a laugh.

"I'm not joking," he said.

That threw me for a second and I didn't respond.

"Goodnight, baby," he said and then hung up.

Keisha and I hustled for the next three days and I was feeling worn out. I got to work late on Friday morning hoping it would be a slower and uneventful day.

"You've got a visitor," Keisha said with an accusatory tone, looking at me sideways as soon as I walked into the office suite.

I frowned back at her looking puzzled and went into my office.

"You still got banker's hours," David said, standing up like he wanted to give me a kiss when I walked in.

I moved over to the window behind him and turned on my radio. Keisha's ear was probably pressed to the door straining to hear whatever was said. I couldn't blame her; with the traffic that ran through here I'd be nosey too.

Chapter Twenty

"I figured out how we can do this," he said, "I rented a timeshare near Opryland, we can meet out there."

"David, I've met someone special and I'm trying to move on in a new relationship and I want to give it a chance, no outside activities."

"I can respect that, but I'm desperate, just once more I swear. I'll even get you some more propofol, whatever you want."

"What part of no don't you understand, the n, the o, what, no, I won't go there again."

"Portia, I really need you, I'm about to lose it."

"You are on my nerves so bad right now. You better be glad I'm not wearing a belt because if I was I would take it off and beat you down right here right now."

"Now that's what I'm talking about," he said, getting excited.

I couldn't do or say anything except throw my hands up in the air.

"Get out of my office; I've got work to do."

"I left the address on your desk; I'll be there tonight around 8:00," he said on the way out.

Google had saved me in more instances than I could count so I sat down and put it to the test again. I typed in 'where to find a dominatrix in Nashville' and pressed enter. Saved again, there was a link to Nashville Dominatrix Professionals. I browsed through the pictures and specialties until I found Mistress Sheba. I punched her number into my cell phone and she answered on the third ring.

"Uh, Hello, I'm calling because I have a friend who is looking for someone with your unique services but it would have to be totally discreet and confidential."

"That's the only way I operate, any other way isn't good for business."

"Are you available to see this client this evening at 8:00?"

"Certainly, I'm free tonight."

"Do we need to deal with names?"

"It's not necessary; most people use an alias anyway."

"What do you need to make the appointment?"

"I need the address and some info about the client."

"He's a professional man, a doctor who works under a great deal of stress, he's semi-happily married, and he gets off on being spanked. I don't think it needs to be severe or draw blood."

"He fits the profile, all I need is a credit card number and we'll work it out. May I ask where you got my number?"

"I looked you up on the internet," I answered, and then I gave her my VISA number.

"Thanks for the referral," Mistress Sheba said.

"No, thank you," I said before I hung up and prayed everything would be okay.

It had been a taxing week and I was physically and mentally drained. I didn't have the energy to cook so I picked up a medium supreme pizza at Papa Don's on the way home. George was out of town, Pam wouldn't be home until Tuesday, and I was feeling out of sorts. I put on some flannel pajamas, put three slices on a plate, and put the TV on the Turner Classic Movies channel. A half hour later, I was full and bored and before I knew it I had the propofol vial in my hand walking up the steps to take a trip.

Chapter Twenty

One part of me didn't want to do it, I had promised George and Raymond that I wouldn't, another part of me was intrigued by the other lives I had lived and my curiosity won out in the end.

I prepared my arm with the alcohol and the lidocaine and before I could give it another thought I jabbed the needle into my vein. The weightlessness in the darkness before the streams of light had become familiar to me. I waited for the colors to emerge within the white light. Then I saw the swirl of vivid shades and felt the coolness in the atmosphere around me. I was free, I drifted in the moment and focused on an image in one of the beams of the light just as I saw the other reverse its direction. I wanted to follow it but I was already falling.

The clang of the fire alarm jarred my senses; I had delayed my exit to avert any attention to myself, but the crack of glass breaking warned me that I was about to cross the line between cautious and stupid.

Down one flight of stairs, I can hear voices shouting, "Get out, fire, fire, get out." I rush down the remaining four flights of stairs trailing behind the last of the older guests as they labor to move quickly to escape the burning building and get to safety. I take a deep inhale when I reach the street with my lungs starving for a breath of fresh air but the area there is already filled with the smell of smoke. I cross the street and join the crowd of spectators fascinated by the destructive power of the flames that glow in the color of a warm sunset. A far away alarm grows closer along with the sound of hoofs clapping against the cobblestones as the horses pull the steam fire engine to the front of the Savoy Hotel.

"Move back, move back," the fire fighters urge as they pull out their hoses.

Four men rush inside the front door in single file carrying a hose and one firefighter aims the other hose into the window from the street while two others hold the heavy weight of the water running through it. I watch in amazement as the flames begin to surrender to the pressure of the water and disappear in clouds of dark gray smoke. A man wearing a black suit, who I recognize as the concierge of the Savoy waves his hands fiercely to disband the crowd.

"Clear out, go home, it's all over, there's nothing else to see, go on home."

I stand there for a little longer watching the smoke rise and then I walk away.

"Blast, thank heaven you're all right, Lizzie," Hildie says, looking distressed when I open the door to our flat. "I was terrified when I heard it was your floor that caught fire."

"No need to worry, my girl, I wasn't in any danger."

"I ran out as soon as I heard the alarm but I didn't see you, and I didn't know what to make of it when you were not here when I arrived."

"Sorry for troubling you unnecessarily, I was making sure the rooms were empty."

"Lizzie, you never let on that you cared about a single soul in the whole building."

"I've gotta heart, Hildie, besides there wasn't much damage save for a row of rooms on one side of the fifth floor and the floor

Chapter Twenty

below where it collapsed."

"It'll be enough damage where the repairs will cost us more than a day's pay and get the landlady on our backs again."

"Don't worry, we'll find another job."

"I don't want to work anywhere else, Lizzie, the folks there are like my family."

"It'll work out I promise," I say, going into my room in the back of our flat.

Hildie will never know but everything went off just like I'd planned. It had been so easy, probably just as easy as it had been for him to take advantage of me mum. How could he possibly be my father and walk by me, not know me or feel anything.

***

My real Papa, even though I never met him, was a fine tailor and me mum always talked about him when she had an especially hard day working for another man's family.

"We lived in a flat above the shop," she would say, thinking back on her better days. "Your Papa had ambitions of becoming rich and dressing all the aristocrats of London. He spent large sums on the highest quality of fabrics, silks, linen, and wool."

"I wish it would have come true," I say.

"You'll only bring more misery on yourself if you fancy things you can't have, remember your place, accept your lot in life," she would say angrily, but I refuse to believe it.

She had told me many times about his unfortunate partnership with a shoemaker and how the debts steadily climbed until they had risen above their heads. Buried in notes and bills and the shop void of the prestigious clients he had anticipated he was forced into debtor's prison. Me mum was then forced into a life of servitude to support herself or starve.

Her beauty and youthful strength was sacrificed to labor for those who don't have any need to dream. She was given a position as a domestic servant in the Northwood Manor with all her meals included. Hunger found us again when she was dismissed from the manor soon after I was born. She took in laundry and sewing until I was old enough to be left alone.

"I don't know why I keep you? I can't feed you or meself," were the first words I can remember her saying to me and they echoed in my ears for years until I started going to school. Then the children teased me in the school yard saying, "Lizzie, where's you Papa?" or "Lizzie who's your Papa?" or a mean boy named Tim would yell, "You're nothing but a bastard." I would hear whispers among the women in the building saying that I'm not my Papa's child since he was put in prison long before I was born. I was ten years old when I stormed home one afternoon and learned the truth.

"Mummy, who is me Papa?" I ask through breathless tears after running home to escape the incessant badgering.

She put down the iron from the shirt she was pressing, "Lizzie, your Papa is my husband, Benjamin Wellsley, but the man who fathered you was my employer, Louis Winthrope."

"You didn't love Papa anymore, Mum?"

"Life is much more complicated than you can understand right now. I was afraid of being out on the streets, so I sold meself for

Chapter Twenty

a warm place to live and a full stomach."

Somehow I got the feeling that she blamed me for what happened. I didn't want to be a burden or add to the hardship she suffered with me mouth to feed so I left home when I was fifteen and took a job as a chambermaid at the Savoy Hotel, the fanciest accommodations in all of London. It was ironic. I had spoiled me mum's life and now I was following in her footsteps.

"Have you worked in a hotel before?" Hildie asked when she was assigned to show me the ropes.

"No, but I learn fast and I won't be a bother," I said.

"Just follow me and do what I do and you'll have this down in no time."

We took the lift up to the second floor and she opened the first room with her master key.

"It's like heaven in here," I said in awe of the beautiful furniture, the electric lights, and the hot and cold running water in the washroom.

"Maybe for the guests, we just get the privilege of cleaning up their mess," she said with a chuckle.

Hildie taught me how to change the linens, fluff the pillows, and make the bed with perfect corners. We cleaned the washroom and put in fresh folded towels. We repeated the routine in room after room until the initial glow of the lavish rooms had dimmed for me.

"Do you have a place to stay?" Hildie asked me at the end of the day.

"Not yet, do you know where I can rent a room cheap?"

"Yep, I do, with me at my flat. We'll go by the fish mongers, buy some fish and chips for supper and then I'll take you there."

I kept pace beside her as we walked, relieved and thankful that I had a place to sleep. Inside the shop, the sound and smell of the fish frying made my stomach growl.

"Vinegar please," Hildie said.

"What for you, miss?" the lady behind the rising hot mist asked as she wrapped up Hildie's food in newspaper.

"A halfpenny of crackling ma'am, I'm not very hungry."

"I've got enough to share," Hildie said, grabbing me by the arm, becoming the first friend I ever had.

That's the way it had been for two years until I saw the name of Louis Winthrope listed as a guest on me floor at the hotel. I pass him in the hallway and I'm invisible to him. It infuriates me and I want to hurt him like he did me mum. When he and the wife go down for tea, I ease inside the room they share and I break the cardinal rule of chambermaids, I go through their personal things. Inside the bureau drawer is a royal blue velvet case. I open it and a wardrobe of fine watches, rings, strands of pears, and other diamond and gem jewelry flash in my eyes.

Then a voice inside me says, "Take it, it belongs to you, it's your birthright."

I hurry and close it, but before I leave I go into his closet and cut a small tear in the fine jacket that hangs there.

During supper in the dining room with the other employees the voice inside my head keeps talking to me, "The wrong you and your Mum suffered must be repaid, providence brought him to you, and this is your only chance."

"Let's go by the pub after work, Lizzie," Hildie says, drowning out the voice as we file out of the room.

"Sure, Hildie," I answer, knowing that things will be different in a few hours.

In the evening we usually turn down the beds while the guests are dining. Inside me father's room I neaten things up and turn down the bed, and then I turn the large perfume bottle on the bureau on its side. Next, I light one of his cigars with the oil lamp and lay it next to her spilled perfume. I take a handkerchief from the bureau drawer and touch one end to the cigar and the other to the widening circle of perfume. I close the door behind me and go into the next room. I clean the toilet, straighten up the room and turn down the bed, and now I can smell the faint scent of smoke in the hallway as I move on to the next room.

It had been bloody easy, a doddle, just like it was for him to use me Mum after she worked her fingers to the bone all day for him. I hum a tune to myself to calm my nervousness as I work. I am in the fourth room when I hear a scream which is soon followed by the sound of the fire alarm. I had done it, I had committed a crime but it was a lesser crime than the one that was committed against me.

I walk for an hour around the hotel before I go back to the flat with my newly acquired riches squeezed in my bosom and twisted in my petticoat. I had filched the money too, no sense in letting good money end up as ashes. Its better use would be the ticket I need to a new life.

***

"I'm still not quite meself, Lizzie," Hildie says, "Let's head down to the pub for a glass of bitter."

"Good idea, we do need to settle down after that hullabaloo."

It was a short walk to the pub, just long enough for me to plan the rest of my life.

Sitting watching Hildie sip from her glass, I say it, "I hear talk they have jobs on the Olympic ocean liner for chambermaids, let's go for it."

"Not me, Lizzie, I don't like the water."

"I want to go, Hildie, there's nothing here for us, and we can travel to America. They say you can change your destiny there. People born poor don't have to die poor."

"I like my life here just fine, Lizzie, I got a good job, and I can take care of meself. I don't need nothing more. It makes me feel good when I can do something that makes someone else comfortable"

"I don't just want to live to do for other people, I want more Hildie. I want to live for meself and I think I could get an education, open up a boarding house, or find some bloke to fall in love with me."

"That sounds like a fairytale, Lizzie, and that's what you deserve. If I were you I'd go down there tomorrow and get me that job."

I wait a few days before I go to the port but when I get there I don't apply for the job. That wasn't part of me plan. Instead I pack all my things in a carpet bag and then I buy meself a second-class passenger ticket. My birthright is still tucked in my bosom and tied in my petticoat except for the string of pearls I left on Hildie's bed as a gift. I had already spent enough of my life tending to the needs of others, now it was my turn. The ship set sail for a two week voyage with me sharing a

Chapter Twenty

comfortable cabin that had four bunks with a woman and her two small children.

"I'm going to join my husband," she tells me as we have our supper one evening, "He left a year ago, he's found work and a place for us, and now we're going to join him.

"That sounds lovely, there's a new life waiting for me there too."

At the end of the voyage, I stand at the top of the Grand Staircase looking out as the Olympic pulls into New York Harbor. A horde of steerage passengers stand on the deck below and cheer at the sight of the Statue of Liberty. If it wasn't for the money, I would be down there with them heading off to Ellis Island. I find my place behind the first-class cabin passengers as we file out down the ramp to the pier eager to be on dry land. I feel light and free, as if I'm walking on air. In my hastiness I get ahead of meself and tumble down on the heels of an elderly man in front of me.

"Are you all right, Miss?" he asks.

"I'm fine, sir, no harm done," I say, laughing to meself.

I turned on my side and sat up. I hunched my shoulders together and stretched out my arms, rising up off of the bed.

"I needed that," I said to myself, feeling refreshed and well-rested.

I thought about the trip to yet another different life in another foreign land. There's got to be somebody else I can trade these experiences with. I know I'm not alone in this. Who wouldn't want to do what Lizzie did, that's all I wanted to do, release the hurt and disappointment and reclaim my life without inflicting pain on anyone else. I slid my feet into my slippers and headed down the steps to treat myself to a big breakfast.

Chapter Twenty-One

I turned on the radio and the Saturday morning blues were playing. I was reaching in the refrigerator when I heard the doorbell ringing. I looked at the clock and it was close to 9:00, probably the Jehovah Witnesses canvassing I figured. I usually don't answer the door for them but I was in a good mood. Why not at least say good morning? I looked through the window and saw it was David.

"Oh Lord," I said, remembering that I had sent an escort to the hotel last night.

My heart starting thumping against my chest and I was scared to open the door.

"Calm down," I said to myself, he's standing out there in one piece so it can't be that bad. At least it was easier to face the music at home than at work with Keisha listening. I twisted the lock and slowly turned the doorknob. I pulled the door back and he was standing there with a toothy smile spread across his face.

"I'm glad to see your happy face," I said, stepping to the side inviting him in. "Come on in the kitchen, I was just making myself some breakfast."

"You know you're something else don't you," he said, following close behind me.

"Yeah, I know, but you pushed me in a corner."

"That wasn't my intention and now I can see that I was wrong to pressure you like that, but you were the only one I trusted."

"So, am I in the doghouse?" I asked, putting some grits on to boil.

"Portia, I came over here to thank you."

"Really, I was truly scared; I didn't know how that was going to turn out, if you would be disappointed or if she might hurt you."

"I was shocked and ready to kill you when I opened the door and saw Sheba and not you, but she took control of the situation and cooled me out."

"Can you sit down and eat?" I asked him with a giggle.

"Don't worry about it; let's just say I won't be needing your services anymore."

"That's a relief," I said, putting some sausage in a skillet, "Pour us some juice to celebrate." When the grits were finished I scrambled some eggs, drained the sausage, and we sat down to eat. The air between us was clear again and we could talk like we used to.

"Be careful, you worry me sometimes," I told him when he got ready to leave, "Everything in moderation."

I closed the door and did the Hallelujah dance, that was one huge monkey off my back. That's was a closed chapter and we were still friends. If only I could manage that feat with Raymond I might be able to live happily ever after. The only other thing gnawing at me was that I had told George I was done taking the propofol and in less than a week I had taken another dose. It wasn't as if I needed it, I just took it because it was there.

"Maybe I should throw the rest of it out," I said to myself.

Chapter Twenty-One

I walked into the kitchen, opened the refrigerator and lifted up the door on the butter compartment. Yet I couldn't reach for vial, I wasn't ready to trash it. It wasn't much left anyway and when it was gone that was it. I closed the refrigerator and I spent the rest of the day and Sunday, despite it being the day of rest, cleaning up my house and getting ready for company. I dusted, mopped, vacuumed, and scrubbed the bathrooms until my hands were nearly raw. With that done all I needed to do was the grocery shopping.

***

I took off from work early on Tuesday, Keisha had already left for the day and both of us were taking Wednesday off. When I pulled into the garage and saw Pam's car parked I started to get excited about the holiday. I rushed inside and she was lounging on the couch watching TV.

"Mama, I was getting worried about you," she said, jumping up and giving me a big hug.

"Why, I'm actually home early today."

"I don't know, the house feels strange when you're not home, I guess I missed you," she said, still holding her arms around me.

"Well, I'm home and I missed you more," I said, giving her a kiss on the cheek. "I'm glad you're already here because I haven't done any shopping and your Aunt Paula and Uncle Charles will be here tomorrow."

"Yeah, she called and told me," Pam said.

"I'm going upstairs to change clothes and then we can head out," I said, "We're getting it done at the last minute so we'll probably end up running all over town to get everything we need."

I changed into some jeans and sweat shirt with the front pocket to hold my coupons and we got into my car and backed out of the garage.

"Let's go to the Green Hills Kroger they're usually stocked better than anyone else," I suggested, heading toward the interstate, "If we're lucky we can do this in one stop."

"Mama, if you need help getting things done sometimes you can just call me and I'll come home."

"Pammy, I'm doing fine, you just make sure you've got your situation under control. I'm ready to see you in that cap and gown in the spring."

"I'm working on it, but I was thinking about staying off-campus at home next semester."

"Okay, what's all this about?" I asked suspiciously.

"Dad's worried about you and this divorce stuff and I want to make sure that you're good."

"First of all, I'm good," I said, getting annoyed that Raymond would try to put her in the middle of our mess. "Secondly, this is between him and me, you concentrate on yourself and living your life. We'll work this out one way or another."

"I told him that he could come over for Thanksgiving dinner," she said, looking over at me wide-eyed. "Is that all right with you?"

"I don't have a problem with it, he's your father and I hope that we will still be family even though I am getting a divorce," I

Chapter Twenty-One

said, trying to hide my irritation with him for going through our child to get a dinner invitation.

"Turkey or ham?" I asked, changing the subject when we walked into Kroger's.

"I can't decide, so can we get both?" she asked, grabbing a grocery cart.

"Why not, we are going to have a full table this year," I said, shaking my head.

"We've got to have dressing, candied yams, macaroni and cheese, greens, and cornbread," Pam said, smacking her lips.

"They don't have any good turnip greens here; let's just make green bean casserole this year."

"We've got to have greens, Mama. What is Thanksgiving without some greens? We can just stop by Farmer's Market and get some on the way home."

"What's for dessert, Betty Crocker, since you're making the menu?" I asked, choosing the seasonings and adding condensed milk to the cart.

"I've got a taste for sweet potato pie and coconut cake," she answered.

"That's why they say don't go to the store hungry. Who's going to cook all of that anyway?"

"Aunt Paula says she's going to bake the desserts."

"I see you all have worked out everything."

"We just don't want to overload you with doing all the work."

"How considerate, all this concern for me lately," I said, "I don't know what to say."

Four hands were better than two and we got all the shopping done including the stop at the market and were home by eight o' clock.

The next morning I picked up my phone hoping to find a message from George and saw a text message from Paula saying that they would be arriving in Nashville at 10:30 on a flight with US Airways and to wait for them at the house. I took a shower and put on some sweat pants and a pullover. It was going to be a long day of cooking and I needed to be comfortable. Pam came down while I was eating a bowl of oatmeal.

"Good morning, Mama," Pam said, giving me a quick hug from behind my chair.

"Well, look at this; I'm surprised you made it down before the afternoon."

"Ha-ha, very funny. What time will Aunt Paula get here?" she asked, pouring herself a bowl of Honeynut Cheerios.

"The doorbell can ring anytime time now," I said, looking down at my watch.

"So what's the plan for today?"

"I think we should prepare everything except for the turkey and ham."

"That's cool, who gets to wash all the greens?"

"You wanted them, you wash them," I said with a laugh, "They're ready anytime you are."

That's when we heard Paula and Charles at the door.

"Thank you, Lord," Pam said, "I've been saved by the bell."

"Don't even think about it," I said as we both headed to the

Chapter Twenty-One

front door.

"Hey, sister-girl and Niecey," Paula said with her arms opened wide as soon as we answered the door. Charles stood behind her patiently holding their bags.

"Come on in, you two," I said, giving her a hug first and then Charles, "How was your flight?"

"They're all good as long as the plane lands in one piece," Charles said.

"Yeah, you're right about that," Paula added, slapping him on the shoulder.

"Y'all know where the guest room is so you can put down your things and get comfortable."

"We had an early start this morning, Charles might want to take a nap, I had mine on the plane."

"Whatever you want to do is fine with me; we'll be in the kitchen."

"Time for round one on the greens and you're the champ," I said to Pam as we headed back into the kitchen.

A few minutes later Paula strolled in to join us.

"Move over, Pammy, you know I'm the one who knocks out the greens," Paula said, coming into the kitchen.

"You only have to tell me once, Aunt Paula, I'm out," Pam said, pulling her hands from the sink full of greens.

"Now you can get started on making the macaroni and cheese and sweet potatoes so we can bake them tomorrow," I told Pam while I boiled the meat and chopped the veggies for the dressing.

"It feels good to be here, guys, I'm so happy," Paula said with her hands wrist deep in the sink.

"We are happy to have you. What made you decide to come all of sudden?" I asked.

"You're doing so much lately, I needed to come and see you; I'm hoping I can meet George while I'm here. Is he eating with us tomorrow?"

"No, he's with his son in St. Maarten."

"That's too bad," Paula commented.

"Tell me about it, I wish he was here."

"This is weird listening to you talk about another man, Mama," Pam said, grating the cheese.

"I know, sweetie, but it is what it is."

"I can smell food and it's getting me hungry. Is there something in here that a man can throw between some bread and make a sandwich?" Charles asked, coming into the kitchen.

"I'll make you one, honey. You want a beer or is it too early?" Paula asked him, drying her hands after her final wash of the greens.

"I'm on vacation, so it's never too early," he answered.

"Why don't you put your feet up in the den and watch the big TV," I said, "Pam will bring your sandwich in a minute."

With the three of us working together we got everything prepared in no time. Paula baked the coconut cake and a sweet potato pie like she promised. The chicken and the ham were seasoned for tomorrow, the greens were cooked, the dressing, the yams, and the macaroni and cheese were ready to be baked.

"Microwave some popcorn, Mama, we can watch a movie

Chapter Twenty-One

together before it gets too late and I fall asleep on it," Pam said, heading into the den.

"Did you all find a movie worth watching?" I asked, joining them with two bowls of popcorn.

"Just a re-run of 'Pulp Fiction,'" Charles said.

"If that's the best you can do, we'll live with it," Paula said.

"It's either that or the 'Wizard of Oz?'" Pam added.

We looked at re-runs switching back and forth between the channels before I called it a night around 10:00.

"I'm clocking out; you guys can work the night shift if you want, I need some sleep," I said, suppressing a yawn.

"Do you want me to come with you?" Pam asked.

"Are you kidding?" I asked, perplexed, "I'm enjoying the company but I'm here by myself most of the time. I think I can go to bed by myself."

Chapter Twenty-Two

"What time do you want to serve dinner today?" Paula asked, peeping in my bedroom door in the morning.

"I think 4:00 is a good time, early enough for us to take our time and enjoy each other. You know Pam invited Raymond to eat with us."

"I heard, I think it'll be nice, like you said, we're all still family. Anyway, I'd like to see my brother-in-law, it's been a while."

"I hope it will set a better tone for us, we're not on the same page right now."

"It's going to be good for all of us to sit down and talk and clear the air."

"As long as he understands there are boundaries that he has to respect."

"Okay, sister. Well, take your time getting up, I'll go down and make everybody a light breakfast," she said, closing the door.

The oven was on nonstop after we finished breakfast as we baked, heated, and warmed our ample Thanksgiving meal. When we were done, Pam set the table in the dining room. It was about 3:30 when Raymond rang the doorbell and Pam rushed to answer the door.

"Hey, Daddy," she said, jumping in his arms.

"Hey, sweetie, how's it going?"

"I'm good. I hope you're hungry, we've got a ton of food,"

Pam said, leading him into the kitchen.

"Don't worry, I brought my appetite," he said, rubbing his stomach while he sniffed the aromas.

"Hello, Raymond, how are you?" I asked, being the peacemaker.

"Hi, Portia, I'm hanging in there."

"What's up, my brother?" Paula said, drying her hands and giving him a hug. "Charles is in the den watching some kind of game. You can either join him or we'll put you to work."

"I'll hang out with Charles; they say too many cooks spoil the soup."

"Who said you'd be cooking? We've got pots that need washing," Paula said, laughing.

"At least you can feed me first before you put me to work."

"That's a deal," Paula shouted behind him as he walked to the den.

"Nothing left to do but to eat it," I said to Paula after I took the cornbread out of the oven.

"Okay, I'll go tell the folks it's time to eat," she said, leaving the kitchen.

I put the food in serving bowls and was placing them on the dinner table when they all walked into the dining room.

"Sit wherever you want, none of you are guests in here," I said, teasing.

Pam took the chair to the right of me at the head of the table and Paula sat on my left.

"Before we bless the food and start stuffing our faces there's something that we need to discuss," Paula said in a solemn voice.

Chapter Twenty-Two

I froze and instantly started praying that it wasn't any bad news.

"Portia, I just want you to listen and don't get upset."

Now I was extremely worried as all the eyes around the table were focused on me.

"Raymond called me and told me about you taking the propofol drug. He's afraid that you may have a problem or be addicted. We all love you and we are all here to help and support you in whatever way you need us."

"I get it now; this isn't a family Thanksgiving dinner. This is an intervention to help poor Portia deal with her drug problem. I'm really disappointed in you Paula; I can't believe you couldn't just talk to me one-on-one before y'all planned this melodramatic moment," I said angrily, feeling betrayed. "And you, Raymond, I can't believe you're trying to use that to manipulate me. It doesn't matter what I do or what you do, we're not going to get back together."

"That's not what this is about, Portia," Raymond said firmly, "I care about you."

"You care about me. You left me, and you did it at the worst time in my life. You left me," I screamed across the table.

"Calm down, Portia," Paula said, "We're not plotting against you; I'm here to find out what's going on with you, that's all."

"Mama, I was scared when Dad told me that he saw you in bed with a needle. I don't want anything to happen to you," Pam said emotionally.

"Nothing's going to happen to me, I'm not hooked on propofol.

This whole thing has been blown out of proportion."

"All right, Portia, but will you take a minute and tell us how this started and then we can eat," Charles said, trying to appease everybody."

"I was still having some problems sleeping and dealing with the loss of Nicholas. I got curious about the drug when I heard how restful the sleep was for people who had taken it. Yes, I have experimented with it a few times but I'm done with that. I've healed a lot since then. As far as you are concerned, Ray, just because I don't want to be married to you any more doesn't mean I'm strung out on drugs. If you want to help me then sign the divorce papers so we can stop hurting each other. I'm sorry I can't forget that you walked away. I forgive you and I feel your pain, but I can't forget it. It will always be there and there's nothing we can do to change it. If anyone else here wants to talk to me they are welcome to do so individually. I'm not on trial for anything so I'm not doing any public testifying in front of a jury. Now, if y'all don't mind I have spent a great amount of time and money preparing this Thanksgiving dinner and I want to eat it while it's hot."

"You're right, sister-girl, we've said enough for now. Charles bless the food so we can eat," Paula said, holding out her arms for us to join hands.

"Lord we come thanking and praising you for protecting and providing for us, continue to bless us as a family and the food we are about to eat. May it nourish us in the name of Jesus, Amen."

"Thank you, Charles, and slice me a piece of ham," I said with a

Chapter Twenty-Two

weak smile, refusing to let the interruption ruin my meal.

"You want some of my macaroni and cheese, Dad?" Pam asked.

"Yes indeed, sweetie, that's the best thing on the table," Raymond answered.

"Pass me the greens, Aunt Paula, and some dressing," Pam said, sounding relieved that the commotion was over.

"Who wants dark meat?" Paula asked with a sly look.

"You know I do, honey," Charles said, and we all laughed.

We all ate until we couldn't hold another bite and Pam went into the den with Raymond and Charles to watch another ballgame.

"I'm sorry for putting you on the spot like that, sis," Paula said while we were putting away the food and cleaning the kitchen. "When Raymond called me it sounded like you needed to be in rehab, ASAP."

"I don't blame you. I know it wasn't the smartest thing I have done in my life but I don't regret it at all. I've only done it a handful of times but it changed my whole perspective on life and living."

"That's real deep, P. In what way?" she asked, stopping to listen.

"When I took the propofol it took me to another level of consciousness where I was able to see that we live different lives."

"You mean that if you die you come back as somebody else."

"Something like that, but not reincarnation where you live one life at a time. I think that the spirit operates in three parts before you go to heaven, the past, present, and the future. I believe there may be something to the theory that says the three dimensions exist simultaneously. Maybe that's the eternal life before the afterlife."

"You've lost me, but at least I understand that you weren't trying to escape to Neverland with Michael Jackson," she said, putting her hand on my shoulder.

"At first, I just wanted to see Nicholas again and then I recognized that it wasn't the past that I wanted, it was the future, but it could never be the way I wanted it. I've accepted it now that I truly believe that the spirit lives on and on."

"Was George the one who gave you the propofol?" she asked suspiciously.

"No, I asked him but he refused to even think about it. I just told him this past weekend that I had gotten it from somebody else."

"Stop, how did he take that news?"

"He was not happy but I think he understood how desperate I was then."

"Why didn't you tell me you were having such a hard time?"

"I didn't want to worry you; it was something I had to work through."

"Portia, can I talk to you for a minute?" Raymond said, coming into the kitchen.

"Sure we can go in the living room," I said, grabbing a cup of water.

We sat down next to each other on the white cloth sofa that we had barely used over the years.

"I wasn't trying to set you up or attack you today," he said, looking down at his hands. "I was worried about losing you, maybe not just from the drugs but as my wife too."

"I know it's hard, Ray, but you lived without me for close to three years, you'll be fine. Don't look back anymore; I've done enough of that for both of us. Look forward and find someone you can make some new history with."

"I don't know if I can, I still love you, but I'll get a lawyer and I'll sign the divorce papers."

"Thank you for not fighting me on this, we've always been best friends and I want us to stay that way for our children's sake."

"We will," he said, leaning over to put his arms around me and giving me a soft kiss on the lips before he left.

I went back into the den and played a couple games of Yahtzee with Pam, Paula, and Charles even though I was exhausted.

"That's enough for me" I said after Pam won again, "I'm turning in." I really needed some quiet time by myself.

"We're right behind you after we finish this game," Paula said.

"Not before I make myself a nightcap," Charles said. "I'm impressed with the company you are keeping, Portia, the bar is fully stocked and its all top shelf."

"I have a friend who appreciates good liquor," I said, thinking about David and thankful that the walls can't talk.

"Who's up for Black Friday Shopping tomorrow?" I said walking out.

"I'm ready to roll out right now," Pam said.

"I just need a few hours sleep and I'm down," Paula added.

"Not me, all I need to do my Christmas shopping is a laptop

and a link to Amazon.com," Charles said, putting his feet up on the sofa.

***

We got out early but the sales in the mall were overrated. We hit the major stores in Cool Springs and a few boutiques in Green Hill, making only a few purchases. We spent most of the time just looking. We gave up the chase for bargains after it started to get dark and headed to the house.

"You all have been gone all day. Where are all the bags?" Charles asked us when we got home.

"They were just pretending today, but I'm very patient, they're going to have to make some real markdowns before I open my pocketbook," Paula said, going into the kitchen.

"Time for leftovers," Pam cheered following Paula.

"Warm up enough for me," Charles added.

"What are you watching?" I asked, sitting down on the sofa beside him.

"He's always watching something far out or boring," Paula said.

"This is for real here," Charles said, pointing at the TV, "It's the History Channel; they're running a mini-series called Armageddon."

"What's it about?" I asked.

"It's about the changes in the world like global warming and what the last days on the earth might be like. I've seen the Revelations part already, this episode is about Nostradamus. He was able to see into the future and wrote his predictions in quatrains."

Chapter Twenty-Two

I kicked off my shoes and sat back to listen. The detail that caught my attention was Nostradamus' study of medicine. They described him as an apothecary, a historical term for a pharmacist or chemist. During his time he formulated medicines from herbs and chemicals. I've always had an open mind about the mysteries of the universe and now I suspected that Nostradamus had put together his own formulation of propofol or something similar that allowed him to see visions of the future that initiated his collection of prophecies.

"It gives you a lot to think about," Charles said as the credits rolled up after the show.

"That's true, anything is possible," I said.

I had hit a turning point. My preoccupation with the past was over; my new obsession was with the future and what it held for me.

"You know Charles and I are out of here tomorrow afternoon," Paula said, bringing him a plate into the den.

"I assumed you two were staying until Sunday."

"No, girl, you know I can't miss church or my Sunday afternoon nap or my whole week will be a mess. Besides we've accomplished what we came for and had a good time."

"I'm going tomorrow too, Mama," Pam said, "Dad wants me to spend a day with him before I go back on campus."

"Excuse me, you all roll in here like the FBI to interrogate me, then you eat me out of house and home, and now you all want to leave before the weekend is over. That's a lot of nerve," I said, feigning indignation.

"When Ray called me I thought you had gone off the deep end for real," Paula said, "I had to come and see about my baby sis. Being here and talking with you has put my mind at ease."

"Good, I don't want you to waste time worrying about me."

"Let me tell you this, if I was worried I would already have your bags packed to take you home with me."

"Paula you are so crazy," I said with a laugh.

"You can laugh if you want to," Charles said, "But your room in St. Louis is ready, she changed the sheets before we left."

"It makes me feel so blessed that you guys care so much," I said, trying to contain my emotions.

"We love you, Mama, and we want you to be happy," Pam said.

"That's what I'm so thankful for, having my family to love."

"Group hug," Pam yelled.

We stood up and held each other and it was a beautiful thing.

Chapter Twenty-Three

It had been twenty-four hours since Paula and Charles had gone to the airport to catch their flight back home. Pam had packed up a bag and had gone to spend some time with her Dad before she went back on campus. The phone rang and I thought it was one of them checking up on me.

It was George, "Come home with me tonight," he said.

"Where are you?" I asked, glad to hear his voice.

"I'm right outside you door."

I rushed to front window and looked out and there was the black Mercedes pulled up by the curb with George inside on his cell phone.

"When did you get back in town?"

"Today, now how long will it take for you to get out here, I missed you."

"Give me ten minutes."

I grabbed my overnight bag and stuffed it with whatever I thought I might need and pulled a suit and shoes out of the closet to wear to work, and rushed out the front door.

"I'm so happy to see you," I said, resting my hand on top of his on the armrest.

"You should have come with me, I want you to meet my family," he said, glancing over at me.

"I probably should have but it was good I didn't."

"Why do you say that?" he said inquisitively.

"Raymond saw the Diprivan and a syringe at my house a few months back, the night I saw you at the club with your date. He was upset about me filing for the divorce and arranged for Pam, my sister and her husband, and himself to be here for Thanksgiving to do an intervention to get me off the drug."

"Are you serious?"

"Yes, I am, I was stunned but I explained everything to them just like I told you and then we sat down afterwards and ate dinner."

"Now for that scene I would have cancelled my trip," George said in amazement. "Anyhow, they're family and that's what they do."

"I know, it just made me more aware of how the things that I do affect other people. I realized that I wouldn't want any of them to do what I did."

"Now that's real talk, I'm relieved to hear that," George said, leaning over to kiss my forehead.

"This is it," George said, pulling up into the driveway of what they call a McMansion.

"George, this is a lot of house for one person, have you ever heard of a condo," I asked, getting out of the car.

Standing in the frosty night air framed in the gleam of the landscape lighting it was very impressive.

"I told you before I like nice things and I like to be comfortable."

"You are obviously very successful at what you do because this is beyond being comfy."

"I try," he said, grabbing my bags out of my hand. "Come on in, mi casa es su casa."

Stepping into the house I was sure that it had been professionally decorated, there was afro-centric art and animal prints and it was filled with fine furniture.

"Follow me and I'll show you around."

George showed me the layout of his home and it was upscale raised up to another level.

"Have you eaten?" he asked when he sat my bags down in the master bedroom.

"Yes, I have," I answered.

"Great," he said, "I want you to take a shower with me," he said, taking off his clothes.

"You know you are more of a mystery than I will ever be," I said, undressing and trailing him into the spa he called a bathroom.

I closed my eyes and I felt like I was caught in a summer rain storm, the water was warm and soothing, pulsing against my body from every direction. We bathed each other and it was the most romantic and intimate experience I had ever had. All dry and moisturized we climbed into his plush bed. George turned on the TV and I turned over and went to sleep.

"You're already dressed," I said when I finally opened my eyes in the morning.

"I've got an early day," he said, sitting down on the bed.

"These are for you," he said, handing me a set of keys, "You can drive anything you want in the garage and we'll pick up your car later."

"Okay, have a peaceful day," was all I could form my lips to say after he gave me a quick kiss goodbye.

That evening after work I went home and got some more clothes to stay with George a few more days. It was good to have someone around at the end of the day, but when he went on call at the hospital later in the week I decided to go home and stay at my own house.

"How are you?" he texted when he got a break.

"I'm good, staying at my house tonight," I texted back.

"I'll come by if I can," he wrote.

"Okay," I texted, and opened a can of soup for dinner.

I inhaled the aroma of the soup through the steam that rose above it and I admitted to myself that I had missed having someone around when Raymond left, but something was making me nervous. I usually have a plan to whatever I'm doing and now I felt like I was out of control, just living, without knowing where I was heading. I had delved deeper in my past than most people ever dreamed about and it fascinated me but now I craved to know what lied ahead in my future. I was never one who went to fortune tellers or palm readers, it used to scare me, but now I just wanted a glimpse, a few hints to help guide me. I thought back to my Friday night travels in time and was tempted.

It was around 10:00 in the evening when I heard the door bell ring. I knew it was George, he had texted me that he would come by when he was done. I opened the door with a set of keys in my hand for him.

"I was hoping I wouldn't have to ask," he said with a smile.

"The word says, 'we have not because we ask not,'" I said, helping him out of his coat.

"Uh-huh, what do you have to eat?"

"I made you a light dinner, Mr. Funny Man, come on in and sit down," I said, walking into the kitchen. "I set you a place in the dining room."

I had sautéed some large scallops in butter, steamed some rice, and made some creamed spinach for a light evening meal.

"There's a bottle of Albarino for you on the table."

"Now this is what I'm talking about," he said, sitting down.

I sat down in the chair beside him.

"I know you've got something on your mind," he said.

"Why do you say that?" I asked, smiling.

"Everything on this table says that," he said, looking me in the eyes."

"I just want to spoil you," I said, meeting his look, "Although I would like to mention my daughter Pam is coming home for the Christmas break and I want you to meet her."

"I'd love to, that's not a problem."

"I'm thinking it would be better for me to be at home, I'm not sure if I'm ready for her to see you sleeping over. It's been a lot of changes for all of us lately."

"So we finally get to the point," he said.

"There's no point, George, I just want you to meet her before she sees you coming out of my bedroom."

"That's cool, I can live with that, but the rule doesn't apply at my house," he said, flashing his sexy smile.

***

Pam came home when the semester ended two weeks before Christmas.

"Hey, Mama," she yelled as soon as she walked in, "Guess what?"

"What?" I asked, waiting for her to walk into the den.

"I got the lead part in the play."

"That's fantastic, a star is about to be born."

"Exactly," she said, dropping down on me and giving me a hug.

"I've got some news for you too," I said.

"Oh no, whenever you have news it's always over the top."

"That's not true, and I'm tired of being the messenger everybody wants to shoot."

"All right, all right, what is it?" she said, stiffening her shoulders and closing her eyes.

"You are so wrong," I said, holding back a laugh. "It's just that I've gotten a lot closer to a man I met early this year and I want you to meet him."

"Is that it?"

"Yes, that's it."

"Now I can exhale. Mama, I'm all grown up and I want you to be happy whether it's with Daddy or not. Life goes on."

Chapter Twenty-Three

"Well that's a load off my mind," I said, relaxing and letting my own breath go.

"Mama, you need to stop stressing so much," she said, walking into the kitchen.

Truer words had not been spoken, but it was easier said than done.

***

I thought it would be a good idea for Pam and George to meet on neutral territory. Pam loves Chinese food so I made reservations at P.F. Chang's.

"I can't believe we got here first as slow as you were moving," I said to Pam as the hostess showed us to our table and handed us menus. "Just order what you know you like, nothing new, I don't want you to waste a whole plate of food."

"Mama, I know what I want, I've eaten here before."

"Excuse me, my lips are sealed," I said, turning to my own menu,

"May I inquire as to how long?" she asked, being facetious.

"Don't hold your breath," I said.

"Hello, pretty ladies," George said, interrupting our exchange just as I was about to remind her which one of us was the mother.

"Hello, hello," I said, sliding over to the left in the semi-circle booth to make room.

"George, this is my daughter Pam, Pam meet George Reynolds. He's a physician at Metro General."

"Nice to meet you, Dr. Reynolds," Pam said.

"It's my pleasure, dear, please call me George," he said,

reaching out his hand in front of me.

Pam shook his hand with a smile and I felt like I had cleared another hurdle. We ordered and when the food came we sampled from each other's plates.

"You know I'm crazy about your mama," George said to Pam.

"I'm getting that feeling," she answered, staring back at him.

"Would us being together be a problem for you to get used to?"

"Not really, I'm about to graduate and I may not be in town anyway. I'd feel better if she has somebody around."

"In that case let me put your mind at ease, I plan to be around all the time."

Chapter Twenty-Four

"I'm stuffed," I said, leaning back from the table of the employee Christmas party.

"The caterers outdid themselves this year," George said.

"You didn't eat much," I said to him as we sat together at a table in front of the quartet playing the music of the season.

"I'm going to be on call all this weekend, overeating slows me down and I don't need that starting off."

"I guess that means I won't be seeing you tonight."

"Not unless you need some intensive care," he said, being playful.

"I do need some," I said, joking, "But it's not an emergency."

"I've got to go," he said, standing and squeezing my shoulder with his hand drifting up the side of my neck, "Get some rest and I'll see you when I can."

It was a just a week before Christmas and all non-essential hospital personnel would be off until after the New Year. I watched George weave through the crowd in his white coat and prayed the next thirty-six hours would fly by.

On the way back to my office I bumped into Keith, the first

prospect of my mission.

"Happy Holidays," I said, not wanting to appear ill at ease.

"Portia, how are you?" he asked pleasantly, standing with a group of his colleagues.

"I'm doing great, how about you?"

"I can't complain," he said, lifting up his left hand around the plastic cup of punch and I took notice of the wedding ring.

"Congratulations," I said, flashing him a sincere smile and wondering how old the new wife was.

He nodded and I made my way back to the office to call it a day. I glanced out of the window while I put on my coat and took in the beauty of the lighter than air snowflakes that wisped across the courtyard decorating the evergreens and rooftops like a winter wonderland. The Christmas spirit was stirring and I was starting to feel it again, I had not experienced the joy of it in a long time.

"Keisha, I would like to wish you a Merry Christmas and a Happy New Year," I said, handing her a holiday bonus inside a card on my way out.

"Thank you, Mrs. Roberts, same to you," she said, sitting at her desk wearing a Santa Claus hat and earrings that rang like bells when she moved.

"Close it down early and I'll see you next year, take care," I told her, pulling the door behind me.

"Be careful," she said just before the door closed.

Pam was standing in the doorway as soon as I walked up the steps from the garage into the kitchen at home.

Chapter Twenty-Four

"You got a special delivery today," she said, looking rather serious.

"What was it?" I asked, putting down my messenger bag and purse in a chair.

She didn't answer, she just handed me a large brown envelope. Inside was the final divorce decree from the County Clerk's office.

"Wow," was all I could manage to say, I was speechless.

"Dad probably got one today too. I'm going over there for a few days. You already have somebody to keep you company," she said, picking up her coat off the other chair and rushing out of the room.

Her small suitcase was packed in the living room and she snatched it up on her way out of the front door.

"Pam," I shouted behind her.

"I'll call you, Mama," she said without turning around, and then she shut the door.

"Damn," I said to myself, "Why am I always the bad guy?"

I plopped down on all the carefully arranged pillows on the loveseat and looked at the papers with mixed emotions. This was a close to the biggest portion of my life. On one hand, I was sad about the way it ended, why it ended, and I wondered if I should have tried one last time to make it work. On the other hand, I was happy to have a fresh start to pursue a relationship with George, yet I was afraid. Maybe I was moving too fast, what if there were some more hurdles waiting for me. I wanted to see my future.

It was Friday evening and I was by myself. I had promised my family, George, and myself that I would leave the propofol alone but at that moment I felt weak and the temptation was so strong. I looked in my hiding place in the refrigerator and took out the vial, went up the steps and pulled out my injection kit. I put on my red silk pajamas to keep with the festivity of the holidays, pulled the covers up to my waist, and prepared the needle. I had second thoughts before I injected but I pushed them out my head as the plunger went down into the chamber.

The sensation of falling started immediately and I just relaxed into it and let my body spin and fall into the atmosphere. Then it was if I wasn't falling anymore, the essence of my being became a whisper of the wind itself. It's in this weightlessness that I can move through time. It's like a trap door or an escape route to another dimension. I think to myself that I don't want to fall back, that I want to fly forward. I reverse the spinning and I start to rise as the beams of light encircle me. They intensify as the light divides into prism of colors. Images bathed in green and brown come into focus but I have the sensation of flying and I feel vibrations surrounding me.

The circling above me begins to slow and I feel myself going down. The helicopter lands and I am directed to the west side of the building and taken inside to the room where Javier is waiting. I'm escorted by four secret servicemen on my every side making me feel like the magnetic needle in the center of a compass. The man in front opens the door and I walk inside.

"Benita, I'm so glad to see you," Javier says, rising from his seat at the table and giving me a hug. I can feel the tension in the

Chapter Twenty-Four

stiffness of his arms on my shoulders.

"I'm always just a phone call away, you know that," I say, backing up and taking his hand to walk back over to the table.

"All hell is about to break loose, threats of missiles firings are coming from all ends of the earth and the panic among the people has set in," he says as we sit down.

"That's why you are here today, my brother; this is your destiny, to be the calm amidst all of the turmoil," I say, rubbing my hand across his back to soothe him.

"What if our adversaries decide to invade our borders and take over our water stores?"

"That wouldn't make sense, what they can take won't last a year; it's the knowledge that they need to continue to survive long-term."

"Thank God, we have it, Benita."

"You were born for this moment, Javier. I have always believed that, and Mama and Poppy would be so proud."

No one else would have believed he could have come this far but I sensed it a long time ago as I watched my brother grow up. I knew that he was born to do great things. I was nine years older than him so I was more of a mother to him than his big sister. He had the brains and the charisma at an early age and I had seen to it that he had the best education money could buy. Times were hard on our family back then when we were kids; Mama and Poppy were laborers picking peaches and tomatoes near Charleston, South Carolina. Seeing them struggle I made up my mind back then that I would work hard and help my family get to a better life.

I studied long hours into the night to make good grades and I was a whiz in math. When I got the scholarship to Temple University in Philadelphia I knew I was on my way to making all of our dreams a reality.

"Benita, why don't you study to be a doctor," my Poppy would always ask whenever I came home for a visit.

"I don't like hospitals, Poppy, I have a weak stomach. The only sterile place I plan to work is in my own office," I would answer.

"You don't have the cold heart it takes to make it in corporate America," my Mama would add, "You're always trying to help somebody; you don't get rich doing that in this country."

"You will be surprised, Mama, you can make a fortune doing the right thing and nobody has to suffer."

It was true, I was on the kindhearted side, but I was a shrewd business woman. My first business class taught me to 'find a need and fill it,' and I focused on the needs of future. I suspected that with the burgeoning populations around the world that pure water would eventually become the new liquid gold. I did my research and an early investment of mine made a ton of money from water filters that purified sea water or contaminated water into drinking water. I made another small fortune buying a company that discovered an economical method to produce hydrogen fuel. Driven as I was, I never married or had a family of my own.

I used a significant portion of my wealth to bankroll my brother's political career after he graduated from law school. It

Chapter Twenty-Four

was money well spent; because now he was the Vice President of the United States, the highest ranking Hispanic in the history of the country, and literally a heartbeat away from being President of the United States with the president hospitalized in a diabetic coma.

"Benita, things are at a boiling point and I'm not sure how to contain the situation. Purified water supplies around the world are dangerously low. Destructive riots or violence could breakout at any time."

"Relax, Javier, this has a diplomatic solution. We have the technology, but we don't have to give it away. The leaderships of these countries have pilfered the money from the people for the last fifty years, they need to go into their pockets and build the facilities to provide the filters for water."

"My concern is how to keep the peace in the interim."

"Trying to police the planet is what broke and bankrupt the United States in the first place and we have nothing to show for it."

"I understand that, Benita, but we have received warnings that missiles are already poised for retaliation."

"Reprisal for what action, Javier, threats and attacks are for those who have no other cards to play. We've got the ace of spades; technology, and believe it or not the free market still exists. The one constant is money, it talks and bullshit walks, my brother."

"I don't want to have to bargain and see people die so that the filthy rich can hang on to their coffers."

"We're in a period of adjustment; money will have to change hands and jobs will be created. We were so close to Civil War twelve years ago and how you handle this emergency will determine whether this country recoups it economic status. You have to make the well-being of the American people your first priority. That was a costly lesson that nearly destroyed this country."

"I have to give a press conference in fifteen minutes and I know they've set virtual traps for me to fall into, so many want to see me fail."

"Don't worry, Javier; you know I'm your chief ally. You dictate the pace and the tone of the press conference," I advise him before we go down.

"They want to see if I'm in charge, Benita."

"That's what you are about to show them, Javier, but don't let them make you think you have something to prove because you don't. You have the right to be here, you've earned it."

When the elevator door opens in the East Wing my brother and I step out and walk into the Press Briefing Room. Cameras began flashing and a low roar of voices grows louder as he moved towards the podium. I looked proudly out into the sea of microphones pointed in his direction. "Relax; stay composed," I repeat in my mind trying to telepathically relay the words to my brother. "Take only one question at a time, keep it orderly, don't let them take the control from you."

"Good afternoon, Ladies and Gentleman, as put forth in the Twenty-fifth Amendment, Section 4, the president has been declared disabled. At 1:00 this afternoon I became the 'Acting

Chapter Twenty-Four

President.' I am here today to put the American people at ease. There is no reason for us to panic or behave rashly due to the challenges before us. We have the resources that we need to function normally for many decades to come. Now I'll take a few questions."

Hands wave in the air and Javier points to a woman from United Press International.

"Mr. Vice President, have you come to any solid decisions concerning the imminent threat of depleting water that is escalating around the world?"

"This is a vital global concern and the world leaders will have to come to an agreement on the direction to which we all shall proceed. We have the technology available to solve the problem, we just need diplomacy. Cool heads must come together and negotiate."

Javier took a question from a major broadcast network.

"Mr. Vice President, will we need to institute a draft to mobilize troops at strategic bases on the major continents?"

"Past attempts to police the world have proven to be too expensive without meaningful returns," my brother answers, "The technology for supplying pure water will not be used as a weapon or withheld from any nation. China and Indian are in better positions to supply any manpower that is needed; the United States doesn't have the human capital to reach around the world."

A man from the New York Times asks, "How do you propose we maintain safety and security for the American people?"

"Our security is not in jeopardy. There is a developing urgency in the world based on our need for suitable drinking water and we have the ability to fill this need. Still, there is the issue of economics. Nonetheless, we are willing to arrange a summit to come to a peaceful solution for the survival of us all."

I nod to Javier after his response to signal to him that he has said enough.

"Thank you very much," he says and we walk out with the cameras flashing at our backs.

Inside the Oval Office I pace around the floor taking in the view of the trees and flowers until Javier finishes speaking outside the door with his aides.

"Well done, Javier, you made your points, now all you have to do is wait for the phones to ring" I say, patting him on the back.

"Reed, keep all lines of communication open, when word of willingness to talk comes notify me immediately," he says to the Chief of Staff.

"Yes, Mr. Vice President," he says, leaving us alone to talk.

"I wonder who will be the first to rise to the occasion and take the lead, Benita."

"I don't know, Javier, India is now the most powerful nation, China is nearly as strong but they are compromised by a host of environmental issues, but they both will have to play the role of the Good Samaritan for a change."

"I'm worried that this could start a whole new barrage of terrorist attacks from the Middle East."

"Don't become preoccupied with what lurks in the shadows.

Chapter Twenty-Four

That region has imploded, they weakened themselves with wars and conflict, and now with the dwindling demand for oil they have made themselves irrelevant. Hydrogen energy is going to be at the top of future energy resources."

"Excuse me, Vice President Planas, there's been an incident on the Canadian border and there's been a change in the President's condition," Reed says, bursting into the office, "You're needed at the hospital right away. I'll brief you on the way, the helicopter is waiting.

"Are you coming, Benita?"

"Go on, I'll wait here for you with Rosalyn and the kids."

I couldn't be with him every moment and he would need to start thinking for himself and making his own decisions without me.

Rosalyn and I sat together watching the news reports. Multitudes were trampling across our borders from the north and the south. The insurrections were beginning and the people were storming the American Embassies around the world.

An emergency interruption in the broadcast announces, "The condition of the President had deteriorated over the past twenty-four hours and we have just received an official report from the Bethesda Naval Hospital that the President has died."

"Oh my God," Rosalyn gasps.

"What have I done," I say under my breath, standing on my feet.

I had wanted so much for my brother but this wasn't what I hoped it would be. He was now in the axis of the world's turmoil. How would he manage under the pressure of increasing pandemonium? "Was it his dream or mine?" I feel my knees weaken under me, my head feels light, and I'm passing out. Everything appears to move in slow motion as I'm falling.

When I came too I laid there for a while thinking. I had come to the understanding that we all have to live our own lives and make our own choices. I was divorced and Pam was grown. I had a fresh start, but now I was afraid of making a mistake. A critical case of the 'what ifs' had me paralyzed like a deer in headlights. I reached for the phone and called Paula.

Chapter Twenty-Five

"Hello, sister-girl, I saw your number flash on the TV screen," Paula said when she picked up.

"What are you doing watching TV this early in the morning?"

"I'm watching some of those 'flip this house' shows trying to get my courage up for Charles' latest venture, what's up?"

"I got the divorce papers yesterday."

"Ouch, and how was that?"

"It freaked me out a little but Pam flew out of here to go comfort Raymond," I said bitterly.

"Girls and their daddies, mommas and their sons, that's how it goes, P."

"I know, it's just that sometimes it feels like I'm the only one who has to stand on their own two feet."

"Do you need me to come back down there, because you know I will?"

"No, I'm just venting, George is here for me, but he's been on call for a couple of days."

"Now that you're a free woman you can go on and say yes to the dress."

"I'm not ready for that yet and you need to change the channel on your TV."

"Ha-ha, you got me; but this is what the rest of us do when

we can't sleep."

"Damn, Paula, that was a low blow. You don't have to hit me, I'm already down. What happened to the ten-count?"

"I'm sorry, that was insensitive and over the top, I was trying to make you laugh."

"Now I'm scared of what you've got when you want to make me cry."

"Pull it together, P, before you catch the holiday blues. Why don't you put up some decorations and trim your Christmas tree or something to stay busy?"

"Excellent idea, sis, I'll do that. Bye."

"Talk to you later."

I went into the basement and brought up the boxes of lights and decorations. I wasn't sure if Pam would spend Christmas with me or Raymond but I decided to do it just for me.

In the evening George called, "Hey babe, I got a reprieve finally, I'm home and the weekend isn't over."

"Why didn't you come by when you got off duty?"

"I don't mind spending time there, but it's another man's house."

"It's my house," I said, feeling insulted.

"It's the house that you shared with him and raised your family."

"Does that bother you?"

"No, but I prefer to be with you where I don't have to be surrounded by your past."

"Is my past a problem?"

Chapter Twenty-Five

"Not for me, but you haven't made peace with it."

"I was having a hard time, but the future is the only thing I have on my mind right now."

"For me, I deal with the present and I still want you over here," he said in the deep sexy voice.

"I'll be over there in about an hour," I said.

"Thanks, babe," he said and then hung up.

"I'd better check in with Pam before I go," I thought, just in case she might drop by the house. "Hey, Pammy, how are you and your dad doing?"

"We doing good, I think we're going to go see a movie in a few."

"I was on my way over to George's and I didn't know when you might be coming back home."

"I don't know, Mama, it depends."

"I was hoping that you would spend Christmas Eve with George and me."

"I would like to, but I think I'll spend it with Dad this time, he needs me more than you do right now."

"Whose opinion is that, because it's not true?"

"Gimmee a break this time, Mama," she said.

"Okay, sweetie, I'll leave it alone."

"I love you, Mama, bye-bye."

"I love you more," I said before I hung up, dumbfounded.

"Where was he when we needed him?" I was the one who had hung in there and now I was being shut out. "Why?" I wanted to know, I hadn't done anything wrong.

The phone vibrated with a text, it was George saying, "Bring enough of your things to stay until after New Year's."

I pulled out a suitcase and packed like I was leaving town. I turned off the Christmas lights, grabbed the gifts I had for George, put on my coat and walked out the front door to my car.

"Hey, Portia, wait a minute," a voice shouted from across the street. It was my nosey neighbor Cynthia.

"Hello, Cynthia, Merry Christmas," I said as I popped the trunk to load up my suitcase.

"Merry Christmas to you too, Portia, I've been meaning to come by and see you; I saw you had a lot of company for Thanksgiving."

"Yes, my sister came down with her husband."

"I couldn't help but notice that Raymond came over too. I thought if you two were working it out he might be home for Christmas."

"No, Cynthia, it didn't work out, and let me be the first to tell you that we are divorced."

"Ooo, I'm sorry, chile, I know that's rough."

"Yes, it is," I said, slamming down the trunk and walking to the driver's side door.

"I see you're all packed, are you going out of town?"

"Yes, I am," I said bluntly, opening the door and dropping down into the seat.

Cynthia grabbed the door before I could shut it, "I know Pam came home for the holidays, is she going out of town with you?"

"No, she going to be staying with her dad for Christmas," I

Chapter Twenty-Five

said, putting my hand on the inside handle of the door.

"Honey, I see why you're leaving; I wouldn't want to spend the Christmas in the house all by myself either."

"Well you have a happy holiday, Cynthia, and I'll see you when I get back," I said, gently pulling the door from her hand and closing it.

"I'll keep an eye on the house for you, chile."

"Thank you," I said, pulling away fast.

I took my time driving over to George's house enjoying the glowing lights of the season that flashed along the streets. It cheered me up to see all the individual expressions of joy for the holidays. I turned up the radio when I heard Donny Hathaway sing "This Christmas" and I hoped it would be a very special one for me too. I just had to stop brooding. I had a tall dark and handsome man waiting to spend the holidays with me. What more did I want?

George, always on point, had his home tastefully decorated when I pulled into the driveway. He met me at the door with a hug and a kiss. I set my bags on the floor and stood in his arms feeling the warmth and strength of his body and the genuine care he had for me and I tightened my arms around him and held on.

***

"Do you want to go to church today?" George asked, rolling over next to me on Christmas Eve.

"I think I would, it usually gets me in the real Christmas spirit, but I want to go to a different church this time," I said, not wanting to chance bumping into Raymond or Pam.

We went to a Presbyterian church about twenty minutes away.

"Is Pam coming over later?" George asked when we got home from the afternoon service.

"No, she decided to spend this Christmas with her father."

"I see," he said, sensing my unhappiness with it. "Why don't we make some snacks and watch a movie?"

"That sounds nice," I said, looking in the refrigerator to make a tray.

I sat down on the carpet in the entertainment room beside the Christmas tree and took a sip of wine from the glass that George had place on the coffee table for me.

"My divorce is final," I said, looking at the perfectly wrapped gifts under the tree.

"When?" George asked, sitting on the floor beside me.

"I got the papers a week ago."

"Is everything okay?"

"Fine, except that Pam chose to comfort him instead of me."

"Join the club," he said, putting his arms on my shoulder, "It's rough but it gets better."

"I'm not going to stress over it, I want us to enjoy this time together."

"That's all I needed to hear," he said, "Now I'm going to open up one of these presents."

It was a magical holiday. It all seemed too perfect. I was so happy that it was scaring me. We didn't have the power struggle of young couples; there were no children to fuss over, and no financial worries. He and I had met so simply. Things never worked out like that for me. Where was the drama, the fly that was always in the soup? When was the shoe going to drop? I felt like I was visiting a beautiful foreign country, having a fabulous time, and soon my glorious vacation would be over and I would have to go home.

***

It was right after breakfast a few days later when George came into the kitchen while I was cleaning up.

"Portia, I've got to go to the hospital," he said, "My staff is shorthanded and overloaded. Hopefully I'll be back tomorrow or at least by New Year's Eve."

"Oh, that's too bad," I said, trailing him to the foyer.

"That's the nature of this business. Stay here, relax, and take it easy. Maybe you can come up with some interesting New Year resolutions," he said, putting on his overcoat.

I walked down the steps to the garage with him and waved until the door closed back down. I went into the entertainment room and turned on the TV but there was nothing on worth watching. George had only been gone a few hours when the house began to feel so big and empty and I started feeling out of place. I'd rather be at my own house where I felt more comfortable. I reached for my cell phone and called Pam but I didn't get an answer.

"Why don't I just drop by Ray's apartment for a visit?" I thought, I wanted to spend some time with my child too before the New Year came in.

I grabbed my coat and headed down to the garage. George's Mercedes was parked behind my car and there was no way I was going to take that fine ride on the slippery roads. I hopped into a small red Toyota pick-up truck and backed out of the open door. At the traffic light I dialed again and still got Pam's voice mail. Maybe she didn't want to talk to me. The last thing I needed was a cold shoulder.

I made a left turn and headed towards my house. I parked the truck on my driveway since I didn't have my garage opener and went in through the back door on the deck. When I got inside and settled down I realized that I had just escaped from one quiet house to find myself in another. The problem was inside of me and I carried it wherever I went.

I had to get myself on track. I made a cup of hot tea and went and sat down on the leather recliner in front of the window in the den. I thought about my life from the time I was a kid until today. I thought about the lives that I had been able to experience. Then I saw it, the common thread that was woven into all the different lives. The year or the land didn't matter, age, gender or status didn't make a difference, there was always discontent, disappointment, or dissatisfaction with their circumstances. These feelings weren't thrust upon me in the different instances, I cultivated them willingly.

The irony was that I didn't need to, God's peace was always there in the midst of all my confusion and chaos but it was up to me to take it into my heart and mind. Why hadn't I taken it, didn't I deserve it? I was responsible for a lot of my own anguish because I held on to it tighter than my own happiness. I couldn't do anything but cry for the time I had wasted. I lay in

Chapter Twenty-Five

the moisture of my own tears and wished I could do it all over again.

I was exhausted and wanted to sleep. I know I shouldn't even think about this but there's enough propofol for one more injection. This is my last shot whether I liked it or not, it wasn't like I could call David and ask him for anymore. This would be the conclusion of my own private exploration of time. My last expedition had gone much farther into the future than I wanted to see. The question foremost on my mind is what the rest of this life has for me. I just needed a glimpse of my own future to guide me.

I go upstairs and bring down my kit because after this shot I will throw it all away. I get the vial out of fridge and take it back into the den. I watch the white liquid as I suction it into the syringe with the normal dose where I could see my own past, but there's a small corner left in the vial, it's probably just a few drops. Why leave that little bit in the bottle I say to myself and I draw it into the needle. I feel really weird taking this while it's still daylight but I'm exhausted, besides I shouldn't sleep more than four hours and then I'll go back to George's house. I pull the curtains and lie down on top of the throw blanket on the sofa and find the vein to inject. Almost instantly I feel the floating sensation of weightless and I see the flashing images. Then the images are fading back out to brightness. I can't seem to connect to anything, I'm moving so fast, I can't see the circling beams, the light is so dazzling and it radiates warmth and peace. I feel…..

Chapter Twenty-Six

I'm flat on my back feeling like I've been in a heavyweight championship fight. My arms are so weak I can't raise them. I must have taken several mighty blows to my ribs because each breath I take is accompanied with a sharp pain to my chest and my mouth is swollen. I open my eyes. Above me I see an IV drip on my right. I turn to my left and it's my neighbor, Cynthia.

"Girl, you had me so worried, I have been through it tonight with you. When I saw that strange truck parked in your driveway I thought somebody had broke in on you. Honey, I called 911 and my cousin Harold was the cop who came. He pushed in the back door and we came in to catch the thief in the act. We didn't see anybody suspicious except for you and when we couldn't wake you we called an EMT."

"I didn't mean to cause you any trouble," I said, straining to move my swollen mouth.

"Chile, you were barely breathing and they had to do CPR on you."

My eyes widened in shock when I realized what happened.

"Oh my God," I said.

"Don't worry, honey," she said, leaning down close to whisper, "I threw all that stuff you had in the trash, nobody saw it."

"Thanks, Cynthia," I said gratefully in a low voice.

"Portia, what did you take?" she asked, leaning in closer.

"It was propofol. I was trying to get some sleep."

"Chile, you almost died, your heart stopped."

My eyes rolled back and I just looked up at the ceiling. All of my despondency and misgivings had nearly killed me.

Cynthia pulled up a chair close to the side of the bed near my head. "Girl, you have got to tell me, did you have one of those out of body experiences that some people have when they almost die?"

"Yes, I did," I answered, thinking about all the trips I had taken. "I was with Nicholas again and I even flashed through some of my past lives. From what I saw the spirit lasts throughout eternity transported from one body to another until it makes its way to heaven."

"Girl, that is so amazing, I've got to hear all about it when you get your strength back," she said, shaking her hands in excitement.

"Yes, Cynthia, we're going to have to do lunch or dinner real soon," I said, surprised that she would be the one I could really talk to about my trips.

Our visit was interrupted when the nurse came in with a doctor behind her.

"Hello, I'm Dr. Tucker," David said to Cynthia.

"Hi, I'm her neighbor who called the police."

"Nice to meet you," he said, shaking her hand. "Would you excuse us please?"

"Certainly," Cynthia said, standing up and moving towards the door. She gave me a quick wink and a wave on her way out.

"You almost took yourself out of the game that time," he said, checking my heartbeat.

"It was an accident," I said to him while the nurse took my blood pressure.

Chapter Twenty-Six

"There was just a little left and I wanted to get rid of it," I said to him in a low voice.

"Have you ever heard of just throwing it in the trash?"

"I should have, it was bad judgment on my part."

"Anyway, you'll be fine, there wasn't any permanent damage done."

"Thank God, thank you," I said, feeling a tear drip down the side of my face.

"Was that the end of it?" he asked, looking at me through narrowed eyes

"Yeah, I'm done playing with fire."

"That's a relief. Anyway, you're still down here in Emergency, we'll get you assigned to a room in a bit."

"I need to ask you for a favor," I asked, trying to raise myself in the bed.

"What's that?" he asked, looking at me sideways.

"I need to be released."

He looked at me with questions written all over his face.

"I don't want to have to explain this to my family; I know you can understand that."

"No problem, my friend. I'll take you home myself. My shift ends in a couple of hours."

"Thank you again, David," I said softly as I reached my hand up to pull his coat sleeve.

"We all have our secrets," he said, turning off the light on his way out.

Lying in a hospital bed I had to face the reality that I had risked everything trying to fill voids in my life that would never be filled and others that didn't even exist. I had to accept that no life is without heartbreak and no life is without hope, and every moment is precious.

David took me home and I went straight to my bed. I slept the whole night, so tired I didn't dream. The next morning I drug my battered body up and drove the red truck back over to George's house. I was lying down in bed when he got home.

"You okay?" he asked, sitting on the bed beside me.

"I got restless here by myself and I went out roaming around town and I took a fall. I think I broke a rib but I'm all right. I just need a few days to get back on my feet."

"I guess this means we'll be spending New Year's Eve at home," he said, touching my still slightly swollen lip.

"You don't mind do you?"

"Baby, not at all, I've been working for seventy-two hours straight," he said, standing up.

"I was wondering if your offer was still open." I asked, watching him change his clothes.

"Which one is that?" he asked, looking puzzled.

"The one about my staying here with you."

"Absolutely, but there are conditions," he said with a stern look.

"Such as?" I asked, leaning up in attention.

"You can't go back, it has to be forever," he said, lying down alongside me.

"That's exactly what I've been searching for," I said with relief.

BROWN REFLECTIONS